DARK RINGS

Dark Things Book One

Lainey Delaroque

COPYRIGHT NOTICE

CONTENT WARNING

Below you'll find a few notes about themes in this story that could trigger certain audiences. Others might view these as spoilers. If you do, please skip ahead.

• Themes of consensual kink (rope bondage, masochism and impact play) throughout the story, from the point of view of a main character
• Discussions of racial fetishization throughout the story, from the point of view of a main character
• Descriptions of domestic abuse, not main character
• Descriptions and discussions of medical malpractice throughout the story, from the point of view of main and side characters
• A few of graphic sex scenes
• Occasional bad language

Now that you've been warned, get a warm drink of your choice, sit back, relax, and enjoy the ride! <3

CHAPTER 1

I have no right to be so excited, especially after all I've seen to-day. But I can't help it. It's the way I stay sane. It's the only way I can be a good social worker during the day. Each step on the wet sidewalk feels lighter and lighter. Work was hard today, but I can't wait to get home now that I'm done. I'm humming '*Singing in the Rain*' as I skip to the parking lot. As I reach to open my car door, I notice a long, uneven line going from the middle of the back door to where I'm holding the handle.

Someone keyed my car. Again. My grip tightens as my stomach sinks. Who was it this time? An angry husband? A scorned pimp? It's undoubtedly a man. I touch the wet white surface of the door, running my fingers along the line as the rain soaks my hair. It's someone at least a head taller than me. He probably thought it would scare me. The tiny female Asian social worker. Ha. He would've been right, five years ago. The first time it was scary. By the fifth time, and my fifth bill to fix it, my fear was replaced with annoyance. Cowards. They would beat their wives and children and then key my car because I dared to help.

No. Not today. I won't allow a dickhead's petty threat to diminish my excitement for tonight. Mathias, Connor, and I have been planning this for a week. I slip my hand in my purse, my fingers curling around the small pepper spray I carry with me. The parking lot is well-lit and empty on quick inspection, so I open the door with my left hand. I peer inside to make sure the spray is in prime shooting position in my palm. There's no one inside, and the familiar smell of my Toyota calms me. I get in the car with the feeling of sexy enthusiasm returning bit by bit. I'm not going to be jumped tonight. Well, not by some sicko hiding in my car.

As I drive to my apartment, I run through what is about to happen in my head. I search for any doubt, for an inkling that I'm making a mistake. My palms are sweaty on the wheel, and I almost run a red light, deep in thought. Maybe I should have agreed for them to drive me instead. No. It's too close to my work. If anyone saw a woman getting kidnapped in front of an abused women's shelter, they would freak and ruin the fantasy. Worse, one of my clients could see it. I wouldn't want to add to their trauma, so home it has to be.

My phone beeps with a message. I shouldn't look at it while driving, but I'm too excited by the upcoming few hours. It's Connor, ever the gentleman, checking in.

Connor: *You still up for tonight?*

I type in a quick response, my sweaty fingers sliding on the screen more than is comfortable. My mother would disown me if she knew what was about to be done to me tonight.

Hana: *Ye.*

The anticipation is going to kill me. Well, if not kill me, then make me run for the bathroom for sure. My stomach is in knots as I pass the last traffic light before my home.

I recount everything agreed for tonight. No blindfolds. No penetration. No visible marks. No calling me slut. Everything else goes. Yes, to fear. Yes, to humiliation. Yes, to being unraveled like a set of nesting dolls. Because I need to peel this professional persona off me. I need to let go of the hours and hours of heartbreaking stories I've heard throughout the week. I need to be stripped down to my essence so I can be reborn as the best version of myself. This is the goal anyway. Whether Mathias and Connor will go that deep, who knows.

I park in my usual spot, but the nerves make me stay in the driver's seat a little longer. I rest my head on the steering wheel, taking deep breaths. Imagining. A reel of violence is playing in my mind's eye. All my clients crying. Shaking in fear as those whom they have chosen to trust betray them, one hit at a time.

That's not me. I bear no trauma of my own. My childhood was good, my relationships - fine at worst, amazing at best. So why I desire the dark things I do, I'm not entirely sure. I have my theories. But at the end of the day, it doesn't matter if it works. The pain, the humiliation, the torture - those feel horrible, there's no doubt about it. But after it's all over, I'm free. I'm empty and content. I'm ready for another week. I'm a blank canvas that my clients can paint with the colors of their suffering. In a way, my whole life revolves around my work. But enough about that. I relinquish my introspection and get out of the car.

My gray tweed skirt and blazer feel tight around every part of me. My excitement has bloated me, but no matter. It's all part of the game. It began the moment I texted Connor back. The stiff bun on the top of my head is begging to be released. My tired eyes itch from hours of looking at case files and trying not to cry on behalf of my clients. I will cry now. I will let it all out.

On the way up, I opt for the elevator. Every other night I take the stairs, making use of the free cardio. Tonight, I don't have the stomach to walk up six flights of stairs. I'm already hot and bothered, wetness pooling between my legs. It's embarrassing how easy it is to get me going. I watch the numbers change in the tiny screen in the elevator, and when the doors open, I walk as if in a trance. This is it. No turning back now.

My hands shake while I take my keys out of my bag. Then I hold the key next to the lock, listening in. I can't hear anything. But they're inside. I know they are. And they will hurt me, just like we planned. Just like *I* wanted.

The turn of the lock takes one second, and I step inside, shaking all over. My body is on high alert, still unaccustomed to what I put it through so often.

The hallway is dark and quiet. For a moment, doubt creeps in. Maybe there was a misunderstanding. I close the door behind me and leave the keys in the little dish on the cabinet next to me. I stand frozen, waiting. Nothing happens. Should I turn the light on? We haven't discussed specifics. The whole point of this play scene was for me to know next to nothing.

I return to shaking as I unbutton my blazer. I will turn the light on. As the familiar space is illuminated, nothing is out of place. Not that I expected to. Mathias lives with me. He wouldn't trash the place for a scene. And Connor? I look around for his shoes, but only my slippers are on the floor.

Well, here comes nothing. I hang my blazer on the coat rack and glance in the mirror out of habit.

My heart does a somersault in my chest as I see them. Dressed in all black, with masks on their faces. But I can't react quickly enough. One of them steps forward and grabs my face from behind, covering my mouth. Then he swings me around as if I'm a feather.

It's Mathias. Tall, handsome, caring Mathias. He pushes me into the bedroom roughly. As I flop on the bed like a sack of potatoes, I forget all about his sweet side.

CHAPTER 2

She's tiny, yet her presence wraps around me like delicious barbeque smoke. Her panting breaths are all I can hear as she struggles against me while Connor ties her in some elaborate tie that will immobilize her fully. I can't wait to see how the rope will dig into her skin as she tries and fails to get away. She will relent eventually. She's been looking forward to this all week.

And I, well, me too. I'm a people pleaser, so knowing that I can give her something she craves makes my cock hard.

The three of us are a pile of bodies on the bed, limbs everywhere and heaving chests and so much sexual tension. It won't dissipate until we've all emptied our heads of work worries. In this time between the three of us, the outside world disappears.

"Done," Connor says, his voice triumphant.

I push off Hana and look at his creation and the breathtaking woman within it. She's like a butterfly in a spider's web, with two sets of exposed wings. Each of her calves is tied to the corresponding thigh; her legs are pulled in place by ropes that connect to each side of the bed frame. She struggles to close her legs, but there's no chance. Connor knows what he's doing. He's spread her out for our enjoyment, and my cock swells appreciatively at the sight. I was rocking a semi as I wrestled her into submission, but now my jeans can barely hold me.

We ripped her black pantyhose and pushed up her skirt. Now, it's sitting on her waist like a belt. I crack a smile behind my mask. Her white shirt is still more or less pristine on her chest, a gross oversight. Her arms are tied similarly to her legs—forearm to upper arm in a tight wrap, and pulled to the side, secured to the frame. No matter which way she tries to pull or shift, the ropes hold her in place. She's our plaything for tonight, and we've got her the way we want her.

The shelves near the door are stacked full of sex toys. I spent an hour moving the books and knick-knacks out of there, so we had a space for the vast collection of implements I plan to use tonight on her smooth skin. I start with the most innocent of all - the safety shears.

When Hana plays, she often goes non-verbal. It's something that took a bit of getting used to, but now as her lips press together and her eyes widen at the sight of me with the shears, I know she's fully here with us. And I would bet my life she's also soaking wet.

I blink at her slowly, a simple move that we've agreed between us, to her at ease and remind her that no matter how intense the play gets, it's all for her. I don't waste any time and settle between her legs. Connor lies next to her and moves her hair out of her face, strand by strand. She starts shaking, and I know this touch, usually gentle and loving, now makes her feel even more exposed. There is nothing she can hide from us. Nothing she can hide from herself.

I run my finger across the thin fabric that hides her modesty. She jolts in surprise and lifts her head in a vain attempt to see what I'm about to do.

"Nah-uh," Connor whispers in her ear and pushes her forehead down with his palm. Now she can look at the pristine white ceiling above and take all we have to offer without warning.

I rip another hole in her tights and cut her panties. They're already damp from the anticipation.

My cock jumps in my pants at the sight of her, aching to be let out, to make contact with her skin in any way possible. For now, I have to reign him in. He'll get to play later.

While I'm keeping busy between her legs, Connor pulls out a bright red lipstick and paints her lips in one swoop. She speaks then as we break her first wall.

"I don't—" she struggles under his grip "—like this!"

"Look what you did." Connor shakes his head. I lift my gaze to look at the result of his beautification. There's smudged lipstick around her mouth and on her chin.

"Not so put together now, are you?" I say with a chuckle, then swipe whatever remains of her panties from under her.

She yelps, trying once again to get free. Fat chance. I stuff the panties in her red mouth, enjoying the look of embarrassment on her face. Her dark eyes are like two black holes, sucking me in with a plea to stop.

I won't stop. Not until I've stripped all the armor she put on for the working week.

Hana is a masochist. I'm not a sadist, and Connor isn't either, but we both get off on her reactions to whatever we're doing. So, if she needs pain and humiliation to reset her brain for the weekend, we will provide it.

I take a heavy leather paddle from the cabinet and test it against my palm. The sound of it cracks like an enticing promise in the air. Hana moans behind the gag.

If she didn't like Connor's makeover, then she is going to like this. I run my free hand up and down her inner thighs, prepping the skin under her ripped tights.

Then I run the edge of the paddle across her legs, building up the suspense. She's lifted her head again, trying desperately to see when the first blow is coming. I nod to Connor. He sits at the top of the bed, offering his leg to Hana as a pillow. She settles her head on his thigh, a thankful expression on her face.

He rips her shirt open in one sudden move, making buttons fly everywhere. All thankfulness is wiped off her features, replaced by offended shock. She hates it when she gets even the tiniest stain on her work clothes. Having them destroyed like this? That must sting.

She doesn't have much time to be upset because I lift my arm and finally bring the leather paddle down on a part of her exposed thigh. It's not a forceful blow, but it produces a satisfying sound and rips the transparent fabric under a bit more.

Her chest jumps in surprise. I wait for her breathing to equalize before hitting her again. Connor grabs her boobs and squeezes. As I rain blow after blow on her reddening legs, he twists and turns her peaked nipples.

The scent of her arousal permeates the room, mixing with the sweat of her exertion to take everything we're giving her. I've worked up a sweat, too, behind the mask. The fact that I'm still fully clothed doesn't help either, but I persevere. If Hana can trust me to bring her to the edge of her being, I can take the discomfort. Connor seems fine as his deft hands work on her chest; kneading, pinching, pulling.

After I've counted to fifty in my head, I look at my work. There's barely anything left of Hana's black tights. Her skin is warm under my fingers, and she shivers every time I touch her. I glance at her relaxed face. Enough priming. Time to make her cry.

I give her thigh a final pinch, then push off the bed and head for the kitchen. I fill three glasses with water and bring them back on a small tray. Connor has left her side, too, so she's alone sprawled on the bed. He's leaning on the wardrobe, looking at his nails like he's bored out of his mind.

The bulge in his black trousers betrays the truth, but the game has to continue as planned. I give him a glass of water and down one myself. The cool liquid is refreshing, cooling my insides gulp by gulp. My ears are burning from excitement and a bit of shame about what we're about to do.

I adore Hana, don't get me wrong. She's a fiercely self-sufficient woman with a difficult but important job. I'm doing this for her. My abuelita used to say, '*Quien bien te quiere, te hará llorar*'. Who loves you well will make you cry.

So I quell the doubt rising in my gut and walk toward the bed with the third glass of water. She is really going to hate this next part.

"You look parched," I say, my last predetermined line of the night. After this, it's all Connor.

Her eyes widen. Her jaw moves as she struggles to spit out the panties I've stuffed in her mouth. She shakes her head frantically.

I'm not deterred. I tip the glass, setting the cool liquid free. I start at her head. When the first drop hits her forehead, she squeezes her eyes and shifts to one side. Some water gets in her ear. I avoid her gag, making sure I don't waterboard her accidentally, and continue down, drenching her boobs and crotch. At the end of it, she's glaring daggers at me, glistening and exposed.

It's like a baptism, a ritual that purifies her soul after she's been taking in the filth of the world. And now she's reduced to nothing. We don't need her to do anything except lie there and take whatever we have in store for her. And we're only getting started.

I shift off the bed and go back to the cabinet of toys, pretending to contemplate what I'm going to do. The cane is next. She wanted a stinging reminder that she was alive, something to pull her attention toward her body and away from the thoughts that threaten her sanity every day.

I go into a trance of sorts as I hit her after the bamboo cane is in my hand. I strike her legs, and Connor soothes her. We find an unrelenting rhythm that occupies all of our minds. In those frantic minutes, we're all empty. Givers and receivers. Of pain, of submission, of undiluted trust. One time I hit her in precisely the same spot I've hit her before, and her skin breaks a little. She whimpers, which undoes the spell of the moment.

She's had enough of this. *I've* had enough of this.

Part of me wants to end the scene here. As I look at her tear-streaked face, at her destroyed outfit and her messy hair, I want to hold her and tell her how well she did. How strong she is. How I want to make her waffles in the morning and spend the weekend cuddling in bed.

But when I look into her eyes, there's still defiance there. She's holding onto a tether of her weekday will. I'm sure there's pure hatred in the way she glares. I hope it's not directed at us. I hope she can still remember what we're all doing here. Maybe she hates the cane. Maybe the water that makes her skin shiver every time the air around us moves. Maybe she hates the pain. Or maybe she just hates the world and how it forces innocent people to endure a similar kind of treatment without rhyme or reason.

I nod to Connor. This next part is not one of my kinks.

"Look at you," he says to Hana. "A drenched rat."

I press my lips into a thin line as I turn my back on them both and face the cabinet. My hand is beginning to cramp from the tight grip I have on the cane.

"Ugh, the state of you," Connor continues. "I know you think you're a smart, independent woman. But I don't see it here."

I use my free hand to peel my fingers off the cane, one by one. My shoulders are tight, my whole body rigid. I've got to relax. Although my talking is done for the scene, I have another important job.

I grab the magic wand vibrator in a determined sweep and kneel to plug it in. It's the powerful weapon of control that we will use to build Hana back up after pushing her off the cliff in her mind.

CHAPTER 3

I should be cringing at my words, but the fact is, it's easy. I say much worse to myself, and I mean it. When I berate Hana about her state, the words ring hollow in my head.

I don't let it show because there's a purpose to this, after all.

She's turned her head so she can look at me as I stand slightly behind her. Her eyes are wide and angry. Mathias is like a highly-strung wire on the other side of the room, facing the wall like he can't bear the sight of us.

He did tell me that verbal humiliation and degradation aren't his things but come on. It's only words. Hana is the most independent person I know. One of the smartest, too. She's far from helpless. Well, maybe a little bit now.

Anyway, I've given her way too long to think—time for another attack.

"All I can see is a wet, dirty plaything." I pause for dramatic effect. "Look at yourself. You can barely move."

She starts wiggling at that, testing the ropes yet again. They will hold strong. She wants to prove me wrong. See, I can move. I can almost hear her through her muffled screams.

"Now, now, my doll. You can only move because I wound you up. Which only proves the fact that you're just a toy for us to play with." I lower my face to hers. I'm so close I can lick her tears.

Mathias is looming over us, a menacing presence that would terrify me in any other situation but this one. He's taller than me, leaner, and has something dark about him that I can't place. It's not exactly like mine, but it's similar. In any case, I don't feel we're close enough to discuss it.

Hana breaks eye contact with me to look pleadingly at him, but his face remains in shadow, unreadable. Only the hallway light illuminates the bedroom, so everything is half-black, half-bright. We've closed the curtains so that nothing can pull Hana's attention from us.

I prod her wet cheek with my index finger to bring her back to me. Mathias won't help her. She growls behind her gag.

"You see? We push buttons, and you make sounds." I chuckle.

She glares at me, and I'm overwhelmed by the desire to suck her trembling lower lip in my mouth. To taste her anger and play with her fear, to bite down until I break skin.

I want to crack her open so her essence can spill into me. Despite what we're doing here and what she does for work, she's pure. The demons that torment me every day, that are lingering at the corner of the room even now, can't touch her. I'm sick and selfish, so I want part of her purity inside me.

But I keep whispering dirty, meaningless words into her ear as my hand slips from her cheeks and my nails dig into the delicate skin of her arm. They leave a blazing trail in their wake. She braces for the pain, her whole body tensing.

One glance at Mathias is enough to spur him into action. He flicks the switch of the magic wand, and it purrs into life. Hana hiccups, her head falling back on the bed as the toy settles on her clit. It's only a slow, teasing vibration. It won't make her cum, but it will jumble her thoughts on another level.

I continue dragging my nails across every inch of skin I can reach. She twitches from time to time, the wand hitting the spot.

Her eyes hood over, and her breathing quickens with pleasure. I'm sure she's not thinking of work now.

"Oh, is this the button that shuts off those pesky thoughts of yours?" I stop touching her. Mathias shuts off the magic wand. The room becomes quiet, like a graveyard. My own demons shift at the back of my mind, ready to push me toward my undoing, inviting me to join Hana and become nothing.

I stand firm against them. Maybe I'll indulge them later.

With two fingers, I drag Hana's panties out of her mouth.

"Please," she croaks between coughs that probably do nothing to soothe her.

"Please what, doll?" My voice is smooth like honey, and my lips quirk up in a smile to match it.

"Don't stop."

"Did you hear that, M? The doll can talk."

"We're taking a break," Mathias says, altogether dropping the ball on the dirty talk. It's okay. We're all good at different things.

"Tell me, doll, what would you do if your microwave asked you to stay with it? To keep reheating your food because it doesn't want to be empty?"

Hana's brows furrow. "But… But I'm not a…"

"That's right, you're not a microwave. But you are a toy. A toy trying to be smart."

"I'm not…"

I don't want her to say 'I'm not a toy' because it will break the flow. It will bring her back to a human, logical mind space, and I can't have that. I'm close to her unraveling. Only a few more lines and a few more denied orgasms. I nod to Mathias, who turns on the vibrator.

"Yes, you're not a smart toy. You're a doll. An empty vessel."

She closes her eyes again, her words stolen by rising pleasure.

"Can you feel how whatever essence there was inside you is leaving?" I grab her breasts, pinching her peaked nipples between my fingers. She arches her back, straining against the ropes.

This time I miss the cues of her upcoming orgasm, too taken

by the softness of her breasts in my hands. My dick begs to be let out, making my black trousers feel like a chastity cage. Mathias is on it, though. He lifts the wand from her pussy, letting it vibrate in the air.

"Nnnhn." Hana lifts her head, a pleading expression directed at Mathias. He shakes his head, seemingly more relaxed. Good. I don't want him to be uncomfortable.

"What are you?" I ask, still kneading her boobs in lazy circles.

"I'm…" She hesitates. I stop touching her. Mathias stops the vibrator, and there is once again a loaded silence.

"Don't leave me," she whimpers. "I can't do it all alone."

I'm not sure what 'it' is, but I know we're standing on a precipice. One more push in the right direction, and she will come tumbling down.

"So much thinking," I whisper. "You don't have to do anything, doll. Just accept everything we want to do with you. Look inside. Is there anything left in this pretty head of yours?"

Mathias starts up the magic wand. She jolts when it's on her again. I caress her cheeks up and down, enclosing her tiny face in my big palms.

"You are a toy made for pleasure. Our pleasure. Your pleasure. We will play with you. We're not going anywhere. So, what are you?"

Tears are now spilling from her eyes, sneaking under my fingertips, dropping down straight onto my heart. I want this to work so badly.

"I'm your toy," she whispers. Those small words uttered from her chapped lips are my victory medal. I will wear them like a crown in my memories.

"Our favorite doll," I say.

"Our favorite doll," Mathias echoes. It must have finally clicked for him because he pulls out a piece of rope and secures the wand vibrator to Hana's pelvis. I taught him the tie, and seeing how confidently he ties it, shows he's been practicing. He's clearly way better with his hands than at talking dirty.

Hana gasps as the wand moves this way and that, teasing her without allowing her to reach her peak. When it's finally in place, Mathias shifts away from her and comes to the side of the bed next to her head, opposite to where I'm standing.

I unzip my trousers and my dick springs free like it's never seen a woman before. I stroke it once, glancing at Mathias. He's done the same.

Hana hasn't noticed yet. With her eyes closed shut, she's focusing on the buildup of her pleasure, having let go of her worries for the time being.

I unravel her clenched fist, one finger at a time. She looks at me through her eyelashes, then at Mathias. Realizing what we want from her, she opens her palms and takes our dicks like the obedient toy she is. She can't move much, so we move instead, fucking her hands while she shakes all over from the assault of the magic wand on her clit.

"What are you?" I ask again, pleasure now seeping into me.

"Your toy," she says without hesitation.

"Our toy with moving parts we get to do what we want to." This is not in the script and comes out as a breathless sentence. My demons have dug their nails in my mind, whispering that I'm a sick fuck who can only get off by degrading people.

CHAPTER 4

There's a shadow behind Connor's eyes. I don't understand it. How can I? I know next to nothing about the guy. Whenever we've played together, Hana was there as a buffer. It strikes me as strange now that I've kissed him and had his dick in my hands, yet we've never shared a drink or talked about life. What does he even do?

Hana's hand tightens around my cock, and I can barely think properly. I crave more, so I lean forward and grab Connor's shirt, pulling him to me. This seems to shake off whatever bad mental energy has gotten him to shut off. He smirks and crashes his mouth into mine, bracing himself on the headboard with one arm and on Hana's breast with the other.

As we indulge in a sloppy open-mouth kiss, we keep pumping in Hana's hands, which get tighter and tighter as the vibrator keeps working on her.

I don't know exactly what the three of us are doing, but it feels so good I don't want to think about it.

Connor and I break apart when Hana squeezes our dicks so hard it causes our breaths to hitch. She cums violently with an arch of her back and a loud, guttural moan that seems to last forever. Then, she collapses on the bed, and her hands go limp. She twitches a few times then tries to wriggle out of the magic wand's unrelenting vibration.

I chuckle and let go of Connor so I can wrap my hand around Hana's and keep my arousal up.

"Get it off," Hana rasps in a small voice. We look down at her like two titans, casting long shadows on her glistening body.

"We're not done playing, doll." Connor pinches her nipple. "We can wind you up until your spring breaks."

"I don't want it anymore," she says with tears in her eyes. However, no safe words are spoken, and she warned us ahead of time that she would try to wriggle out of the scene when things got too intense. So, we continue as planned.

Pumping into her hands, both of us return to making out on top of her. Connor's lips are ferocious, biting mine like he's been deprived of something fundamental for so long. I like how easily he fits in this trio, without any conditions or expectations. *You're both my type*, he said, and that was the end of it.

I don't know what my place is in this dynamic yet, and I'm too afraid to ask. After harboring a one-sided crush for years, I don't necessarily trust my feelings so easily. I can't tell my types of love apart - what is friendship, what is romance, and what is just sex? Hell, if I know.

Hana's hands clench again. She's cumming for the second time. They're both so into this. And their reactions are what I need to push me over the edge.

I moan into Connor's mouth as my balls tighten up and my mind goes blank. I erupt like a volcano, my whole body tensing for a few agonizing seconds. Then my head spins, and my knees can no longer support my weight.

Connor is there, though. He puts both his hands on my chest to prop me up.

"Wow," he whispers with a wicked grin. "Your orgasm face is so hot."

I chuckle, suddenly very awkward and unaware of what to do with myself. So I give him a quick peck on the lips and collapse near Hana.

She's deep in her own world, her teeth digging into her bottom lip. I lick her exposed nipple. She shivers, close to her third climax of the night.

"Are you broken yet, doll?" Connor says through gritted teeth, still using her fingers to stroke himself.

"Hnh." Hana can't form words as she cums again, pulling on Connor's cock so hard for a moment she forces her pleasure onto him. He shoots his load with a groan, covering half of her face. As she writhes, her other cheek glistens with my cum.

"Stop this," she says after she's ridden the last wave of her pleasure. "No more."

Connor nods at me and wipes the sweat off his brow. We've reached tonight's rock bottom. The only way is up.

It takes a surprising amount of effort for me to get up and walk to the foot of the bed. I remove the magic wand from Hana's crotch, and she gasps once, then relaxes. For a few moments, all is still and quiet. Connor smooths the hair at the top of her head, and I look at the state of her and let a sliver of shame into my mind. I did as she asked, but I'm not sure if I'm proud of it. What if she hates me for this? What if I've somehow misunderstood?

Hana's first sob cuts through my heart like a dagger. Then she lets out a hiccup and a tiny wail. Connor unties her arms from the bed, and she doesn't wait for all the rope to be off to bring her palms to her face and cry into them.

I untie her legs from the frame too, and she curls up into a ball, still partially restrained. Her shoulders shake as she hides into herself and lets the tears flow out of her.

"I'm sorry we broke you, doll," Connor says in a tender voice. He wraps his arms around her and starts gently pulling the ropes away, untying her one strand at a time. She nestles into his embrace, still crying.

I tug at her legs and scramble to get her free.

Connor touches my arm. "Slowly."

Right. This is important too. I want to get to the point where she will reassure us we did great, but she can't do that if we rush this bit and leave her broken.

"We'll put you back together now," Connor says into her hair. "We'll fix you so you can be whole again."

He's untied one arm, and as it hangs limp in his grip, he brings her hand to his lips and kisses her tenderly. I'm sure there's my cum there somewhere too, but he doesn't seem to mind. He flips her gently to untie her other arm. I'm still on her first leg.

"Your beautiful hands are yours again," he whispers and pushes her palms to her chest. "Use them to hold your compassionate heart."

Hana whimpers at that. She's listening. Good.

Her leg is finally free, and as I start untying the other one, Connor keeps building her up. "You've got strong limbs, legs that take you wherever you need to go."

The last strand of rope slips between my fingers, and nothing is restraining her but Connor and her own will to be here. I run my hands across her legs, caressing the marks.

We stand like this for a few long moments. I'm unsure again of my place here, so I shift on the bed awkwardly.

Then from somewhere, Hana's arm extends toward me, grasping my hand and giving it a reassuring squeeze. She's here with me.

"Yes, doll," Connor says. "We're not going anywhere. Take your time. Awaken and come back to us."

His words ring true inside my head too. I feel like a mirror, reflecting the feelings of both of them, giving them opportunities to express themselves.

Connor takes Hana's face in his hands and looks into her eyes. "I see you. The fire in your eyes and these gorgeous life-saving lips. You did so well."

She blinks back tears. The last few drops roll out of her eyes, in rhythm with her deep breaths. She's stopped crying and is now looking at Connor, listening to his voice pulling her back to a self-aware mind space.

In the end, the three of us hug on the bed. Connor and I peel off our masks and clothes until we're only in our underwear. We help Hana out of the remnants of her work outfit then take her to the shower.

The hot water washes away all my doubts about tonight. Hana and Connor are happy and satisfied. Which means I am too.

CHAPTER 5

Monday comes way too soon. And as amazing as the weekend was, this morning is mundane. Mathias is in the shower, and I'm putting the final touches on an outfit that will not be destroyed at the end of the day. A gray pantsuit that makes me look taller than I am.

I glance at my watch. If Mathias doesn't come out right now, I will be late. I need to put my contacts on, and they're inside the steamed-up bathroom.

I'm about to shout at him to hurry up when my phone rings. It's Connor.

"Hello?" I pick up as I'm on my way to the kitchen. The sandwich I prepared last night is cold and a bit soggy, but it will do. I kneel down to rummage in a cabinet for a travel mug. There are unpaired chopsticks, bento boxes, and scary amounts of plastic storage containers.

"Hi." His voice is clipped. "Did I leave my ring at yours?"

I give up on my search. This mess will be organized soon. "I don't know. Did you take it off here?"

"Might be in the little jewelry box next to the shower where Mathias leaves his rings."

"Hm." I go to check, and sure enough, Connor's sleek black band is there. "Yep. When do you want to pick it up?"

"I will drop by sometime this week. God, I feel really stupid for forgetting it." He huffs a laugh that sounds strained.

"Don't worry about it. We'll keep it safe."

"Thank you. I'm an idiot."

I want to tell him to stop berating himself, but he's ended the call before I get the chance. I can't figure him out. I thought *playing* was meant to make you closer to people.

The black ring between my fingers has a date inscribed on the inside. There's gold showing through the dark layer like the band has been worn a long time and maybe touched a few too many times.

Analyzing it like this feels intrusive, so I leave it in the box, picking up instead one of Mathias's stainless-steel rings. He makes them like people make popcorn, a dozen at a time, together with other metal things. He usually mixes and matches them until there isn't a finger without a ring, but recently he's been leaving them at home. All of them but his fancy rotating ring. I suppose it's too much trouble to take them off in the hospital.

My watch beeps with a travel update. I'll be late for sure. As I call to push my first appointment back, Mathias comes out of the shower looking like a snack.

Only with a towel wrapped around his hips, I want to forget the week ahead and dive straight back into the weekend the three of us indulged in. His big chest tattoo, a realistic owl spreading its wings, judges my staring with its inky black eyes.

I smile. Memories of play, cuddling, and trying new food projects in a reel in my mind's eye.

"I made you late, didn't I?" Mathias's voice, smooth like velvet, wraps around my core. I get an urge to throw my arms around him and lick the little beads of water off his neck, but I resist. We don't do stuff like that. We are roommates and occasional play partners.

"Connor forgot his ring here. He'll pick it up at some point this week." I get straight to the point, refusing to be distracted by his toned stomach and the little happy trail that invites my eyes to the bulge under his towel.

He runs his hand on top of his head, drying his short hair in one swipe. His blue eyes scan me and stop on my fingers, and he chuckles.

"Want me to make you a few of those?"

I look down, realizing in horror that I've put on some of his rings while I was thinking. My soggy sandwich is even soggier on the side of the jewelry box.

"Well, I just wanted to see what the fuss was about. They're not actually that comfortable." Why am I so flustered? I take them all off in a hurry and they clink with each other as I toss them back in the box.

"Did you try on Connor's ring too?" He stands next to me, peering at the small pile of metal. The smell of my soap mixed with his natural scent makes me a bit dizzy.

"No."

"Looks like a wedding ring," he continues. "I've been meaning to ask him about it, but…"

"It feels like prying." I close the box lid and pick up my lunch.

"Yes."

We leave it at that. As I finish my morning prep and rush down to my car, I think about how significant rings can be. And how insignificant too. My own fingers are bare. Passing down rings over generations isn't traditionally Japanese. And wearing random rings isn't traditionally me. I'm more of an earring kind of girl.

One thought leads to another. The rings are nothing but a reminder of how little we all know each other. There's a pearl necklace deep in my sock drawer, and they don't know it exists. Just like I have no idea what happened on the date engraved on Connor's black ring or why Mathias is so compelled to create his own.

The working day brings about another depressing realization, one that I have every Monday. And then day after day. With all their rights and privileges in our time, women are still mistreated. Still more likely to be abused, controlled, and taken advantage of.

As Lucinda, my last client of the day, sits next to me on the sagging couch and tells me about her forced abortion, it takes every ounce of control I have not to scream in frustration.

"I'm just the side piece, you know. He didn't want no baby from me."

She's slim, with big brown eyes, dark skin, and gorgeous natural curls. But her face is sunken in, like she's ill, although she swears she's fine. She sits almost curled up in a ball, with her arms covering her empty belly.

"Where did you have this procedure?"

"It was a good hospital. I didn't see a name, though. I just remember gold curtains. And one nasty woman that was a midwife or a nurse or whatever. She kept making me drink something that made my head all fuzzy."

I shake my head, unable to hide my distaste. "Did you agree to the abortion?"

"Yeah, of course. My man is rich, and he takes care of me. I understand."

If he took care of you, you wouldn't have to sit here with me, I think, and adjust my grip on her folder. This is her third time with us.

"But I didn't agree for no one to take my uterus out," she continues.

"Excuse me?" I must have misheard.

"I had a lot of pain after the abortion because it was late stage, you know, where they take the baby out of you like it was almost born. So I went to the STD clinic, and they said I had nothing there. They did a scan. I paid for it with the money I had collected from my man so now I don't have a lot. Can I still be here? You know, if he hasn't hit me yet this week?"

"You always have a place here with us. We have a free bed in one of our emergency accommodations. You can stay there for a bit until something more permanent opens up," I say, trying to keep my voice steady. Which hospital allowed this to happen? And why aren't they at least taking care of her after the operation?

"That's good. Great. Cause everything hurts, you know, and I think I will yell at him if I see him today. Sometimes I can take no shit, so I get smacked for it." She chuckles like her situation is the most normal thing in the world. As part of my job, I have made it my mission to show women like Lucinda a different 'normal'. One where respect, safety, and joy are all around. They can't always see it easily, however.

"Lucinda," I start.

"Cindy," she interjects. She's relaxed now that she knows she won't be turned away.

"Cindy, I know we talked about this a bit last time, but I wanted to repeat that your feelings and opinions are just as valid and important as those of your partner's." I almost choke on the word 'partner'. 'Abuser' is more like it.

"Yeah, yeah. But it doesn't feel it, you know. Cause I can't smack him back as good."

"Well, ideally, I want you to be in a place where no one has to resort to violence to get their point across."

"Ain't no place like that around here."

We are silent for a moment. The familiar guilt that haunts me after every play session is there at the back of my mind again, eating away at my confidence as a social worker.

I should be doing more. I'm educated, I should have something better to offer to build up her self-confidence. She can leave this asshole; I know she can. The fact that she's with me means she's at least a little bit aware.

I don't say anything. Pestering the victims to do therapy or stay with us longer or give up on their bad habits doesn't work. I tried it when I was young during my vain attempts at forcing the dream of a better life on my clients. I wasn't very popular back then. One feedback report had 'out of touch' written across the page.

So now I measure my words. But so much professionalism means I need to resort to my unconventional methods of release. What would Cindy think if I told her I get 'smacked around' by choice? That I get degraded for free? That I got not one but two men doing it because I need it to be as intense as it gets to make it to the next week?

I sort out the paperwork, and we make small talk. Nothing of it genuinely registers; I'm on autopilot, ready to be done with the working day. When I go to the toilet before my drive back, I stare at my almost-healed thighs and wish I was back on my bed again; tied up, aching all over, and feeling absolutely no shame about it.

Cindy's case lingers in my thoughts. I play with a dangerous fantasy in my mind. I imagine finding out who this guy is, and which doctor agreed to such an abhorrent surgery. Then I see my-self calling my best friend Sophie and telling her to sort it out, which she can do because she's part of Chicago's underworld. A gang queen. Then she would send her people forward, like rabid dogs, and they would destroy in Cindy's name. For her safety and comfort. I'm not sure if resolving things this way truly brings in-ner peace. I've never tried. Sophie's world is nothing like my own. I can help my clients because I do everything by the book. She can't really help because she stays in the shadows. Killing off abusive boyfriends isn't exactly low-key.

Outside in the parking lot, I stare at the scratch on my car, get-ting angrier with each passing second. I throw the door open and rummage in the glove compartment. I pull a purple permanent marker out, one I carry for when the crazy gets the best of me, and trail the scratch, adding more lines, then stylized leaves and flowers.

Fuck you, ugly world. I will make you pretty somehow. I don't know how or when, but I will never stop trying.

# CHAPTER 6

I change into scrubs and put my doctor's coat on. It doesn't even have my name, as if I'm not supposed to stay long.

It's been three weeks since I went undercover in this hospital, and I've achieved nothing. Most of the staff avoids me, from the technicians to the attending physicians. I feel like a medical student - invisible and replaceable.

I rotate the middle element of my ring, reading the engraving over and over. Memento mori. Remember you must die. The first ring I created when my medical license was suspended. The first of many, as I'm still not technically allowed to practice medicine.

Sometimes the stars align in just the right way, and the gang you're accidentally part of needs a doctor to go undercover to appease another gang and avoid a gang-on-gang conflict.

Not that it matters to my patients. I do my best every day. I give them my all because, God, I have missed it. The beeping of the machines, the chatter in the waiting rooms, even the occasional emergency. It makes me feel alive. No amount of metalworking can replace the feeling I get when a patient I have put under wakes up all better.

I place the ring inside my locker with my other belongings and set off on my morning rounds. Unlike the previous hospital I worked in, I have more patient interaction here. It was to help my investigation. I've been hired as a Physician Anesthesiologist though my current practices are along the lines of Criminal Emergencies doctor.

I go to the Maternity Ward first because Hana's story yesterday about her client who got her uterus removed without consent makes me deeply uncomfortable. It sounded so much like this hospital. I'm here to uncover its shady dealings after all. How many hospitals are run by a son of a gang boss?

I did two Cesareans yesterday, so I go straight to those women who seem to be recovering fine. It's all so normal. Too normal. The ward leaves me with the impression of a horror film - you know, the one where happy guests check-in only to find out one floor of the hotel is just full of murderers, ghosts, and dead bodies? I can't shake the feeling, so I go to Reconstructive Surgery and check on the septoplasty patient, my last operation yesterday. I find their bed empty, which surprises me - the patient was vomiting, and the drainage wasn't good, so she was supposed to stay with us for monitoring.

"Where is the patient?" I ask the nurse who is passing by. She looks sternly at me like I'm a little child.

"Discharged."

"Who discharged her?"

"Her file is in the system." She shakes her head. "I don't have time for this."

I blink while I watch her back as she leaves in lazy strides. I sigh. No one said this was going to be easy. Checking files, it is, then.

But before I leave, I see a cluster of orderlies and nurses gathering stuff around a patient and then moving the bed, equipment and all, out of the room.

"Where are you taking her?" I ask as they pass me.

It's a young woman with a bandaged head, probably a burn patient. Why would they take her away from here? Surely, they can't be discharging her.

I don't get a response, only a few glances and a glare from one of the orderlies. He's tall and fat and looks more like a bouncer than a healthcare worker.

My feet move of their own accord, and I follow them until the big guy turns to me and says in a gravelly voice, "You're not her attending. Mind your business."

I swallow hard. Do I push on anyway and risk breaking my cover, or do I accept that I can't help this patient and keep investigating quietly?

'I want you to find out what my son is doing and why he's struck this deal with Comet International. Don't forget you're not a doctor. You're a spy.' The Arcana Empress's words flutter in my mind. Did she know this would be hard for me when she gave me the job?

She promised she would get my license reinstated if I did well. She promised Sophie and the gang to stay away from their territory. But she didn't even hint at what I might find here. I'm guessing things that go against my oath. She would have hired a real doctor otherwise.

I storm outside, the cold air making my lungs constrict. Will the patient be okay? Where is she being taken to? Did I fail her as a medical professional? Or did I succeed as a spy?

At the end of the day, I'm exhausted. So instead of driving straight home, I stop at a flower shop. Maybe Hana also had a bad day. I scratch my head as I look at the display, colorful and full of hidden meaning between the petals of each flower.

"Can I help you?" The florist smiles at me as she puts a sunflower in an elaborate bouquet.

"Can I have one of those?" I say after a sudden bout of inspiration. The middle of the sunflower reminds me of Hana's big, dark eyes and the petals are bright like her personality. "Let me make it into a small bouquet." The florist takes some random foliage, but I shake my head.

"No need, just the flower, please."

"Not even a ribbon?"

"Not even a ribbon."

I pay and leave in a slightly better mood. I hope this small thing will make her smile. When she smiles, I smile too.

A vaguely familiar smell hits my nostrils when I walk into our apartment. Like corn and chicken. A little bit like my house where I lived with my abuelita when I was small.

"Oh, good, you're home." Hana waves me in, her hair in a messy bun at the back of her head, her face flushed like she has been running. She points to a heap on the table.

"I tried to make tamales for dinner. I had a crappy day at work and needed a bit of a break. I know you like them."

A warm feeling spreads in my chest. I want to hug her, but we don't do that. Outside of playing together, we're roommates. Almost strangers.

"Are they wrapped in baking paper?" I peer closer at the food, which looks nothing like the tamales I'm used to. Behind my back, I hold the sunflower, a little bit unsure if it's appropriate to gift it to her.

"Yes, I didn't have leaves to wrap them in. Do you think it matters?" She bites her lower lip, a look of confusion spreading across her face.

"It adds to the taste, but I'm sure they will be delicious even wrapped in paper. I smell chicken."

"There's some inside. I'm not that bad, and I can put fillings in things." She chuckles, and I chuckle back.

"I had a tough day at work, too, so I got a sunflower for the table." I cringe a little bit as I say this, but it's a safe statement. It won't make her feel burdened.

"Oh, is this for me? I love sunflowers. Mama is obsessed with them and puts one in every painting." She points to the artwork on the wall behind her, depicting a girl with various flowers growing out of every crevice in her body. There is indeed a sunflower sticking out of her ear. Next to it is a painting of a poppy, but I don't like looking at that one. It makes me uneasy. Hana's mother is a mystery to me. Her artwork is everywhere in the apartment, but she's never physically around. I've never even heard Hana call her.

"Okay, I lied. I got it for you, not for the table." I hand the sunflower to her, a nervous laugh following my words.

"It's pretty. Should be able to stay fresh until the weekend at least. It will help us get through the week." She sighs. I need to tell her about the hospital, but Sophie and Hana agreed she'll know as little as possible so she could stay clear-headed for her very legal job. The updates on my very illegal investigation remain inside me.

"Can I give you a hug? You look sad." Hana opens her arms after she's put the sunflower in a tall, slim vase under the sound of my silence.

"Of course." I grin. Am I sad? I don't think it really matters as long as everyone around me is happy. I can borrow their happiness.

She wraps her arms around me and squeezes, her head resting on my chest. I bring my hand to her hair, petting it absentmindedly.

"Hey, I'm comforting you right now." She looks up at me, amusement in her eyes.

I chuckle. "Petting you comforts me. You're like a cute little pet who made me tamales."

"Hmm." She narrows her eyes, considering something. Which part? I tense a bit, but she gives me another squeeze, helping me relax. "I can live with that. Pets do bring inedible food into the house from time to time."

"I'm sure they're not that bad." I give her a little kiss on the head before letting her go. I can't help it, and it's done before I can think if it's appropriate or not. The smell of her perfume is comforting. Her jokes make me forget it's only Tuesday, and that there are three more days of undercover work before we get to play.

As she brings plates out and I get us drinks from the fridge, I imagine what it would be like to sweep her off her feet and bring her into the bedroom, where I would worship her until she begged me to stop. A little part of me feels guilty that I don't include Connor in my imagined scene. It's not like I don't like him. He's hot enough to keep my dick hard, but there is a wall around him, an air of unapproachability I can't seem to breach.

"Did Connor come to pick up his ring?" I ask Hana.

"Not yet. Not sure when he'll stop by, but I hope it's not tomorrow. I don't want him to feel awkward about not being invited."

Wednesday nights are when we have dinner with Sophie, Damien, Tanya, and the kids. The whole setup is a bit weird, but we've formed a sort of strange family unit, and Hana was adamant we should catch up every week. I get to see my best friend and his girlfriend, so I embraced the idea.

As I peel the paper off my tamal and bite into Hana's rendition of the dish, I'm reminded why we order takeout for those dinners.

"What happened to the spices?" I tease as I chew.

"I was very careful in following the recipe." Hana tries her own, then stands up and gets some spices off the rack. "Okay, maybe I was too careful. Let's get creative."

CHAPTER 7

There's a mistake in the code. I know there is, but I can't find it, and that drives me slowly, but surely, insane. I've been at it since last Friday. And yes, the weekend with Hana and Mathias completely wiped it off my brain, but today is Wednesday, and I'm struggling to think about anything else.

It works until it doesn't. The meeting with the client is next week, so I better figure it out by then. My fingers go to my left hand, and I rub the naked skin where my ring should be.

Laura would be able to find the error within seconds. She was three times the programmer I am. I try to imagine what she would say if she were just over my shoulder, but my memory of her gets blurrier with every year. It both hurts and feels numb.

A pop-up announces a new email. When I peep the sender, I roll my eyes. Comet International. What do they want? Their software, and all the code within it, is perfect. Unlike this mess that I'm dealing with at the moment.

Dear Mr. Jones,

After running the program on a few computers, we are still seeing the lines of data we asked you to remove. It is essential for our business to be able to sort the data appropriately and then present it according to our standards. Get in touch with me as soon as possible and rectify.

Yours Sincerely,

Ken Rogers

Hale-Bopp Health

Comet International

Was I a criminal in my past life? Why am I so unlucky with my clients? Despite the professional tone of the email, implying that there's something wrong with the software, what they want is shady.

Their original request, made by phone, was to add an option to easily erase a record to prevent it from appearing in specific searches. What are they trying to hide in a hospital?

I drag and drop the email into a folder called 'red flags' where I keep rude correspondence or things that I might need as evidence should the legal system get involved. It only has a few items, but it will grow fat and full if Comet International keeps this up.

I look up at the wall clock in the office. It's almost seven. Why am I still here? I slam the laptop shut and collect my things in a frenzy. Suddenly I can't stand to be here, annoyed at the broken code, the demanding client, and my missing ring. One of those, at least, can be fixed.

I ring the intercom on Hana and Mathias's apartment. When someone picks up, there's laughter that dies after a loud shush. I maybe should have called ahead.

"Hi Connor, come on up." Hana's voice crackles from the wall.

Upstairs, she welcomes me with a little wave. Hugs seem to be reserved for when we're playing; before, after, during but never outside of those times.

"I came to pick up the ring, but you're busy." I fiddle with my car keys.

"Of course, just a moment. Come in, though. Are you hungry?"

"I—" I don't bother finishing my sentence because she's already left to look for my ring. I step forward into the dining area and see a table full of people. I press my lips into something like a smile as I see familiar faces.

Sophie is here with her boyfriend - I know both of them from the Moon Garden Club, where we played one time. I never got his name. Next to him is Mathias, then two teenagers and a strikingly beautiful woman with a blonde bob haircut and piercing blue eyes.

"Connor!" Sophie stands up from the table and gives me a quick hug. Then she wraps her arm around my shoulders, despite being shorter than me, and starts pointing people out.

"This is Melanie, my sister. And Thomas, her friend." The two teenagers look up but don't stop chatting, clearly not agreeing about something.

"You know Mathias and my boyfriend, and that there is Tanya."

Tonight is not the night I will learn the guy's name. He's one of the types that I prefer to avoid anyway, tall, big, and always scowling. I heard he'd been hurt in the Moon Garden fire a little over a month ago, but he seems to have recovered.

I nod at the beautiful woman, Tanya, and she smiles back, revealing a row of perfect white teeth.

"Do you want to grab a chair? I will get you a plate," Mathias says.

I look at the table full of tacos, and my mouth waters. Yet compared to the laughter I heard coming through the intercom, everyone is quieter. I'm an outsider, and if I stay, they will act reserved around me. That irks me, so I shake my head.

"I've just come to pick something up. Already had dinner."

Hana comes back and gives me the ring. "You sure you don't want to stay?"

Warmth spreads through me, like Laura's presence is back around me the moment I slip the ring on my finger.

"Thank you, but I'll go. See you on the weekend?" I open the front door.

"That's the plan," Hana says, something like relief in her tone.

In the elevator, I feel a bit lonely. That table full of food and people reminds me that when I come back home, I will eat in front of the TV, with a Netflix show as my only company.

Well, maybe not. Laura is always with me. I rub the black band sitting on my left ring finger, and for a precious moment, I can picture her smiling face, clear as if she's in front of me.

CHAPTER 8

Water drips down my elbows as I once again let work thoughts in my resting mind. Cindy didn't make her appointment today. I found her a lovely one-bedroom property which I hoped would entice her to stay away from her abuser longer, but she didn't even call to say she was okay.

"Okay, talk," Sophie says, her reddish-blond hair spilling every which way from a messy bun. She's waiting for me to pass her a plate. I pick up the pace and rinse the one I was holding onto for too long.

"It's nothing."

She cocks up an eyebrow. "Is it Connor?"

"No. Connor's great. Not sure where this three-way play is going, but that's not an issue." I start soaping up another plate. Everyone else is still in the dining room, chatting and laughing and making me feel stupid for being unable to stop worrying.

"You sure it isn't, Mathias?" Sophie nudges me with her hip.

I sigh. She's my best friend, but ever since she met Damien and fell head over heels for him, she thinks all problems originate from

37

misunderstandings in relationships. It doesn't help that she is right most of the time.

"It's just work. A client missed an appointment."

"Does that happen often?"

"Yes and no. That client is very punctual. If she confirms, then she is always there at her allotted time, or she calls to reschedule. I'm afraid something may have happened."

"Does that happen often?" she repeats, the question now sharp like a knife.

"Well, more often than I would like. These women are always in danger."

She presses her lips together. "Like you."

"I'm not in danger." My brows furrow.

"I saw your car art."

"Oh." I look down at the soapy mess in the sink. I don't know what to say.

"It hasn't even been three weeks since the last time it got keyed. I know you don't have money problems but come on. Someone is clearly out there trying to hurt you." She gets angrier and angrier with each word, drying a plate in ferocious circles.

"You will break it." I put my wet hand on her dry, pale one. "I'm not in danger. People who do that are cowards. Why key my car when they could key me?"

I wiggle my eyebrows and grin. Sophie shakes her head, but her features soften. She likes using her new power to protect her friends and family. She's always looking for ways to get involved, but breaking and entering, threats, blackmail, and violence are a set of problem-solving options that I don't want to entertain.

"What's her name? I can get some guys to go and check out her address; see what her boyfriend is doing," she says.

"You know it would be unethical to tell you that."

We continue washing dishes in strained silence. I'm back to worrying about Cindy.

"I can get Lu-Na to see if there are any cameras around the domestic violence center. If you give me a timeframe, maybe we'll be able to see something."

I hesitate. I want to know what happened. Or maybe if someone has been loitering outside. We don't have cameras for privacy
reasons, but the shops around might. Maybe a car with a black box
drove by or something.

"Can Lu-Na even do that?" I ask. "Are they like a team of hackers or something?"

They've been a mysterious force assisting Sophie and Damien
on their quest to reclaim the gang they currently run. Everyone has
evaded all my questions so far about Lu-Na. It's almost as if they
don't exist.

"Something like that. Just think of them as the IT fairy."

"Okay. Ask them to have a look."

I'm still anxious about Cindy, but my tacos don't sit so sharply
in my stomach anymore. I can finally relax a bit and digest.

CHAPTER 9

Tanya is playing that annoying match-three game on her phone. Damien is swirling some wine around his glass like he's a connoisseur, which he's not. Hana and Sophie are laughing in the kitchen. The kids are scrolling social media together. It all sounds utterly fine, but I'm on my last tether.

"I need to tell Hana," I blurt out after I can't hold my words anymore.

"She doesn't want to know," Tanya says. Her confidence has reached a new high after she became the manager at Love and Err, the club that is the base of Sophie's gang operations.

"Did something happen?" Damien finally takes a sip of his wine, making a face like it's too bitter as he swallows. He's, as always, straight to the point.

"I noticed people being moved around when they should stay put. As well as discharged patients who were in no condition to be out of the hospital." I rest my head in my hands, my elbows propped up on the table. The tacos I convinced everyone to get tonight left a bitter taste in my mouth. Not because the food was terrible but because I had to endure an hour of chewing noises and small talk when all I wanted was to talk about my undercover work. But everyone seemed so calm and content to be together that I bit my tongue and almost swallowed my tacos whole.

Hana didn't look too enthused either, but maybe that's because Connor decided not to stay. I'm happy he didn't. He's not one of us, really, no matter how well he kisses. The core of the gang will always stay the same. Sophie and her sister Melanie; Damien and his son Thomas; Tanya; Lu-Na and me.

Hana knows what we do but doesn't want to be part of it. But as Sophie's best friend, my play partner, and a former guardian of the teenagers, she gets a sure seat at the table. Connor doesn't.

"You look like you're having grumpy thoughts." Thomas walks past the table and grabs an apple from the fruit bowl.

I try to relax my face. "Get one for Melanie," I say, sounding more like a stern teacher than a fun uncle. This undercover shit is going to give me an ulcer.

"Already asked, doesn't want one." He gives me another once over. "Do you want one? To keep the doctor away and all that?"

I chuckle. "Why would I want to keep myself away from myself?"

Thomas shakes his head, but a smile is playing on his lips. He never fails to cheer me up.

When he's away from earshot, Damien speaks. "So you have patients that are not supposed to be out and about?"

"Yes, seems so."

"Are you sure they're out?" he asks.

"No," I reply, drawing out the 'o', his conclusion slowly coming to me too. "They're still inside the hospital."

"According to what the Empress told us, the top three floors are for the VIP clients and management. The basement isn't ac- counted for either, but Lu-Na found that there should be an old crematorium down there somewhere from when the building was a psychiatric asylum."

"Spooky," Tanya says without looking up from her phone.

My tacos lurch in my stomach. "You won't make me go down there, right?"

Damien smiles one of his gorgeous smiles, reminding me of the one-sided crush I harbored for him for years.

"We'll try to find more on our end, but for now, maybe check out some records. See what trail those missing patients leave on file. If there's restricted access, take some photos, and Lu-Na will sort it out."

"Okay, that sounds doable." The ache in my stomach doesn't go away. "Are you both sure it's okay to keep Hana in the dark for this? Maybe she could offer some insight too."

"Anyone can offer insight," Tanya says, finally making eye contact with me. Her piercing blue eyes meet mine. "Not anyone has the courage to ask their friends to keep them in the dark so they can uphold their morals and be the best advocate for their clients. Respect that."

I press my lips together, feeling like a child who just got told off. I nod, although Tanya has already gone back to her game.

Damien pats me on the shoulder. The touch that would have sent shivers down my spine before is distant and unfamiliar. I understand what I should do and why I should keep the details of my investigation under wraps. And yet I want to reveal it to Hana because not talking about it feels like I'm erecting a wall between us, each day is a brick, and each week is a row complete. And why would I build a wall when all I want is to keep seeing her beautiful smile?

CHAPTER 10

It's Friday night, and my mind is split in two. Usually, I leave work thoughts on my way out of the office. Not today. I'm at the Moon Garden, the BDSM club which boasts it can help people loosen their grip on reality. Most Fridays, it works. Most Fridays, I can think about nothing else, imagining how I'll be wrapped up tight in rope and pain, my senses assaulted by loud music and the smell of naked bodies moving together.

"My client didn't come to the rescheduled appointment today either," I tell Sophie as I slip out of my shirt and bra. "I'm truly starting to worry. Her phone goes straight to voicemail."

Sophie is already changed into a little black skater dress, barely covering her ass. She nods and narrows her eyes. "You might want to finish dressing up before I show you this."

She waves her phone in the air with a grave expression.

"Oh, no." I kick my trousers off and slip into a black bodystocking, intricate weaved patterns making me look covered while I feel anything but. A chill creeps up my spine as I close the locker and look at Sophie. *Please don't let her be dead.*

A trio of women comes in, giggling and poking fun at one another, their mood in stark contrast with our own. I grimace as Sophie takes my hand, leading me to one of the bathroom stalls. We shuffle in, and she plays me a video.

At first, there's nothing, just the parking lot and the unmoving cars in various shades of gray. Then Cindy goes out of the building and lights a cigarette. I glance at the time stamp. Monday, right after our session. Smoke billows around her as she smokes, her foot tapping on the ground faster and faster. She shouldn't be smoking after such a big operation. She should be in bed resting.

"Is that it?" I ask, my patience wearing thin.

"Keep watching," Sophie says.

Another minute of rhythmic smoking passes, then two men approach Cindy. I gasp as one of them catches her by the back of the neck, like a scruffy kitten, and pushes her toward the edge of the frame. The other one takes her bag away and throws whatever is left of the cigarette to the ground without putting it out. Then they disappear off-screen.

"Did they take her?" I rewind the video, rewatching the last few seconds again and again.

"Lu-Na believes they did. But we don't have a plate number or a car description. There's no sound. But I sent some men over to your workplace, and they had a look around. There are no signs of a body there. We have to treat her as a missing person."

"I must call the police." I scramble to my feet, feeling stupid in my sexy outfit. "Can I give them this video?"

"Look here." Sophie pauses on a video frame and enlarges the image until a pixelated hand with a distinctive tattoo shows. It looks like an 'x' with little triangles at the end of each endpoint.

"Is this one of your rival gangs?" If it is, the police probably won't be able to help much.

"No, we're not sure what it is. But it is definitely some organized crime shit because check this out." She shows me a picture of three men sitting at a bar, all three of them sporting the same hand tattoos. "This was in one of the Arcana bars. We asked the

Empress if she knew anything, and she said she would look into it too. Apparently, they caused a scene and were kicked out that night. Whoever they are, they're bad news."

"Shit." I'm at a loss for words. So far, I've logged Cindy's absences and notified the center director, but other than that, no one knows she's missing. "Will alerting the police help or put her in more danger?"

"You know my opinion on the police," Sophie replies.

"What about those nice detectives that worked with you and Damien on the case of the missing girls last time?" I don't trust the police either, but if there's a chance they could be helpful to Cindy, I am obliged to exhaust all options.

"Carl retired, and Ayisha got moved to some other department as a reward for solving that case. But you know, it's worth a try. I will send you their details." Sophie pulls me into a hug. I stare at the cubicle wall as we both try to relax. Someone has written, 'Lose your fake nails in my cherry pie' and it makes me smile.

"I don't know if I should stay tonight or if I should call the detectives right now and try to arrange a meeting," I say into Sophie's soft hair.

She squeezes me tight. "How about you call them, arrange a meeting for a hospitable time, then stay and unwind. I've got people already looking for your client, and Lu-Na and the Empress are looking into the tattoo guys. My phone's on me, so if anything changes, I will let you know. You've had a tough week and deserve to have your weekly reset. Your other clients deserve you at your best too."

"And this is why you're my best friend." I poke her in the ribs as we go out of the toilet.

She jumps a bit and shoots me a mock glare. "And here I thought it was because I was good at rope."

"That too."

The locker room is once again empty. I take my phone out of the locker and dial Ayisha Montgomery. If anyone on the police force would be willing to listen, it would be her.

I'm dangling in the air, my hands behind my back, my head bowed under its own weight. When Connor pulls the rope attached to my ankle, I grunt in relief. My leg flying high takes the pressure off the intense hip harness that digs into my legs' insides and bends my lower back at an impossible angle. The chest harness limits my breathing so that all I can focus on is that rhythm of getting air in and out of my lungs. Mathias is sprawled on the floor below me, watching us. He's running a flogger across his palm in a promise of pleasure and pain. His eyes bore into mine, and I drown in his gaze, his blue irises darkening like a turbulent sea in a summer storm. The way he's looking at me makes me feel exposed, seen in an intimate but intrusive way, so I close my eyes and continue breathing. That's all I have to do right now.

Not much happens in my mind as I get lost in the scene. It's not as intense as last Friday's, so I wrap myself into the sensations that Connor and Mathias bestow upon me and stay warm and safe. Nothing penetrates the bubble of contentment of just being physically alive.

I breathe in and out until the clouds of my mind part, and I'm covered in a blanket, given water and shoulder rubs. Cradled and snuggled and stroked like a small child. My high is slowly replaced with tiredness, and the bubble doesn't burst but evaporates like it's never been.

I run through next week's appointments in my head, which is a bad habit. On Monday, I have another appointment with Cindy. I've arranged for Ayisha to come visit at the same time. If Cindy comes, she can share her experience with another Black woman. I doubt she'll show, though, so I can use the hour to fill Ayisha in and look at legal options. And if she can't offer me anything, maybe I'll take Sophie up on her offer and have her gang visit Cindy's guy.

I've had clients miss appointments before but never like that. Never have they been kidnapped minutes after they were sitting next to me. My mind runs away with this, and I start imagining stuff. What if I had gone out earlier? Maybe I could have stopped them or alerted someone. What if I had stayed with her longer? What if I was smarter and didn't let her leave until I checked the parking lot was safe? What if she didn't stop for a smoke but instead went straight to the accommodation?

"Is that okay?" Connor's last three words register, but not the few sentences before. I have no idea what he's asking about. I'm lying across Mathias's lap while he plays with my hair. Connor puts his ropes back in his rope bag, looking like he's about to leave.

"I wasn't listening," I say, my filter gone as per usual after a scene.

"Daniel wants me to spot him while he ties Hayley. He's brought a new friend and wants to impress him, apparently. But, like, safely."

"Ah, that new guy Callum, was it?" Mathias brushes a stray lock of hair out of my eyes. "They're quite the trio."

"Not as hot as us, though." Connor winks and I smile at that. We're pretty hot.

"We'll be fine here. Go," I say.

"Don't have too much fun without me." He bends down to give me a little forehead kiss and hug Mathias.

After he's gone, I'm instantly aware of the quietness of the room. It's so small, like a box with a soft green carpet in the middle and a horizontal bamboo pole above for suspension. It's one of the first private rooms renovated after the fire blazed through the Moon Garden a few weeks ago.

Its simplicity as if amplifies every movement Mathias makes next to me. His chest rises and falls in time with his lazy head pets. Sometimes he takes some hair in his hand and twirls it around his fingers. He seems so relaxed that it makes me tense.

He feels it instantly, and his fingers hover in the air above my head, an unspoken question between us. I don't want him to stop touching me, though, so I reach for the first thing that pops into my mind.

"So, Hayley got two of her professors to be her play partners. Scandalous." I smirk.

His hand returns to my hair, and my muscles relax. I shift a bit and wrap my arms around his waist, inhaling the scent of his body around mine. He smells both like black pepper and vanilla.

"Kinky relationships are amazing. There's literally no combination of partners or kinks that's too weird or unheard of. I like that," he says.

I nod. I'm not interested in talking about Hayley. Or anything. Surprisingly, my eyes drift to his clean-shaven chin, then up to his full lips. I want to kiss him. More than that, I want him to kiss me back and then push the blanket down my shoulders and take me right here on the green carpet. I want him inside me, and I don't know why.

It's such a simple desire, it knocks the breath out of me. I haven't let a man fuck me in years.

"What are you thinking about?" Mathias must have noticed the change in my breathing.

I wrap the blanket tighter around me, trying to hide my peaked nipples. I shuffle away, self-conscious about the dampness between my legs.

"About you," I say. He looks puzzled, so I quickly add, "and Connor. About us three."

"What about us?" He stretches, giving me a full view of his intricate owl tattoo and the smooth skin on his torso. He only has a tuft of hair in the middle of his chest, and it matches the owl's dark feathers perfectly, making it appear 3D.

"We're quite unconventional. Like Hayley." I reach for the bottle of water, sipping slowly, trying to buy myself more time to get my sex drive under control.

"We all should just do what makes us feel happy and fulfilled. And if that's playing in threesomes, I give my enthusiastic consent." He extends his arm toward the bottle, and I move to give it to him. "No, silly, come back so I can keep cuddling you. This bare-bones decor is making me cold, and you're the best portable heater I have access to."

I chuckle, and some of the pressure dissipates. It's just my body chemicals doing god knows what to my brain after a difficult suspension. I shuffle back into his lap, and we fit like two puzzle pieces. He embraces me, and this time, his hand finds its way inside the blanket. He draws circles on my thigh, his fingers sometimes catching on the webbing of my bodysuit. The times his hand brushes along my bare skin send small electrical currents straight to my pussy. I give up on ignoring it. It's impossible because he won't let me go without asking me what's going on, and actually, I'm content in his arms.

As that feeling builds up inside me and I finally decide to take a risk and kiss him, he speaks.

"Can I ask you a question?" His voice is a whisper across my hair. "You don't have to answer, but I've been meaning to ask it for a while, so might as well."

"Sure." It comes out like I'm not sure.

He asks anyway. "Why do you limit your sexual play to no penetration?"

Oh, boy. I intake a sharp breath.

"I don't mean it like I want to do it, I just want to get to know you better and see if I can help in some way. You don't have to tell me, in fact—" His words come out like a Gatling gun.

I put a hand on his mouth, silencing him.

"I'll tell you. I don't mind talking about it." I flash him a brave smile.

He relaxes around me, but I already know I won't be able to talk about this if I'm curled up in his lap like a pet. So I stand up and sit on the opposite end of the room. It's not very far. If we extend our legs, our feet will touch, but it gives me enough physical distance to start getting the words out.

And they're not easy words because I have to speak about my mother, my race, my ex, and the dozen schoolgirl uniforms that I burned when I swore off sex with men.

MATHIAS

CHAPTER 11

When Hana leaves my side, the air around us moves, chilly and full of floating rope fibers. I can sense she needs the space between us, so I don't follow. She looks like a Hershey's Kiss as she brings her knees up to her chest and covers herself with the blanket, her head the only thing sticking out.

"You know I'm half-Japanese." She begins her story. I nod. I won't interrupt her until she asks me an open-ended question. "I'm going to spare you the details of me growing up. It was mostly fine. I didn't have a great time being different as a child, and when my parents separated, I was sent to boarding school. In there, I was just another rich kid. They didn't care much about who my mother was as long as she paid, and she paid well. Without her around, I grew up a proud American."

She pauses then, expecting me to react. When I nod to encourage her to continue, she takes my cue.

"It was a girls academy. It was jarring after my co-ed primary school but not unwelcome. As a teenager, my first experiences with boys were pretty tame. Holding hands, sharing drinks, the occasional kiss. In the meantime, I was also 'practicing' with girls, which made me feel a certain way that boys didn't quite achieve. Now I know it's because I like both, but then I thought it was because boys my age were stupid, and I had to date men if I wanted to feel a woman."

"Oh…" The word slips from my mouth before I can stop it. I mean it like 'oh, honey,' but it comes out a bit harsher.

"I know, teenagers are dumb." Hana chuckles nervously. "We snuck out to a bar one time and met some guys there. One of them was pretty, almost like a girl, and I instantly liked him. He was very polite and had eyes only for me. Long story short, we started dating. He surprised me one day with a lotus origami. He said it looked exotic, like me. I was flattered. Then he brought me a Hello Kitty keychain. Then wrote me a letter in kanji, which I couldn't read because it had been years since I'd gone to Japanese school. The other girls started making fun of him for being weird, but I was ensorcelled. It was like he had taken a hidden part of me and brought it up to the surface. Not only that, he loved it. So when his ideas dried up, I picked up my old Japanese textbook and started teaching him about our culture."

She inhales sharply, then exhales in one loud sigh. My legs are starting to go numb, so I shift my position.

"I'm sorry, I know this is long. Like I've started from the beginning of the universe."

"I'm listening," I say, breaking my intention to be quiet. I feel like she needs reassurance.

"I was a stupid, stupid girl."

"The power of hindsight makes everyone look stupid. You were just embracing a part of yourself. But he ruined it, didn't he?"

"I still can't quite tell if it was him or me," she continues, "but it did unravel in an ugly way. We had gotten to a point where we were making out every time we were together. He started buying clothes for me, nothing kinky, just skirts and T-shirts. They were always related to some aspect of Japanese culture. We started having sex. I wasn't sure how to do it, having minimal previous experience, so I let him arrange me on the bed. I would lie there, and he would comment on my noises, telling me I sounded just like a Japanese girl. I thought it was a compliment then, but when I think about it now, I cringe."

Hana shivers, and my arms ache to hold her again. But she's close to the tipping point in the story, so I just look at her, afraid that any movement will scare her into silence.

"He went to Japan on a work trip and came back with a bunch of costumes. And you know I like dressing up, so every time we had sex, I was wearing some modified schoolgirl uniform or a Sailor Moon costume. It wasn't all happy roleplay, though. He bought me a wig one time, but I wouldn't wear it because it felt too tight on my head, so he said I was an ungrateful brat. That made me feel powerful for some reason, so I kept doing things to annoy him. He would often just spank me and tell me I was a bad girl. But once I dressed up as the woman from the 'Cherry pie' video, you know, with the small denim shorts and the non-existent top? He lost his shit, pushed me onto the bed, and said I wouldn't come that night as punishment. He kept edging me until he made me cry. 'That's what you get for acting like an American whore,' he said and left. After that, things didn't get much better, but I was resigned to acting like the young submissive Japanese girls he so clearly liked. I was in a bad mood on the night it all fell apart, and he made me wear this ridiculous cat costume. It was just black lingerie with ears and a belt with a tail. As he was grunting on top of me, he kept calling me 'neko-chan', which irked me. When we were cleaning up after, I asked him to call me by my name. And guess what?" Hana's hand comes out of the blanket in the heat of the moment. She swipes it across like she's doing a magic trick. "He didn't even know my name! And we had already been dating for a few months at that point."

"Wow." I roll my eyes.

"And when I got angry about it, he said that it was unladylike to shout like that at your lover. He said the girls he'd met in Japan would never speak to him that way and stormed out." She pauses, her eyes focused on the middle distance. "I stopped seeing him after that. He left me with an identity crisis and the firm belief that I was only good to men if I behaved like a 'proper Japanese lady'. I tried going out with guys for some time, after I thought I had gotten over most of the experience, but every time a guy would start grunting on top of me while he was inside me, I could hear 'neko-chan' in my head, and all my insides turned. Thus, I made my 'practice' buddies my priority and slept with girls exclusively."

I don't know what to say. Her story sits so big between us that I have no clue how to proceed. Do I ask her more? Do I steer the conversation in another direction? Do I keep quiet?

My mouth makes the decision for me.

"I'm sorry that happened to you. I could have never imagined it was something so twisted."

She rubs her eyes as if she's waking up from a long dream. "It's in the past. I've learned to cope. Oh, and I burned all those uniforms and costumes he bought me. It was all Polyester shit, so it stunk up the neighborhood for a week."

Maybe she needs to try again. I'm sad that her sexual experiences with men are defined by that horrible memory. But I keep quiet. She hasn't asked me for an opinion, and if she decides to try again, the decision has to come from inside her.

"Names and nicknames can be triggering. I don't like being called Mat or Matty. It's not my name. How do you prefer people to call you?" I ask.

"Hana is fine. It's familiar, and people don't have issues understanding it."

"But you're called Hanako."

"It means 'flower child'. When people call me Hana, they essentially call me a flower. It's not so bad."

"But you didn't answer the question."

She presses her lips in a thin line. Not in anger but in amusement at my persistence. "I prefer Hanako."

"I will call you that from now on. It's a beautiful name. Do you know my last name is Flores? That's 'flowers' in Spanish."

She smiles. "I didn't know that. It seems we're right at home here in the Moon Garden, happy and thriving."

"Can I give you a hug?" I ask.

"Yes," she says with a soft chuckle.

I don't move toward her, only open my arms, and let her come to me. Which is how this thing between us will always be as far as I'm concerned. I want to override her bad memories with good ones, whether sexual or not. I want her to want to take a step in my direction and know I will be there, ready to welcome her.

There is a slight sting in my heart as my conviction plays out in my mind. I waited so long for Damien, and he took a step sideways toward Sophie. He never did make it to where I was standing with my open arms. Why do I think this will be any different?

Hanako crawls on all fours to me, the blanket making her look like the cutest turtle ever. She settles down in my lap and covers both of us. Is that a step in my direction, or is it wishful thinking?

I don't tend to use the word 'perfect,' but there is no other way to describe tonight. The scene with Hanako and Connor exceeded my expectations, the memories of it keeping my dick in a semi-hard state all evening. And while the image of Hanako's lithe body is etched in my mind's eye, her honesty has branded my heart. I thought I liked her before, but now, I'm sure. This affinity toward her is now a full-fledged crush. And with the pace of how my feelings have progressed, I run the grave risk of being the willing participant in a one-sided love again.

As we climb the stairs to our apartment, I debate telling her all of this. I never told Damien about how I felt, and maybe that's how I wasted my chance. Maybe Hanako likes me too.

"Wasn't it funny to watch Connor facepalm when that new guy just wasn't getting his instructions?" Hanako's voice is bubbly, with a lightness that comes from a time well spent.

"To be fair, his explanations sucked. He should never teach anyone anything." It's a joke, but I feel guilty about making it. I feel more guilty about excluding Connor from our bonding time. I've been so intoxicated with Hanako's story and this new level of connection with her that I didn't consider where Connor factors in. As far as I'm concerned, he's someone fun to play with. I'm not sure how much we actually have in common because he never volunteers up anything and I don't ask. Though, I will ask something next time. Something mundane that I'm already supposed to know. Like his profession or where he's from.

The door to the apartment opens smoothly. I oiled it yesterday because it was making a creaky noise. We shuffle in, and my eyes stop on the small black Oxfords that are neither mine nor Hana's. Before I can comment on how odd it is for there to be unfamiliar shoes in our house, I hear a female voice with a heavy accent.

"Oh, good. You are finally home. I thought I was going to fall asleep at the kitchen table."

I look up. A petite Asian woman about twice Hanako's age is looking at us. Everything on her looks expensive, from her fluffy slippers to the shawl thrown across her shoulders. Pearl earrings and fat pearl bracelets. A hairstyle that must have been done professionally and recently. A smooth, small face with minimal make-up. Her manicured hand is holding a glass of wine, lazily swirling it around as she leans on the hallway's wall, the same wall that I pinned Hanako to only a week ago.

"And you have brought a date." The woman's resemblance to Hanako is uncanny.

"Mama?" Hanako is frozen in place. "What are you doing here? Mathias, this is my mother, Tomoko Yagi."

I extend my hand, and she looks at it like it's a piece of garbage on the street. I pull it back and do a slight bow, looking at Hanako for aid. She's not looking at me at all, fumbling with her bag instead and taking out her phone.

"You didn't say you were coming," Hanako says as she struggles to unlock her phone.

Her mother lifts a drawn-on eyebrow. "It was a surprise. Clearly an unwelcome surprise."

My ears burn. I've lost my ability to speak, so I give Hanako's shoulder a light tap in encouragement and shuffle past Mrs. Yagi, aiming for my room.

When I go in, I see three suitcases and a few transport packaging tubes. I don't think this is my room anymore. *Shit.*

HANAKO

CHAPTER 12

My post-play brain can't process this. I get the urge to walk up to my mother and embrace her. Then I get the urge to scream. It has been years since I last saw her. Months since I heard her voice. Weeks since I got a message.

I take off my shoes. I take more time than I usually do. I'm stalling. A spark of anger makes me glance her way. Why does she think it's okay to let herself in unannounced in my home? Yes, the apartment was initially hers, but she did gift it to me. My name is on the deed.

She's looking at me with a relaxed face, still leaning on the wall like she hasn't got a care in the world. I know it's just a facade. She will have a lot to say in a minute.

After I put on my slippers and shed my overcoat, we go to the kitchen wordlessly. No hugs. I make myself a cup of mint tea preemptively. I will need to be calm for this.

"So, who is this man?" She starts the second my butt touches the seat of the chair.

The desire to embrace her is long gone, replaced by a dull fear.

I don't know what I'm afraid of. Everything, honestly. There is nothing in my life that my mother would approve of.

"Mathias. He's my roommate."

"Do you need money?" Confusion paints her face. She sends me money every month despite me telling her I don't need it. It goes into a savings account, for I don't know what. Rainy days, I suppose.

"It's not because of the money," I say, reaching for words that will make her not ask questions. I reach and fail. "He's not a lodger. It's complicated."

"Is he your boyfriend?" She raises a disapproving eyebrow.

"No."

"You said you were focusing on your career last time we spoke." She takes a small sip of her wine without breaking eye contact with me.

"I am."

"Is this man part of your career plans?"

I sigh. "His name is Mathias. He needed a place to stay."

"For what reason?"

"Personal reasons." I roll my eyes. How can I tell her it was so we could look after two teenagers while our respective best friends were busy with a gang war? I can't even tell her it was because we wanted to see what it would be like, whether we could live together while playing with Connor.

"Hanako! You know I don't like it when you roll your eyes."

"Why are you here, Mama?" I change the subject before we fight.

"I wanted to come see my child. I did not expect my child would not be happy to see me." She stands up to top off her wine.

"I *am* happy to see you." My voice is quiet, so she probably thinks I'm lying. I'm not, though. I just wished she'd warned me. It's not like her to show up like this, so I wonder if there's anything wrong. I want to ask, but the words won't come out. My thoughts stray to Mathias, who is hiding in his room, usually the guest room. Is he okay in there?

"We discussed you dating a Japanese man before," my mother says. "It is not proper for you to be living with a man who is not your husband or partner."

I try very hard not to roll my eyes again. "And I thought we agreed that I'm focusing on my career, and I'm not interested in marriage."

She purses her lips in obvious displeasure. As the silence stretches and I sip my tea, tiredness tugs at my shoulders. I'm slouching in my chair, my legs crossed, my arms tucked close to my body like I'm a sad shrimp.

Here are three things Mama doesn't know about me: that I'm pansexual, that I'm kinky, and that I don't do closed monogamous relationships. And here are three things that she believes I need in order to have a good life: a self-sufficient career, a Japanese husband, and respectable, culturally appropriate hobbies, like ikebana or shodo. I don't think shibari would qualify, but I haven't asked.

In any case, we agree on very little when it comes to the direction of my life. I know she wants what she thinks is best for me, so I mostly let her have her dreams as long as she leaves me alone. But coming here unannounced and scaring Mathias into his room pushes that boundary.

"I do not think you want to talk to me tonight," she concludes out of nowhere.

"Is everything all right?" I finally get my question out. "You know, with your art and health. The galleries?"

"Everything is fine," she responds quickly. "I missed you. But I have to admit I was not expecting any of this. I'm disappointed."

"By what?" The words slip out high-pitched. I'm gripping the now-cold mug with a familiar tightness in my throat. I'm about to cry, like a child.

"Coming home late with a man, looking disheveled." She runs a hand through the air in my direction. I'm dressed in an oversized hoodie and leggings. Comfort clothes because my whole body aches. My chest aches now too, but it's nothing to do with the rope I did tonight. She takes my silence as an invitation to continue, ignoring the tears welling in my eyes.

"When I was looking for a glass, I saw the state of your cupboards. This is not you. You are tidy. And there is stuff all around that does not belong in this apartment." She points to the wooden rack of Mathias's collection of tumblers. "You do not drink spirits, do you?"

I'm lost for words. One traitorous tear slips down my cheek. My mother follows its path, then flicks her gaze back to my eyes.

"I'm going to sleep in the hotel across the street. I hope we can speak tomorrow after we have both calmed down."

I manage a nod. I won't be able to convince her to stay, and I'm not going to kick Mathias out so she can sleep in the guest room. The cabinet in my room is still full of sex toys, so I can only hope she hasn't been there yet. If she had, she would have added it to the list of reasons for her disappointment.

She hesitates on her way out of the kitchen. For a moment, I think she will come and give me a hug. She doesn't, she just shakes her head and goes to collect her luggage.

She exchanges a few curt words with Mathias while I sit frozen in my chair.

My eyes stray to the painting on the opposite wall. A massive poppy flower takes center place in it, each of the petals depicting a different scene. It's a replica of the painting that was my mother's breakout success.

In the first petal, a girl in a yukata is playing with a kite, surrounded by fireworks. In the next petal is a woman with thick black hair standing next to a man taller than her, painted with pink skin and yellow hair, sakura blossoms all around them. Next is the same woman with a torn kimono, curled up in a ball, threatening hands pointing at her from each direction.

The critics assumed this depicted a broken marital relationship, maybe abuse, maybe some cultural misunderstanding because the last petal features the woman alone with a baby, a sunflower painted behind them.

I know that interpretation is wrong. She never corrected them because it elevated her standing in the art community. The universality of the experience of a woman suffering because of a man was more relatable than the truth.

I stare at that third petal, feeling every bit as alone as the dark-haired woman. After my mother fell in love with my father, an American, and agreed to follow him to the USA so he could keep his job, her family disowned her. She never went back to Japan. I never met my maternal grandparents.

After she separated from my father, she told me sunflowers symbolize hope. She talked about the painting while sipping on wine. Proud and happy and free. On an evening much like this one. She told me I was her flower child, the one that brought her joy when everyone abandoned her.

Then she abandoned me.

My eyes leave the painting to look at the drooping sunflower at the windowsill. Not looking very hopeful, but that will change in the morning. So when I think about Mathias and how much he cares, about how he hid away like this wasn't his home too, I'm embarrassed by my mother. Embarrassed, and disappointed, too.

CHAPTER 13

I have no idea what to do in this situation. Hanako didn't mention at any point during our few months of cohabitation that her mother might be in the picture. She was in Europe somewhere until she wasn't. Now she's here.

I pace back and forth, turning every couple of steps and making myself dizzy because the room is small and I'm tall. I navigate around Mrs. Yagi's luggage, careful not to move it even an inch. She seemed stern, and while I'm way past the age where others can tell me what to do, I feel like if she told me to get all my things and move out tomorrow, I would do it.

I sit on the bed and stare at the door. I stand up and look at the painting on the wall opposite, a big red cross with some flowers blooming on it and happy and sad faces instead of petals. I lean against the wall. The walls are pale beige, so the red cross and its blue background stand out. I press my palms to my face; it feels hot under my touch. I can't stand to look at that painting, so I turn my back on it and stare at the door again.

During all this, I could hear the Yagis talk in the kitchen. Nothing I could make out, but the few words and long pauses told me it couldn't have been a happy chat. Should I go and check? I'm lucky I went to pee before leaving the Moon Garden; I've been hiding here a while.

I move to the desk where I have all my metalworking works in progress. I used to have a separate room with the large equipment back in my house, but now all that is in a room in Love and Err's subbasement. I haven't created anything extensive and elaborate since I started spending time undercover in the hospital.

I have a few raw rings, so I pick up one and rotate it in my fingers while pondering what I want to put on it. I prepare my handpiece as an image takes shape in my mind.

Just as I'm about to start, the door swings open, and Mrs. Yagi comes in. She doesn't look happy.

I stand up, knocking my desk and sending parts flying everywhere. Her face softens. Does she pity me?

"You live here?" she asks.

"Yes, nice to make your acquaintance, Mrs. Yagi." I don't offer her my hand this time though I do bow my head a bit. It's almost a submissive gesture. I don't know if she notices because I'm already looking down at her, almost twice her height.

"What do you do?" She glances at my desk.

I'm unable to reply for a moment. What should I say? Something that won't make Hanako look bad. "I'm a medical doctor by education."

Mrs. Yagi looks pleased. "Which hospital?"

"I'm between jobs at the moment." I scratch my head. I should have said I was a locum or something. It's not like I can give her the name of the hospital I'm trying to destroy from the inside out.

She looks less pleased now, one of her brows raised. I'm beginning to get very familiar with that expression.

"Are you and my Hanako together?"

"No, ma'am."

"Don't call me that."

I think I've offended her, but before I can apologize, she raises her hand, palm open, and stops me.

"What do you prefer to be called?" I ask instead.

"Does not matter. I do not expect we will see much of each other after tonight." She shakes her head and bends down to grab a suitcase.

Her words sting but I don't show it. I reach down to help her. She shoots me a look that stops me in my tracks.

"I understand that you're not happy with my presence. Still, let me help you move your luggage. If not for me, then for my parents. They always taught me to respect and help my elders, no matter the circumstances." As I say this, an alarm bell goes off inside my head. They told me that when I was ten. I'm not ten anymore, and this scary lady is not that old.

"Good." She crosses her arms in front of her chest and looks at me expectantly. Okay, that didn't offend her. I'm so confused.

"Where do you want them?" I take one with each hand. They're not very heavy, probably only half-full.

"Down to my car." She walks out of the room, stopping any questions before they are even asked.

I have many. Like, where is Hanako? Why is Mrs. Yagi leaving? Did I cause this?

"I can free up the room for you," I say to Mrs. Yagi's back.

"No need." She doesn't turn around.

Hanako is in the kitchen, sitting at the table still as a statue. She felt so close to me tonight like our hearts were beating to the same rhythm. Now she's far away, an unspoken issue growing between us.

I want Mrs. Yagi to like me so Hanako can be herself again. I go down twice and fill the trunk of an expensive hired car with suitcases, only to receive a curt 'Go back up'.

I take the elevator, unable to shake the feeling that I'm lacking something fundamental. I've seen adults and children open wide at the operating table, people dead and people dying but never have I felt so inadequate as when Hanako's mother raised her eyebrow at me. For a little lady, she's terrifying.

CHAPTER 14

The first sip of my caramel macchiato tastes divine. There's nothing quite like treating myself to a nice cup of coffee on Monday morning. I hope for a quiet day as I walk into the office.

My boss is perched on my desk, his ass almost pressing on the spacebar of my keyboard. There is a chair in front of him and one next to it, but no, he wants to assert his dominance by sitting on my things.

I take another sip of coffee, bracing myself for whatever manager bullshit is coming. *I love my job*, I tell myself. And it isn't a lie. I simply don't love who I work with.

"I know you haven't booted up yet, but don't bother. I was just on the phone with the Comet International IT team."

"They don't have an IT team, that's why they hired us." I can't help myself.

"They do now. Maybe you spurred them into action by ignoring their request for reasonable adjustment of the software," my boss says.

I ignored their email last week, and they've decided to get my boss involved. Clients from hell, that's what they are.

"It wasn't reasonable," I mutter under my breath.

"It's in the contract that we will endeavor to make any changes they need, so the software meets their business needs." My boss points his meaty finger at me and wiggles it in time with his words.

I get the overwhelming desire to turn around and leave. Instead, I try to explain my inaction.

"They want to delete medical records. This is illegal. I gave them the option to archive them, but they weren't happy."

"Code it so they can do whatever they want with their data."

"It's medical records, though. People's health. Not their data. It doesn't sound right." My ears burn now, anger rising to the surface. I should research what protections I would have as a whistleblower. This isn't okay.

"Are you the moral police?" My boss inclines his head like he can't believe what I'm saying. I don't respond, and he nods. "Didn't think so. So grab your hot chocolate for adults and drive to the hospital."

"Is there anything I can say so that you take my side on this one case?" It's barely nine in the morning, and I'm already exhausted.

"Nothing." My boss looks triumphant. Can I quit? I probably can, but he'll just make someone else go and include that ridiculous option in my code. Hell no.

Hale-Bopp Health is a hospital I knew nothing about until a few months ago when I started developing their records system. I asked to see their existing IT infrastructure, and the Director only smiled. He presented it as a big, exciting project that would propel Comet Healthcare into the hospital business.

As I walk through the main doors, I don't see anything that would make them that interesting. It's a hospital. There's a reception, staff, and patients.

Two men in suits come to greet me, both with short buzz cuts and bulky bodies. They look like businessmen on steroids.

"Mr. Jones, right?" The one on the right says, placing a hand on my back and navigating me toward a staff elevator before I can confirm my identity

"Yes. And you are?" I don't like the look of them. Laura always said I'm a jumpy guy, always ready to see danger where there is none. But right now, I really want to jump away from these two.

"We work for Crossfire Security. We're helping Mr. Rogers with various projects around the hospital. Currently, we're overseeing the implementation of the IT system you have so kindly developed," the one on the left says.

Big words, but I'm not feeling them. Both men look like they work more with their bodies than their minds.

They force me into the elevator with the sheer force of their presence. Both are taller and bigger than me, and I'm not too fond of that. When they press the minus-three level, my stomach drops. I don't like going into basements with scary-looking people either. I should've quit my job today. I don't want to quit life, instead.

I make a wise decision to keep my mouth shut all the way down. When the elevator doors open, there are bright lights, a hallway, and more doors than I can count. We walk forward, and I'm thankful nothing is flickering because I'm already on my last tether.

The journey inward is long enough for the shadows around the doors to start looking like the faces of my usual demons. Their twisted expressions remind me that I deserve whatever is coming. That this day is a result of my actions so far.

I rub my ring with my thumb, rotating it like always while summoning a memory of Laura for comfort. I remember how she went into a whole academic discussion about why she doesn't like pie, and I'm halfway through her argument about the texture of the crust when I'm pushed down to sit in front of a computer.

I'm in the hospital server room, an environment so familiar it should have been soothing. But no, it's unlike any hospital IT infrastructure I've seen before - it's sleek and modern, perfectly organized. It's discordant with my expectations, and that stresses me even more.

"You didn't reply to the email from last week, so now we will encourage you to use your deft fingers and write a deletion option into our software," says the man who's clearly more eloquent. Not that I like what he's saying.

"There is a robust archive algorithm." I don't know where I find the balls to speak back.

"It is not what we want. Do what we say, and you'll go home," the other man says.

"Are you threatening me?" The fact that this stupid question rolls out of my mouth is embarrassing enough. The fact that I also try to stand up and leave crosses a line.

They both reach for a shoulder and shove me back onto the chair. Their hands are still on me as one of them presses his foot lightly on mine.

"We don't have to make this more complicated than it has to be," he says.

I look down at his steel-capped boot. Is he going to step on me? I huff a laugh at the mental image, then instantly regret it. He doesn't just step on me. He crushes my foot under his with all his strength. I try to weasel away, more from the shame of being tortured in this pathetic way than the actual pain.

"In case you thought that was all my strength, it wasn't," he continues. "If you do what we want now, you will go back with a bruised foot. If you decide to be a smartass again, it will be broken."

My mouth is so dry it hurts when I swallow. "I'll do it. Please let me go so I can use the keyboard."

They let me go. I can breathe a bit easier now, but a shake has started in my torso. I don't bother hiding it as I boot up my program and get into the code.

"Don't think of doing anything funny because we will check. And if we find something weird, you won't walk out of here." This is said by the more brutish of the two, but I'm numb now. I've reached peak fear. What more do they want from me?

As I start working, my mind fuzzy with a mixture of coding problem-solving, Laura's pie hang-ups, and terror, I get into a sort of a zone. It's why I do what I do - because I'm good at it and because it silences my demons and the world.

From that haze, questions flood my thoughts. What does it mean that I won't be able to walk out of here? Because my feet would be broken or because they would kill me? How would they check if I did something weird? Probably run a few reports and see if the records they want to be deleted come up. But how would they know if they're truly deleted?

They wouldn't know. Because if they could do this themselves, they would have. They wouldn't be torturing the IT guy. They won't know. Not if I don't tell them.

My fingers start working faster, the lines of code blinking to life, character by character. This might never matter. But maybe, just maybe, if someone like me needs to find information that is supposed to help justice be served, for whatever reason, it will be there, hidden.

I don't know what is going on in this hospital, and I don't want to know. But I'm not going to be part of covering it up.

I keep shaking, but now the adrenaline of fear mixes with that of excitement and rebellion. They won't know because I know what I'm doing, and they don't.

"It's finished," I say in a quiet voice, trying to keep my pride out of it. The solution was so simple and so perfect that I could literally cry. However, I keep my emotions bottled up. Hell knows it's something I'm very good at.

The eloquent guy proceeds to delete several records in front of me, using the shiny red 'Delete' button, which only archives records and makes them inaccessible for the search and report functions. It means if the patient comes back, the hospital won't ever find their history – yet it also means that whatever they want to erase is only hidden. Ready to be uncovered should someone with code knowledge investigate it.

I try to remember the names of these people. It strikes me as odd, that they're all female names: Maria, Penny, Lucinda, Elisaveta. They don't remain on the screen long enough for me to remember their last names or birthdays.

The guy runs a few reports and types in the search bar. Nothing comes up, as expected.

He pats me on the back. "Good work. Let us escort you upstairs."

I start to get up and tell them that I'm fine on my own when shooting pain in my foot makes me stumble. The brute catches me, grinning.

"Maybe you should use our service and get that checked, just in case."

Bruised, my ass. I can't put any weight on my foot. There's probably a fracture there. But I keep quiet and let them help me up.

By the time I've made it into the elevator, a thin layer of sweat has coated my brow. I can't drive like this. I will have to call a taxi, but I sure as hell refuse to stay in this creepy hospital a second longer.

HANAKO

CHAPTER 15

Cindy isn't here. I'm not surprised, but I am upset. Detective Ayisha Montgomery is sitting next to me on the same sofa Cindy sat on last week. After I finish recounting what has happened, Ayisha takes a pointed sip of her drink.

She's dressed in dark jeans, a tank top, and a plaid shirt on top, too trendy for my office. The last time I saw her, she had her hair in cornrows but has since styled it in a high puff. She looks approachable and helpful; two things I don't find in most police officers I deal with. Despite this, her expression is now thoughtful, bordering on grave.

"Is it that bad?" I ask.

"Well, I'm struggling with what to advise you here. As a detective, I want to tell you to submit a report and let Missing Persons handle it. I work in Homicide, so I really don't want a case involving your client. But that's the thing - if you add the institutional racism I'm trying to fight against every day, I know we don't have the time to have her case go through the motions. She will likely end up in a bad state before we get anything done."

I bite my lower lip. I'm about to be angry at the world again, but I stop my outburst in its tracks. It won't be helpful. Making a decision would be helpful.

"What would you do if you were in my place?" I ask. "I don't want Sophie and the gang to make things worse for my client somehow with all the stuff they might do."

"I thought they stopped that illegal business." Ayisha raises an eyebrow.

I draw a hand in front of my mouth. Shit. "I mean, um, Love and Err is fully legal, they just—" I scramble for words, "have connections, you know."

Ayisha releases a loud sigh. "You know what, I haven't had a gang-related murder in this area since things changed, so don't tell me anything more."

She takes her gun holster off and places it on the table, then she does the same with her badge and ID.

"This is me speaking as Ayisha, who grew up poor in West Chicago." Her eyes slide to one side. "If Sophie and her connections can find your client quickly and get her out of whatever trouble she's in, I would use that opportunity.

"If you genuinely think they will make things worse, sabotaging your client's rights to get protection from the state and the law, then leave it to Missing Persons and I will try to make them work faster." She takes a deep breath, then releases it loudly, unable to hide her exasperation. "But keep in mind that after my partner Carl retired, I'm not very well-liked there. I'm a woman, and I'm Black. Microaggressions are my daily life, but they can cost someone's actual life if fellow officers decide to be petty."

My eyes are wide as I listen to this. I can't help my next question, which has nothing to do with Cindy. "Are you safe working there?"

"I am," Ayisha smiles. "Thank you for asking. I'm sorry I can't help more."

"No, you've given me options, and I respect that. But the decision isn't easy. Can I do both?"

"You can, but you might have Missing Persons sniffing around the same places as Sophie's people - wouldn't that be troublesome for them?"

"This is ultimately about finding my client. We should do our best even if it makes us uncomfortable, right?" I scratch my head, no longer sure what I'm saying.

"Just check with your friend if that's what you want to do." Ayisha starts putting her stuff back on.

After she leaves, I pace around the room with the phone in my hand. My next client comes in fifteen minutes.

I dial Sophie and tell her Cindy's details. I ask her about getting the police involved, and she's quiet for a moment, then tells me to do it.

"The stakes are too high," she says. "We know very little and if we're too slow, we'll fail Cindy. So, let's have everyone look for her. I want that guy to start feeling like there's a fire under his ass."

"Don't leave any karada, you know," I whisper into the phone.

"Any, what?" she asks. I give her a second. "Say it again."

"Karada." It means bodies in Japanese, and I don't want to say it in English because I don't know who's listening. Phones, doors, spaces in general - not as private as one might think.

I can hear her typing, probably Google translate. "Oh, okay. I wouldn't do that. Let me speak to Lu-Na and get back to you. When's your next break?"

"In an hour. Send me a message when you're ready, and I'll call you."

We hang up, and I do my hardest to concentrate on the issues of my next client. She's having problems finding work, and my not being there fully isn't helping her. I chastise myself every few minutes as I look into her case and try to find her any job opportunities. In the end, she agrees to interview for a maid job and leaves happy. I'm barely keeping my nervousness in check.

There's a message from Sophie on my phone, so I dial her number.

"Your client is at a mental hospital right now," Sophie says.

"What?" My word is a high-pitched yelp. Why would Cindy be in a mental institution? She didn't have any indication that she would benefit from such care last week. She needed real medical help and to be away from her abuser.

"I'm going to check it out today," Sophie says in an even voice. She's not losing it as I am. She's also really good at sneaking around and picking locks. I'm good at filling out forms.

"I'll come with you." I'm also good at talking to people. Maybe we can talk Cindy out of there.

"I'm not sure what the situation is there. Lu-Na couldn't hack their system. It might be dangerous," Sophie says.

"I'll bring my pepper spray."

"Okay then," she says with a chuckle. It wasn't meant as a joke. Seeing how she doesn't continue dissuading me, my determined tone must have been enough. "We'll go after you finish work. I'll meet you outside."

"Deal," I say.

The adrenaline of the decision has me pacing again. I collate all of Cindy's details and go out to bring them to the office staff so they can file a report with Missing Persons, as per protocol. I don't find anyone, so I head to the staff eating area. I can hear way too much noise coming from there. What is going on?

I'm expecting someone has a birthday, maybe an engagement. Perhaps a victim won the case against her abuser and came to give us all cookies. Maybe— No, what I see doesn't feature in my wildest imaginary situations.

My mother is here, fussing around my colleagues and some clients, urging them to eat and enjoy. At the tables in front of them is a selection of dishes from a taken-apart bento box. It's massive. I wonder if she cooked all that herself or just ordered it at some crazy expensive Japanese restaurant.

"Hanako, come," she says as she spots me in the doorway. Everyone turns to me. Faces stuffed with food and eyes full of gratitude or confusion meet mine, and I'm at a loss for words.

"What is this?" a secretary asks, pointing at one of the sections in the box in front of her.

I peer at it. "It's potato salad. Also, I need you to file a report asap, so can you do that first."

I hold out Cindy's folder, and she takes it reluctantly, getting up slowly like she's expecting someone to tell her to stay. I nod my head sideways to urge her to get a move on, and she scuttles away, glaring at me.

This whole situation reminds me of when I used to bring bento lunches to school when I was in middle school, just before I got transferred to a private boarding school, and the Japanese part of me was put to sleep.

My mother used to make me one every day, but I felt embarrassed to eat them in front of my classmates. My lunch looked nothing like theirs, and all I wanted was to not be different. In the beginning, everyone used to ask me what this is, and what that is, until I couldn't take it anymore and started eating in the toilets.

I can smell that memory, and I don't mean the food, so I take my mother's arm and drag her out of the room.

"Why are you here?"

She grimaces. "You keep asking me that. It sounds like I could be anywhere as long as it is not where you are."

I let go of her. "I didn't mean it like that. I just keep being surprised, and I don't like surprises like these."

"I only wanted to see where you work and treat your colleagues to a meal," she says, still looking offended.

"We don't do that here," I say with a sigh.

"Here where? In this workplace? In this city?" She looks me straight in the eyes. "In America?"

I look down. "I don't like to be singled out as different, Mama. Different isn't good. Different makes life difficult."

"But Japan is part of you. It is my homeland. It is yours too. Are you ashamed of me?" She takes my hands in hers.

I don't like it when she does this. It's emotional manipulation. I want to tell her that if she wanted me to love that culture, she shouldn't have left me to grow up alone in my formative years, but I keep quiet. It's not the time nor the place for this conversation.

"I'm not ashamed of you. Please don't do stuff like this behind my back in the future. This is my place of work. It's not professional to bring food in for everyone and puts me in an awkward position." I recite this in a monotone voice before guilt shuts me up. I want to be nice to her, I genuinely do, but it's not working out. Not when she keeps appearing in places when I'm not mentally ready.

"I do not like the double standard you have." She crosses her arms in front of her chest. Her expensive pearl earrings bobble as she shakes her head.

"What?" I have no idea what she's talking about.

"I heard you. With your Black lady friend and then on the phone. You are going to do something illegal."

My back goes stiff, and I grab her arm again, this time dragging her to my office and closing the door.

"Did you eavesdrop on me?" I hiss.

"It wasn't on purpose." She waves my anger off with one hand. "But I didn't raise you to be reckless like this. I do not want you to get hurt."

"You don't know the whole picture," I say. "Someone's life is on the line, and I'm responsible for them. It wasn't an easy decision. Please back off."

"Women do not charge into danger like this. You will not help your client if you get hurt, too," she says with genuine concern in her eyes. It's the only thing that keeps me from lashing out at her.

"Trust me, Mama. I'm stronger than you think. You taught me to run and hide, to accept misfortune and shrug it off. And it was a good lesson, but it's not applicable to every situation. I don't want to live like this. It doesn't serve me." I'm breathless as I finish my argument.

I feel again like I'm eleven years old, trying to get her to give me Lunchables instead of her tasty bentos. Just like then, she isn't convinced.

"I missed a lot. I barely know you anymore, so I will try harder. I cannot stop you but please, be careful, Hanako. Be smart, and if you need to run away, do not let these modern ideas about fighting stop you. Just save yourself." She strokes my arm up and down, her tone soft and motherly. There is also an undercurrent of disappointment, so I drop the subject.

"Come back to the apartment. I've freed up some bedroom space so we can sleep together," I say instead. After she left on Friday, she never came back and didn't call. I was too stubborn to do it either. I used the time to tidy up and hide away all the sex toys from my cabinet. The bedroom is so empty of anything kinky now; it's basically a virgin.

She smiles. "Yes. Wonderful. Is Mathias still going to be with us?"

Her question is loaded with something yet I'm not sure what. So, I say it as it is.

"Yes, it's his home, too."

"I see," she replies.

She's not warm about it, but she doesn't argue with me. I call that progress. Next on the agenda is saving my client and convincing Mathias not to be terrified of my mother. It will be a busy Monday evening.

CHAPTER 16

I wait until the nurse isn't looking over my shoulder to pull up the report for recently discharged patients. I open one or two, and it all looks fine. There isn't a single patient on the screen that has been discharged too early or for dubious reasons. I frown and enter the name of the patient I knew shouldn't have left the hospital. Nothing. Nothing at all. Like she was never treated here.

So I reach for my inner detective and go to the paper files, locked in a cabinet behind me. Only the most recent would be here. Every day they are moved in and out according to who's in the ward. Most are on the records level upstairs with the offices.

I look for the key, but it's not here. I'll have to wait for a nurse or admin member to return. It's lunchtime, so most of them are reheating their food in the staff area. A bowl of paperclips gives me a wild idea.

I pull out my phone and ring my lockpicking expert and current boss.

"I'm popular today," Sophie says instead of a hello. "How can I help?"

"Walk me through picking a simple cabinet lock?" I whisper into the phone.

"It will be my pleasure. Do you have a bobby pin or something you can bend?"

"Will a paperclip do?"

She chuckles. "Perfect."

Less than two minutes later, I'm shuffling through files, looking for my patient from yesterday. I didn't get to speak to her before or after the operation. She was already sedated when she came to the OR, which I thought was extremely weird.

Her file is there, on the side marked for taking upstairs. I double-check her name and enter it in the system's search bar. Nothing comes up. Is it glitching? I look for today's patient, and his record pops up without a problem.

I hear staff around the corner, chatting about church stuff. This is my cue to stop snooping. I try to lock the cabinet, but I'm not good enough, so I leave it closed and unlocked, hoping they would blame each other for the oversight. I clear the search and report history then leave before they can spot me.

The secret level. Where did they take the patients whose records got erased?

Up or down? I get into the closest elevator and stare at the buttons. Could they be VIP patients, taken up? But if they are, why would they be down here with the usual patients first?

I press the button to the top floor. I don't want to entertain the idea that they're taken to the basement levels instead, where Lu-Na think there should be a crematorium.

The doors open on the level before that, and a doctor I've never met before steps in.

"Who are you?" he asks.

"Dr. Flores, Anesthesiology." I show him my ID.

"Should you be up here?" He looks me up and down. His eyes stop on my chest as if he can see my tattoo showing through the scrubs. Or maybe he notices I'm not wearing a stethoscope. Perhaps he knows my aura is off, and I'm an impostor.

"I have a meeting with Ken," I reply, keeping my voice steady. My expression is stuck in what I hope is nonchalance.

He doesn't say anything after that. Name-dropping the Director works in typical hospitals, so I'm happy to find out it works in this damned place too.

I pretend to be replying to a message when the doors open, letting him leave first. I have no idea where I'm going. Definitely not to Ken Rogers's office, the Arcana Magician, and the son of the woman who hired me to do this investigation. She asked me to be discreet. I assume this means not bumping face to face with him.

This is precisely what happens when I finally leave the elevator and step into a corridor decorated with plants and artwork.

"You," he says as our eyes meet. "My mother's special hire."

Fuck. What do I do now?

"Come to my office." He waves for me to follow him as he passes me.

I run through potential explanations of my appearance on the top floor like a slot machine.

'I pressed the wrong button.'

'I have a message from your mother.'

'One of my patients called for me.'

'I wanted to meet you.'

I cringe a little at the last one. He's two heads shorter than me and dressed in the most boring corporate attire - a dark gray suit with a white shirt and a dark blue tie. His hair is slicked back with something that makes it look hard, like plastic. There are little specks of white on his hair and shoulders - he needs that dandruff treated soon.

When we go into his office, it smells exactly like I expected - of something heavy and expensive, overpowering to the point of sickening. It's in sharp contrast with the bleach smell of every other hospital floor.

There's a sleek glass desk in the corner of the room and a coffee table with leather sofas in the middle. He sits at the top of the table, in the only armchair in the room, and motions for me to sit on his left. The floor-to-ceiling windows reveal a stunning view of Chicago.

"I want to treat VIPs." This is what my thought slot machine stops at. Not too bad, though risky. If he asks me how I know about it, god be with me.

"My mother put you up to this?" He scratches his chin.

"No." I shake my head. He doesn't look convinced. "She was doing me a favor. I have a suspended medical license, so I needed a job that wasn't picky about that. You can check."

This sounds believable enough, right?

Ken nods. "What did you do?"

"Got into a fight with a patient's guardian." My answer comes out smoothly. It's not a lie, though not entirely the truth.

"Wow." His eyes light up, something like admiration in his expression. I thank the Empress's foresight in telling us he has a penchant for violence. "So, you want to work with the VIPs."

"Yes."

"I don't see why not. I've heard good things about your operations so far. Oh, don't look so surprised. Of course, I'm going to keep an eye on my mother's new present to me. But tell me, what does she get out of your little deal? You get to work and get paid. What about her? Are you her good little spy?"

He smiles the most sinister smile I've seen. I don't know how he came to be so creepy-looking - his mother is a lovely woman, albeit formidable. If she weren't a gang leader, she would have been perfect as a strict teacher or a grumpy baker. She's the opposite of creepy, more like a tough-love motivational person.

"I'm not a spy. I saved three of her underlings that got hurt in a recent explosion. She offered to repay me by doing me a favor." Now, this is a lie. Will he be able to tell?

"Hm. This does sound like my mother. She always did care for the little man." He continues scratching his chin and the red, flaky patch on it. Eczema, probably.

"You should see a dermatologist for that." I narrow my eyes, distracted. His numerous skin conditions put me at ease.

"Oh, I have. But it's so itchy. It will sort itself out. Anyway, if I let you work with the VIPs, you can't beat them up." He winks.

I force a chuckle out of my throat. "I won't."

"Because our VIPs are not actually the patients, more often than not they're the guardians. And their wish is our command." He raises his eyebrows, expecting me to assent to this too.

Slowly, it dawns on me. All of the patients that went missing on me were women. One trans male who had just transitioned. And they all didn't seem to be lucid enough to consent or be checked in with.

"I have had time to reflect on my suspension. I'm not an aggressive person; I won't hit anyone." The words taste bitter on my tongue. I definitely don't want to be involved in whatever this is. If my hunch is correct, it's something that will be in breach of all my doctor oaths and regulations. But I need to stay undercover. I can't fail this mission, especially if so many lives are on the line.

I need to leave this situation and report to Sophie and Damien. The Empress wanted me to discover what was happening in the hospital after it merged with Comet International. Well, the definite answer is, nothing good.

"Okay, okay. I'm not worried. Some of my best friends are violent people." He winks again, and I want to rip his eyelids off. I huff a laugh, not because I find his joke funny but because the image amuses me. Maybe I can be aggressive given the right motivation.

"Great. When do you want me to start?" I put my hands on my legs, preparing to leave.

He leans in and whispers, "Tonight."

What the hell?

"You mean after work?"

"Too soon?" He returns to scratching his chin.

"I'm not going to be in great shape. I've been working long days recently." This is an outright lie, and I hope against all hope that he doesn't pick up on it.

"Hm," he narrows his eyes, and I hold my breath for a few agonizing moments. "I respect that. Work-life balance and all, right? Sleep in tomorrow then, and come for six in the evening. One probation operation, and if the staff like you, you're in. How does that sound?"

I nod, eager to leave. "Perfect." I shoot him a fake smile.

Ken grins from ear to ear. "It would be great to have another Sleep Inducer!" He burst into a hearty laugh. "Get it? Because you induce sleep?"

I laugh with him, forcing the sound from my belly. I understand the joke, I just don't think it's amusing. I'm sure this will be the first of many disagreements between me and this walking dandelion.

Get it? Because that's a lot of dandruff. My laughter turns genuine.

HANAKO

CHAPTER 17

Sophie is in her battle clothes, all black, chosen for maximum comfort in case she needs to be bendy. Leggings, a t-shirt, and a puffer jacket. Her strawberry blonde hair is in a high ponytail with a pink cap on, covering her face from view. I'm in a black skirt and blazer two-piece, and a beige shirt. My usually comfortable pumps make my legs feel wobbly as we approach the reception of the mental hospital.

"I don't understand why we have to use the front entrance," Sophie whispers in my ear.

I shoot her a look which shuts her up. We will try the legal way first.

"Hello, how can I help?" The receptionist is a friendly brunette our age. Hope blossoms in my chest.

"I'm here to visit one of your patients. I'm her social worker and believe she may be in distress." I rummage in my bag for a business card.

"Can you let me know her full name and date of birth?"

I tell her Cindy's details. She types furiously, then frowns. "You can visit her, but she has been sedated for her safety and that of others."

"What do you mean? When I saw her last week, there were no indications of this." But as I say it, doubt creeps into my mind. She did say she wanted to fight with her partner. Her abuser. But why would then those men drag her away? This isn't adding up. The only person who can tell us what happened is Cindy herself.

"How sedated is she?" I ask as the receptionist hands us a note with the room number.

"I can't say, you will have to see for yourself. Visiting hours are going to end in 45 minutes. Please make your way out of the building when asked."

I nod and pocket the note. The room is on the third floor. As Sophie and I board the elevator, I stand next to her, stiff as a board. I don't know what state Cindy will be in, and I'm terrified. It feels both like I'm overreacting and that I've failed her. My mind jumps from one imaginary scenario to another, each worse than the previous. I hope she's whole. I hope she can speak to us. I hope we're not too late.

We stand in front of a private room. This can't be it. I'm sure Cindy can't afford insurance. She can't afford to be here, sedated.

"That's not a person who's agreed to be here." Sophie voices my concern as she slides the door open, and we take in the room.

It's bright, clean, and smells of fresh flowers. Cindy is lying on a bed, staring at the ceiling. She doesn't turn when we come in. There is a nightstand next to the bed. On top of it are a bible and a gorgeous bouquet of white lilies.

"This kind of stinks," Sophie whispers. "Like it's covering up something."

"Like what?" I whisper back. "Why are we whispering?"

She taps her ear. Has she spotted any hidden microphones? I feel out of my depth, so I stop talking.

I peer at Cindy's face. She wears a blank expression, a bit of drool escaping from one side of her mouth. I touch her hand, expecting her to react, but she doesn't.

"Cindy?" I whisper first, then call out her name in my normal voice. Her eyes shift to me finally, and she makes an unnatural sound like she doesn't know how to speak. There's no recognition in her features. There is a damp curl stuck on her forehead.

I press my lips, anger simmering somewhere deep in my blood. They took her baby, her uterus, and now her ability to speak? To move? Or did they take her personality? I walk to the foot of the bed and look at her chart. She's due to be discharged tomorrow.

"Come on." I pull Sophie after me as I storm out with Cindy's chart in my hand, furious. Someone better have a good explanation for all this nonsense.

I bump into a nurse. He starts to apologize, but the words die in his mouth as he sees my face.

"Is there a problem?" he asks instead.

I wave the chart in front of his face. "Why is my client here sedated? Bring her to a normal state and let me talk to her."

My request is unreasonable, but I should try.

The nurse gently takes the chart from my hands, his facial expression soft, like he's used to dealing with outbursts like mine every day. Maybe he is.

He scans the chart then shakes his head. "Lucinda is sedated for her own safety. If you can identify who you are, as well as your relation to her, I can show you the consent documents she signed a few days ago."

"She—what? Yes, I need to see those documents." I pull out one of my business cards from my bag. "Here. I'm a social worker. You can check my license online."

"But how do I know you are working with the patient?" He only glances at the card before handing it back to me.

"You want me to go get government documents that prove our involvement?" I turn around and look at Sophie, who's been quiet. She returns my look but shrugs her shoulders. I understand, she can't help me with the legal stuff. "By the time I bring you any documents, she will be discharged. I saw the date on her chart."

He only stares at me.

"Level with me. When are you discharging her tomorrow exactly? Why? I will be here with the documents before then."

"Listen, you seem to really care for Lucinda, but so does her current guardian. We are only looking after her the best way we can. I will tell you one thing, it's important that we keep her relaxed because she has an important procedure scheduled in another hospital. If you are truly looking after her, you would know that." His face is no longer friendly. He judges me. He thinks I'm a terrible social worker.

I judge him right back. How can he not tell the difference between informed and forced consent? Whatever documents Cindy signed must have been signed under duress. She was reluctant to leave, but she was not stupid. She wasn't delusional.

I open my mouth to say something and start an argument because I have nothing to prove that Cindy is my client. Do I even want to do that? Who is good, and who is bad here? Everything is suddenly twisted, like a house where you walk on the ceiling and the floor spans above you.

"We want to take our complaints up with the hospital that is responsible for her treatment." Sophie slides next to me and touches my upper arm.

"You do that." The nurse pushes past us and reattaches the chart to Cindy's bed. "We work with lots of hospitals and pride ourselves in providing the best secondary care."

"Can you tell us which one it is?" Sophie continues.

"Hale-Bopp Health. You should know that," he says.

Sophie lets go of me and walks up to him. I'm afraid she will do something rash and stupid, so I step after her. She stops me with an arm across my chest.

"We know plenty. But do you see these marks?" She points to Cindy's wrists that have fading bruises. "She was restrained."

"It happens with patients who are a danger to themselves and others." His voice isn't too assertive now.

Sophie still has her cap on low, protecting most of her face, so when she smiles, her grin looks sinister. "It happens. Like a snowstorm or burning your toast?"

"Look, ma'am, we haven't done anything outside of our primary medical duties. As you can see, the patient is not restrained now.

We've had no complaints about Hale-Bopp from the guardian, and we're essentially only providing a bed and care."

"Of course, but who gave you the right to judge her social worker? Your patient was abused and probably will be again. Yes, it seems like she's safe here with you. But what about tomorrow when you hand her over to that hospital?" She turns around to leave, grabbing my hand on the way. "Just because you refuse to see something, doesn't mean it's not there."

She pulls me down the corridor after that, and we leave the hospital in a rush that is suspicious even to me. I didn't even get to say bye to Cindy. I wrench my hand out of Sophie's and stop in the middle of the parking lot. Reluctantly, she stops, too.

"What's going on?" I ask.

"Let's get in the car, and I'll tell you."

The darkness, kept at bay by the sparse lamp posts, swirls like a predator. A sense of danger has crept up around us. I nod stiffly and follow her to the orange Honda Civic, parked right at the end, where black half-covers it like a protective blanket.

Sophie is more attuned to these situations where the tone changes. Whatever she felt back in that room, I missed. But I feel it now, looming over us like an open mouth, its dreadful stench chilling me to the bones.

We shiver inside the cold car as she starts the car and the heating.

"You don't want to know about my shady dealings, right?" She narrows her eyes at me and presses her lips together. She's uncomfortable.

"I prefer not to, but if it's important or I can help, you can tell me." I knit my brows together. Does this have to do with Cindy? Is she involved in her abduction somehow?

"Did Mathias tell you which hospital he's working undercover at?" Sophie reaches and takes my hand in hers. She hasn't said anything, but I already know where this is going. It's how she delivers bad news.

"No, but it's this Hale-Bopp hospital, isn't it? Where they took Cindy's uterus and will do god knows what tomorrow?"

Sophie's eyes widen. "They did what?"

I tell her Cindy's whole story. Some of the words feel like lumps as they come out of my mouth. I know there's no need to hold anything back. Not if the gang is involved in the dealings of that hospital. But still, breaking confidentiality makes me feel uncomfortable and icky.

After I finish, she sighs. "We need to figure out a way to stop this operation from happening."

"I have to talk to Mathias first. He's been distant these past couple of weeks. I don't think he likes working undercover," I say.

Sophie nods. "He wanted to tell you so much, but he respected your decision not to get involved. We all did."

"It was a stupid decision," I whisper. "What you said to that nurse, it was meant for me too, right?"

She starts shaking her head, but I pat the top of her hand with my palm.

"Just because I refuse to see it doesn't mean it's not there. Who knows how many of my clients have suffered in that hospital? And will continue to do so until your gang and the Arcana put a stop to it." Tears well up in my eyes. Hot tears of frustration. "You will end it, right? That's the point?"

She shoots me a sad smile, which is quickly replaced with pity. "Let me talk to the Arcana Empress. I don't think she has any idea how deep the corruption goes in her territory. I will do my best to convince her to give us more creative freedom. Mathias's mission is a recon only, but that won't cut it. We'll help Cindy, Hana, but we need to be smart about it. Chat with Mathias. He has all the inside information, after all."

We drive off, slicing the darkness with the Honda's headlights. I imagine Mathias in Hale-Bopp Health, alone, held together only by his doctor's oath, and returning home to me only to be tortured by my indifference.

We're roommates, I tell myself. We talk via exploring kink with Connor. We show our true selves then. We share food, like a family. But we are not a family. We're roommates. My mind goes round and round in circles as Sophie drives me home. I can't shake the feeling of being a horrible human for putting up this boundary between us. Yeah, we're just roommates, but it breaks my heart all the same.

CHAPTER 18

An awkward conversation with Hanako's mother is not what I need after the most stressful Monday of my life. It's not what I need, but it's what I get.

"Tell me about your parents, Mathias." She pronounces my name in a way I haven't heard in a while, similar to how my abuelita used to pronounce it. Matti-as. Like how Americans pronounce Patty. I warm up to her instantly, like she's used some sort of password that I didn't even know existed.

"I like how you say my name," I reply, which makes her frown. I didn't answer her question. "My parents and I are not close. We had a falling out some years back, and I haven't heard from them since."

I say this with a soft, rehearsed smile. That part of my life is a closed chapter. I've accepted who I am, and the price of that was accepting that my parents will never do the same. I forgave them a long time ago for my own sanity.

"That's not good," Mrs. Yagi says. She rests her chin on her fist, observing me as we sit on the table where a few nights ago I ate paper-wrapped tamales. That night seems like a lifetime ago. "Do you have siblings?"

"No, Mrs. Yagi."

"Savings?"

"I have savings." My tone is even, not because I'm happy with her intrusive questioning, but because I'm too tired to care.

"Do you have a girlfriend?" Mrs. Yagi is fast like a Gatling gun.

"No."

"What about my Hanako?"

"We're roommates." The answer comes too fast. Will she be able to tell it's a practiced answer?

"Are you sure?" She narrows her eyes. I think she can tell.

"She isn't my girlfriend." I'm too tired to lie.

Hanako and I aren't just roommates. I catch myself thinking recently, what if I started doing random little things around the house, like leaving her small presents or giving her hugs from behind while she was doing something else, like washing up or just standing there, contemplating her mother's paintings, like she does a lot. What if I put my arm around her shoulders while we watched TV or let her rest her pretty head on my lap?

I want to do it all, but a cowardly part of myself replies with vicious strength every time I get brave enough to think it. *Try it, and you'll lose her. She was clear about her boundaries, step over them and see what happens.*

As I get bitter about it all, sudden courage swells in my chest, and I ask Mrs. Yagi a daring question of my own. "What exactly is it that you dislike about me?"

She cocks her head to one side like she's giving me a chance to backtrack and apologize for my words. But I only stare back at her, waiting.

"I do not dislike you," she says. "I just do not want my Hanako to make a bad decision."

"What kind of bad decision?"

"A woman's choice in a partner is one of the most important decisions she would make in her lifetime. I am here to guide her in the right direction. I was not expecting she would have a 'room-mate' who can sabotage her future." She takes a loud sip of her coffee, the one I made her like she's proud of her answer.

Blood rushes in my head. I can feel its rhythmic swish in my ears. "And we circle back to my original question, what is it about me, specifically, that you think relates to your statement?"

Mrs. Yagi rolls her eyes. "She lives with you. No man will like that. And you are not suitable for her because of cultural differences. Hanako needs someone who will help her connect with her dual identity."

"That person should be you," I say, skipping over her other arguments. "Where were you all these years when she was supposed to be figuring out who she was?"

She gasps. "You have no respect for your elders. This, right here, is a cultural difference."

"Respect goes both ways." I sigh. My anger has given way to tiredness again. It feels silly to have this conversation without Hanako.

"I will repeat myself, Mathias. I do not dislike you. I just do not understand your place in Hanako's life and wish it was occupied by someone else." She talks slowly and gesticulates as if to drive every word home.

Despite everything, I still like how she says my name. Even Hanako doesn't say it like that. Nor does anyone else, really. Only my family used to say it like that. So I grasp onto that little positive feeling.

"I will clear out the guest bedroom for you, Mrs. Yagi, so you and your daughter can catch up in peace. I have a place I can go to."

"I appreciate that, Mathias."

I don't really have where to go, but I will crash at Love and Err. I go to pack a few things, as my heart is torn in two. If Hanako was here, would she have let me go? It would be unfair to make her choose sides. We are, after all, play partners and roommates.

I steer my thoughts in another direction as I push clothes into a large rucksack. I think of Hanako's warm body and sexy moans, of her exposed neck, and how she smells like fear and arousal.

And as if those thoughts summon her—the front door opens, and tiny feet shuffle across the corridor. She stops by the kitchen for her post-work glass of water. She's late today.

She talks a bit to her mother. Then, as I'm stuffing my phone charger in my backpack, she storms in.

"Don't leave because of my mother, please." She's upset. I freeze in place. I had thought my initiative would make her happy.

"It's okay. I will crash at Damien's." I leave the backpack on the floor and go to stand in front of her. I want to hug her but then remember her mother's words and only pet her head. Am I a bad decision? It doesn't feel like it.

"It's not okay. Listen, Mama goes to bed early. We will have dinner, then you'll come to my bedroom because we have to talk about something important." She glances at the door, then goes and opens it abruptly, as if expecting someone to be eavesdropping. No one is there. She sighs and continues. "And after, if you want to go and sleep at the club, I won't stop you. But we can share my bed."

My brows arch up, and the usual question is on my lips. Are you sure? But I don't say it because I don't want her to reconsider. I want to sleep wrapped up in her warmth.

"Should we talk now?" I ask instead. "If it's important?"

She shakes her head, points to her ear, then in the direction of the kitchen.

I nod, and after precisely two seconds of internal debate, I open my arms, inviting her into a hug. She doesn't hesitate. Nuzzling my chest with her nose, she relaxes, and I relax with her.

The dinner was awkward. I could see Mrs. Yagi's unspoken question in her strained expression - *why are you still here?* I pretended I couldn't tell and ate the food she made. I can't lie, it was great.

Mushroom fried rice, miso soup, gyoza, and jasmine tea. It's probably a part of her crusade to bring Hanako back to her roots, but I'm not complaining—a warm, home-cooked meal after a bad day is a treat no matter the intentions. And it seems we all needed it. After, there were no arguments, just a couple of curt goodnights.

Now Hanako and I sit on her bed, hugging a pillow each, a little bit apart. I want to jump her and wrestle with her until we're sweaty and horny, but the mood isn't right.

"Tell me about Hale-Bopp Health and what you do there." She gets straight to the point.

I frown. "Did Sophie tell you?"

She nods.

"Do you really want to know? What changed?"

"A client of mine disappeared. No, she was kidnapped. Actually, before that, something horrible was done to her in that hospital. And another something horrible is coming, I'm sure of it." She tells me about Cindy. Her story is fragmented as she goes back and forth in time, rushing to get to what happened tonight when she was with Sophie. When she gets to that part, my blood runs cold. She's left her name with them. They know where she works, her license number. 'They' being the mental health hospital, but they work very closely with Hale-Bopp Health. I don't know yet how involved they are.

I keep quiet while she whispers, but at some point, I let go of the pillow and inch closer to her. At the end of her story, she's sitting in my lap, clutching her hands together, her knuckles white.

"So how bad are things? What have you found out?" She looks up at me with fierce eyes.

It's my turn to talk.

"Well, you know how Chicago has a few gangs that are more or less doing their own thing in their territories? Sophie and Damien have most of central Chicago, but the Arcana shares a boundary with them. One of their people helped Damien escape when he fought with the Jesters, the gang that his ex-wife rallied against him." I pause. She seems to be following. She was around us all at the time, so Sophie must have told her some of this. "The leader of the Arcana, the Empress, had a problem of her own in the meantime. The hospital that her gang used to treat gang-related injuries was changing. She had left the management to her son, Ken Rogers, the Magician, and all was great until he struck a deal with a healthcare company, Comet International."

"Oh, I know them. They have pharmacies all around Chicago, don't they? And their own line of supplements?" Hanako asks.

I nod. "It would seem they want to get into the hospital business, so they got into some agreement with Ken, rebranded the hospital, and opened it up to non-gang patients. Made it legal, apparently. But the Empress isn't convinced. Her underlings are being charged for medical procedures that were free for them before; however, her son doesn't want to open up about it at all."

"So why doesn't she just barge in there and get it all sorted?" Hanako says, confused. "She's his mother and the leader. It's her territory."

"Sophie asked the same question," I reply. "The Empress gave us three reasons, which was pretty impressive because I expected her to dismiss us. First, she's preparing Ken to be her successor, so she doesn't want to go against him openly. Second, despite her reservations, the hospital brings in a lot of money. And third, now that there are non-gang patients there, she doesn't want to get them caught in any crossfire."

"And this is where you come in." Hana puts her index finger on my chin. It's not meant to be sexual, but my cock twitches underneath her. "Sophie told me it's a recon mission. Are you gathering evidence against this Magician and Comet International?"

"Partly. It's not exactly evidence that I'm looking for. I need to find out what is raking in so much profit and if there are any worrying practices." I adjust Hanako's position, pulling her closer to me.

"There are," she says with conviction in her voice.

"Yes." I nod slowly. "And I might have just gotten in the middle of it all. Let me tell you what happened today."

She intakes a sharp breath. Her heart gallops with mine, our chests pressed together. I force the words out with a lot of effort.

It's hard to concentrate when all I want is for my mind to go blank, like a page covered in black paint. It's what it does when I kiss Hanako and when Connor and I torment her.

Opening up to her feels like a dam breaking. The subject is heavy, like a stone pulling us both under deep waters, but there is a release of pressure that feels cathartic. The wall I've been building between us with all the withheld information crashes down, destroyed by honesty. I want to kiss her so badly.

HANAKO

CHAPTER 19

Sophie was right to tell me about Mathias and Hale-Bopp Health. My client's disappearance and the undercover work are connected, and in some twisted way, I'm happy about it. This connection extends and ties Mathias and me together, too. We're not running away from each other, chasing two different enemies.

We're here, in my bed, entwined. Not only physically but mentally, too. We share a common goal.

As he finishes telling me about his day, I'm so overcome with emotion that I don't know what to do with myself. I'm aware of his heat, of the hardness of his chest, and the stirring of his cock under me. He's feeling it too—this charged silence.

I stop playing with his Memento mori ring and twist in his lap to look into his blue eyes. When he is this close to me, it's hard to remember our complicated roommate-play partner arrangement. My body only knows how his attention feels. I crave him.

But as my attraction grows, clouding my senses, an alarm in my head shouts Cindy's name while I'm standing in the halfway.

"It sounds like the operation you have tomorrow could be Cindy's. We have to stop it somehow," I whisper.

"If she makes it to the operating room, it will be difficult to help her. I could risk exposing myself and the Empress's plan. We have to get her out of the mental hospital and away before Hale-Bopp's people come." He runs his hand across his brow.

"I can ask Sophie for help. She's the best at arranging covert stuff like this." I reach for my phone without leaving Mathias's side. "We don't know when they're moving Cindy. Hopefully, Lu-Na can try harder and hack into the system."

"They can do it," he says. "Hospital transfers and other logistics usually use another system. Will be easier to hack than the patient files."

I type a message to Sophie and put my phone aside. "We have our next steps," I say. I gaze into his face again, his straight nose, his high cheekbones, and the shadow of stubble on his tanned skin. My eyes drop to his lips. With the worrying side of me somewhat satisfied, only the pull of his closeness remains. I put my palm on his cheek and let my thumb explore his skin in gentle strokes.

"Do you want me to stay the night?" he whispers. His arms circle my waist, pulling me in.

"Yes." My voice is a breath across his lips.

"Your mother says I will sabotage your future," he says.

My eyes flick to his, my brows knitted in confusion. "Sabotage it how?"

"I might scare off your future Japanese husband." A smile is playing on his lips, but I'm too close to be fooled. There is a flicker of hurt in the blue of his irises.

"You won't. I'm not sure what I want for my future. It might be a Japanese wife. Might be three American husbands." I wink, and he huffs a laugh. Good. "Mama is here for a reason. I don't know why but I will find out. She's trying to force some traditional family stuff onto me, but I'm not feeling it. She was never a traditional Japanese woman. She left my father, then she left me. She lives on creativity and praise. Nothing about that is traditional."

Mathias takes my hand away from his face and kisses my knuckles. "Take your time figuring it all out. I'll be here for as long as you want me around. I don't want to be a burden to you or your future."

"My mother is wrong about that part. I know this much. The jury is still out on a few other things, but I want you here with me." I pull him into a hug, running my hands up his neck and resting them at the back of his head. His smell comforts me as I close my eyes.

Mathias won't ruin my life. If anyone will, it will be me. Uninvited, the image of Cindy lying in front of me sedated plays out in my mind. Beaten, restrained, non-verbal. All familiar things to me.

Mathias cups the nape of my neck, burrowing his fingers in my hair. It hangs loose, dark, and heavy on my shoulders, begging to be played with. He tugs at it gently, and we're again looking into each other's eyes.

Then we kiss, one of those movie kisses where both leads lean into one another at the same time. We start slow. Our exploration is shy because this kiss is not like the others. It's not part of a scene. It's not a confession of love. It's a confirmation of connection for me. A deep understanding.

And it's so damn good. I shift around his lap, breaking the kiss for a second to straddle him. His eyes are half-closed with desire, his dick hard under my wet pussy. Two sets of fabric separate us, my pajamas and his sweatpants. It's too much. I want it all off, so my skin can stick to his, and we can be one.

I pull his T-Shirt over his head, revealing the intricate owl tattoo on his chest that I explore every time I get to see him undressed. Today, its open wings look as if they're embracing my attention as if it's about to land on my arm and snuggle up with me. I run my fingers across the lines, feeling the muscles underneath. Mathias shivers under my touch.

"What are we doing?" His face is a battlefield - confusion, desire, hope. Emotions shine in his features, open and honest, catalyzed by the conversation we finished minutes ago.

"I don't know," I whisper as I lean in close again, wishing him to take my lips and spare me the need to reply.

Whatever it is, we're breaking my rules. My boundaries twist and slither away like yellow snakes. The world opens up with its possibilities and its endless dangers.

'I didn't raise you to be reckless like this.' My mother's words mess with my head, mixing with the scent of Mathias and the taste of his lips.

I slide off him, so I can remove my clothes, pushing through the mental discomfort. He does the same.

But when I reach for him now, the spell has been broken. Uncertainty stands between us. No matter. We've been naked together enough times for me not to ruin this. I climb back into his lap and press my lips to his.

He responds with a half-hearted peck before he breaks away to speak. "What did you think about just now?"

"Nothing." I smile, but he tilts his head to one side, not convinced. "Just something Mama said. She's messing us both up, huh?"

"What is it? Is it about me?" He hugs me in that safe way that makes me relax. It seems like the heat between us has subsided, yet the warmth remains.

"No. She said that I was reckless. Running into danger."

He smiles. "Have you met Sophie? That's a reckless person."

"Well, she's my best friend. I guess it rubbed off?" I chuckle, but the knot in my stomach doesn't ease.

"Do you agree with your mother?" He starts petting my hair.

"I didn't until I saw Cindy today. She seemed broken. And I shouldn't talk like this about my clients, but she reminded me of myself a bit. The things that her abuser did to her, what many abusers do, overlap so much with what I like in kink. The beatings, the torment, the control. It feels wrong to want it when so many are suffering." As I'm talking, I can feel Mathias's subtle shifts and reactions; I can tell he disagrees with what I'm saying.

"I understand why you feel this way. The psychology of kink

is complicated. But I know you, so let me give you a straightforward example to put your mind at ease. Imagine you're building a crib. You need to use a hammer to get the nails to stay where they should. You use it. A child sleeps happy and comfy. On the other side of the city, someone uses a hammer to bash someone else's head. You read about it in the newspaper. Are you going to stop using hammers?"

I blink at his ridiculous scenario. "No."

"The beatings, the marks, the mind games are only a tool. In kink, we use them after gaining explicit consent and within the boundaries set for the scene. In abuse, they're utilized by the abuser in any way that helps them reassert control over their victim. The difference is context." He takes my chin gently and turns my face toward his. "The issue of recklessness is the same. Crossing the motorway with your eyes closed is reckless and dangerous. Wanting to help a client and getting your gang friends to help you is just dangerous. There is always a risk with everything we do. Every decision we make can come back to bite us in the ass. Doesn't mean all decisive people are reckless."

I sigh after he stops talking. I don't have anything to say in response. I feel stronger somehow, supported by his beliefs. I rest my head on his chest, the owl's feathers tickling my cheeks.

"Can you stay the night and just hold me?" I whisper.

"Of course."

"Do you truly believe everything you said just now?"

"Wouldn't have said it otherwise."

We spoon under one blanket, sharing our body heat. Mathias's heartbeat is steady at my back, and under its rhythm, I fall asleep.

CHAPTER 20

I'm floating somewhere between dream and reality. It's a beautiful place, all in pastel colors, smelling like jasmine and home. The air is warm, and everything is light, defying gravity.

A loud crash pulls me out of it. A rude awakening if there was ever one.

"You will be late, Hanako." Heavily accented English pins me back into reality.

I'm awake now. I am. I rub my eyes. Hanako is waking up next to me, her soft, naked body still pressed to mine.

"Close the door, mother," she croaks. She did warn me she's not a morning person.

The door closes with a soft click. Seconds pass slowly as we cuddle. I'm still holding on to the tether of that pastel place. Mundane thoughts break through, however. One is particularly loud.

Mrs. Yagi saw us.

I detach myself from Hanako and assess the situation. We're naked. Snuggled together. If I walked in on us, I wouldn't assume we were roommates. Fuck. Someone will have to explain something. I don't want to be the one.

Hanako sits up, her eyes still half-closed. "I need a coffee," she says. "What time is it?"

I look at my phone.

"Oh, shit."

"Are we late?" she grabs her own from the nightstand. "Fifteen missed calls from Sophie? What the hell? And I'm late!"

She jumps out of bed, looking for clothes, her phone still in her hand. She struggles to get her arm through the sleeve of her shirt because of it.

I pull my boxers on and go to her side, plucking the phone from her grip. I hold her shoulders and make her look at me.

"One thing at a time," I say. I try my best to be calm, but there are a dozen missed calls from Sophie on my mobile too, and about as many from Damien and Tanya. Something has happened with Cindy or with the hospital. Whatever it is, we slept through it. We muted our phones yesterday so that they wouldn't disturb Mrs. Yagi during dinner and her sleep prep.

"I was supposed to arrange something with Sophie for Cindy today. I have a client in an hour. And Mama saw us. Will I be able to have coffee before I go? I have to hurry." Hanako jumps on one leg as she puts on some dark blue trousers.

"Okay, okay, but listen." I sit her down on the bed so she can get properly dressed. "We need to call Sophie back. After that, we will come out and sort out the situation with your mother. Then, we will set off. You will have time for coffee. Can you call and push your first appointment?"

She finally stops for a second. She considers my words, then nods.

"Do that first." I adjust the buttons on her shirt and her collar.

After she's bought herself a bit more time, I dial Sophie. Hanako goes to the door, opens it, and looks up and down the corridor. I frown. Does she think Mrs. Yagi will eavesdrop on us?

After her check, she sits on the bed next to me. The line rings, long and damning. We're so bad for muting our phones.

"Where the fuck are you?" Damien's voice booms

from the speaker, and I scramble to lower the volume. "We overslept," I say. No excuses, just the truth.

"You *overslept?*" He sounds like I've told him that water is dry. "Well. Glad you had a good time. Is Hanako okay? She's not picking up her phone either."

"I overslept, too," Hanako says in a small voice.

"Uh, okay." Damien isn't stupid. He will pick up that we overslept together. Won't make him less angry, but still. "Whatever, Cindy is with us at Love and Err. She's still not responsive, so come to check on her if you can. Wait, why aren't you at the hospital?"

"I have a surgery booked for the evening, so Ken told me to come late." I scratch my head, feeling very naked in my boxers. "Tell us about Cindy."

There's a shuffling sound, and the phone goes back to its owner. Sophie speaks. "So, you know how Lu-Na were supposed to hack the transfer records?"

"Yes?" Hanako draws out the 'e'.

"Well, they were supposed to be moving her right after lunchtime. But there was an opportunity for us to take her when night and day shifts changed, so we took it," Sophie says.

Hanako's face drops. "You didn't need us?"

"Well, we did, but neither of you picked up. In my defense, we called *a lot.*"

"Okay. Give me the short version? I'm late to work," Hanako says, still looking dejected.

"Lu-Na sent a forged early discharge order, and Damien and Tanya dressed up as hospital staff. It was actually really easy. It seems other than dealing with Hale-Bopp, this hospital is all proper and legal."

"And what will happen when the actual staff from Hale-Bopp come to pick Cindy up?" I ask.

"Nothing, I assume. Lu-Na hacked the reception phone line, too, so we can intercept any calls we want. Outgoing and incoming."

"So if they call to clear the mix-up, Lu-Na will pick up?" Hanako says.

"Me or Tanya. Lu-Na don't do phones. But I don't anticipate this will come back to us in any case. So our priority is getting Cindy to a safe, comfortable place." Sophie sounds like a real gangboss lady. I can't believe she has only been doing this for over a month. The job fits her like a glove.

"Okay. Okay. Okay." Hanako is up and pacing the room now. "There's still that housing that I got for Cindy. We can take her there after I finish work. Can you look after her until then?"

"Yes, she's in one of the private rooms," Sophie says.

"I will drop by on my way to the hospital," I say. She needs an IV at least. "If you still need me to go to the hospital?"

A part of me jumps at the opportunity to stop doing the undercover work. If the Empress meets with Cindy, they can talk, right? One can tell the other about her experience with Hale-Bopp. The Empress can then safely bring it up with Ken and make the hospital safe again.

"I think you should continue for now." Sophie's words are gentle. "I know it's hard for you. But we don't have enough information. You've only just gained access to the VIP wing."

I press my lips into a thin line in quiet assent. Sophie takes my silence as agreement. Hanako will talk to her later, they decide and hang up.

I feel a little bit out of control. It's time to face the fact that I'm going to Hale-Bopp, and I'm participating in their VIP work. If they're doing something abhorrent, and I don't stop it, I will become an accomplice. I will stop being a doctor for real.

"You can call in sick." Hanako takes my hand and places it against her cheek. I'm still in my boxers. As if being half-naked will save me from going out.

"I can't." I let my thumb caress her skin.

"Maybe it won't be as bad as we think," she says, but she doesn't mean it. Her client's case rattled her, and she doesn't get rattled easily.

I remind myself why I'm doing this. For my license, for the safety of patients, to keep Sophie and Damien's gang out of trouble with their neighbors. I strive to do good still. It must be enough. If I don't unveil what is happening there, who will?

But I still feel like a balloon drifting toward the endless sky. So I pull Hanako close and press my lips to hers.

After yesterday, I'm done with this whole roommate thing. We're allies now. Partners. Maybe not romantic partners but, in every other sense of the word, we're together.

She responds to me instantly, her lips opening and her tongue darting out to meet mine.

A knock on the door startles us both, and we break away. The semblance of control I had regained dissipates.

"Should I talk to her now?" I ask as I rush to put on clothes.

"You just go and check on Cindy. I'll deal with Mama." Hanako says, determination in her eyes.

I press a kiss to her forehead as I escape the apartment, ignoring the perfect Japanese breakfast laid out on the table. Damn it.

After rushing across Chicago's city center, the quietness of the private room is jarring. Damien has decorated it tastefully in pastel yellows and greens, like a lemon-lime combo. Cindy looks like a woman from a Renaissance painting; she has thrown the sheets covering her to one side, and her gaze lingers somewhere in the upper right corner. Instinctively, I look there too. Maybe there's a cobweb or a spider?

However, there's nothing. Just like the nothing that is in her eyes as I ask her a few questions, trying to figure out what happened to her. I put an IV in her vein, conscious of the fact that she could be dehydrated if they've been keeping her sedated for a long time.

She doesn't move as I insert the needle. I do a few more checks, testing whether her reflexes work. Her eyes flick to mine as I'm checking her elbow. She moves her head slowly.

"Don't hurt me," she whispers.

I sigh. Her spine is fine, and the fact that she's speaking is a great sign as well.

"You're safe," I say. "I'm Dr. Flores. I'm Hanako Yagi's partner. Do you remember her? Your social worker."

My heart flutters as I utter the word 'partner'. It feels… right.

Cindy nods. "She's nice."

"Yes, very nice. She worked tirelessly to find you. You will see her tonight." I hold Cindy's cold hand and massage it, inviting circulation back into it. "I have given you fluids, which will help you shed the effects of sedation. Please keep the IV in."

I move to her other hand as I watch her face, looking for signs of fleeing or aggression. But there's none.

Tanya comes inside just as I head out to look for her.

"Make sure she has water, and if she wants food, give something bland to her. Help her to the toilet if she wants it. The more she pees, the faster she'll regain her lucidity."

"No problem." Tanya winks, and I give her a quick hug.

"Time to go pretend to be a horrible person," I say on my way out.

"You know how I dealt with it? When I worked for the Jesters?" She puts a small, encouraging hand on my shoulder.

"You helped plan and deliver a coup twice?" I grin.

"Well, yes, but while all that was in the making, I just separated myself. So I didn't lose what was important." She points to my doctor's bag with a nod of her head.

"Thank you," I say because I don't want to disappoint her by starting a discussion about it. But we're different people. I can't have two of myself. I can barely maintain my one stressed existence.

No, my way is simpler. Always go toward the good. I have to believe that's what I'm doing tonight.

CHAPTER 21

My foot hurts like hell. It's bruised and swollen, and I'm pretty sure there's something cracked inside. I need to check it out, but I can't actually *go* anywhere. I worked from home today. I'm a little bit scared to go outside. Okay, fine, I'm terrified.

When the adrenaline wore off after my momentary bravery and the pain in my foot settled in, I regretted my actions. My stupidity. I could have done all I did without trying to convince those gorillas that what they want is immoral first, without getting stepped on.

I swallow some painkillers and hobble to my couch. I'm clutching my phone like it's my lifeline, but I have no one to call. The ring that I had blackened after Laura's accident shines more and more. I've been rubbing it a lot these days, calling on her incorporeal support for anything that rattles my confidence.

She's quiet now. As if the pain numbs my memory of her. She's far away when I'm physically occupied. She doesn't like my pain or my pleasure.

I can't say the same about my dark demons, the ones always ready to tell me how fucked up I am.

Tonight, they chant 'coward' over and over while I'm curled up with my swollen foot, afraid to leave my house.

I unlock my phone and scroll through the pictures. It's all memes and photos of rope I've done. There's not a single one with my face on. It's like I'm a ghost in my own life.

No, that's not true. There is one photo—

My phone lights up with a call. It's Comet International. Maybe it's the email guy, Ken. Or maybe it's one of the two men who took me to the IT basement. Maybe it's a third someone who specializes in telephone torture.

My hand shakes. I toss my phone away, scared I will answer it by mistake. It lands screen up on the carpet next to the coffee table. I side-eye it as it keeps ringing. When it finally stops, I allow myself to breathe. I'm dizzy from holding my breath.

The photo I was looking at before pops up, and I take the phone back, ignoring the missed call notification. The photo is the one I took last Friday at the Moon Garden. Hana is dangling in the air, her face full of concentration. Mathias is next to her, his hand in her hair, smiling like an idiot and making a peace sign. And then there's me, well, my forehead and my left eye, at the bottom of the picture. I remember I was smiling. Hah, I was supposed to delete this photo. It was part of the scene; we were poking fun at Hana. But then I went to help Hayley and the guys and forgot. I don't think I even said goodbye to Hana and Mathias.

Should I call them? Hana can't help. She's tiny. And she's a sweet, quiet woman. How can she help? I would hate it if I somehow got her in trouble with those guys from the hospital.

What about Mathias? He's tall. And he has that scary friend I don't know the name of—Sophie's boyfriend.

Maybe I should call Sophie? There's something dangerous about her. I can't put my finger on it, but I know not to cross her. Perhaps they can get me to safety.

For fuck's sake, what even is safety? What do I want? It's not like I have anyone coming after me. I'm just the dumb IT guy who got stepped on.

While I think, I let my demons demean me. I repeat what they call me, reinforcing it, making it real. My fingers scroll through my contacts list, full of clients, play partners, and forgotten acquaintances. Who the fuck is Charlie Green Ford? Or Marie (Second number)? I don't even have a first number for her.

My thumb hovers over Mathias's contact. Would he think I'm pathetic if I tell him what happened? I circle back to the fact that I have no idea what I want to achieve - get someone to protect me? To deal with those people? Maybe I want to switch jobs and disappear.

Maybe I just want to share. No, fuck that, I don't do mushy feelings.

You did plenty of feelings with me. Laura's voice is sing-song in my head. I close my eyes and let the mirage of her comfort me.

I lie down on my couch, still shaking a bit. I stretch out my legs and put my arm over my face. The painkillers are working because Laura is back.

And for the moment, I set aside my fear and lock up my demons somewhere dark and damp in my brain.

I reach for a golden memory, one that's filled with sunlight, the smell of the lake behind Laura's parents' house, and the sound of her laughter. We're skinny dipping, and despite the heat of the air, the water is cold. I touch her skin, covered with goosebumps, and she shivers. It's a shiver that has nothing to do with fear.

CHAPTER 22

The VIP wing sparkles. From the immaculate floors, walls, and windows to the shiny potted fern leaves and shimmering humidifiers. It's lush, like a hotel lobby. When I follow the attending physician showing me around, I act as a silent observer, taking in the decadence of something that has gone so far from its primary function that it's unrecognizable.

Here, I see the missing women from the mundane wards below. They are all sleeping peacefully, recovering. Their guardians, if present, are dressed in pressed, branded suits. All of them are men.

In many ways, it reminds me of Lavender, the corrupted sex club which Sophie and the gang fought so hard to destroy. But that was about taking advantage of women's bodies. What is happening here?

In the last room we visit, there's a wealthy-looking old lady. She's sitting on the golden leather couch, reading a newspaper. There's a cup of tea on the table in front of her and a Danish pastry. Her posture is relaxed like she's enjoying a break in an exclusive cafe, not sitting in a hospital.

She doesn't pay any attention to the bed at the foot of the massive room. A woman lies there, sleeping or unconscious, her machine strangely silent.

Then, it hits me what made this floor feel like a coffee made with salt. It looks good. It smells good. But it doesn't *feel* good. The taste it leaves in my mouth is one of stomach-twisting anxiety.

"Madam." The attending goes to shake the old lady's hand. Thick golden bracelets jingle on her frail wrist. She turns to me, looks me up and down, and grins. Her eyes turn predatory.

"Who's this lovely doctor?" She coos, and I imagine her tongue coming out of her mouth two-pronged like she's a venomous snake.

"The new anesthesiologist. He'll be making sure your Delilah wakes up tomorrow after we fix her."

"Make her pretty, new boy. Like you." She winks and extends her hand to shake mine.

It takes all of my doctor training on bedside manner not to retch at how she looks at me and the feel of her leathery skin on mine. She brings her other hand to the top of our handshake and slides her fingers to the back of my hand, up my wrist, and into the sleeve of my doctor's coat. I jerk my arm away.

She continues grinning. "I'll be staying over tonight. I hope to see you after hours."

I frown and look at the attending next to me. He doesn't meet my eyes. His plastered smile and enthusiastic nod tell me he's not on my side. Maybe there are no sides here. There's simply surviving on your own.

"We will make sure to send him over," he says.

My eyes widen, and I finally find my words. "I have a difficult surgery tonight, so I will be going straight home after work. Need to get that valuable shuteye, so I'm fresh for tomorrow."

I hope this will appease her. Her… relative?… is the one going under the knife then, after all.

She waves me off. "Suit yourself, pretty boy. But you'll be missing out."

I smile because if I don't, something unprofessional and mean will slip out from between my lips.

The doctor and I head out. It's almost time for Cindy's surgery. I hope I will be told to go home. My heart skips a beat at the prospect of watching the chaos unfold because of Sophie's actions this morning. What will they do? Send someone to look for her? How will they handle her VIP guardian, whomever they are?

I don't have to wonder long because the attending's phone rings, and he straightens before picking it up. What a sleazeball.

"What? How can a patient disappear?" He pauses, his face turning red. "Well, I'm not going to be the one breaking the news to Mr. Rogers. It's your mess. Deal with it."

I take deep breaths to keep my face from breaking into a genuine smile.

"You want me to give you orders? I'm a surgeon, not a fucking manager. Go ask security for help if you're so scared to go to Mr. Rogers. No, no. I'm here to operate. It's your job to get me the patients to operate on. Don't fucking talk back to me. Yeah. Well, good luck and thank you for nothing." He rolls his eyes.

I arrange my face in a concerned expression. "Something wrong?" I ask.

"The patient we were supposed to be operating on tonight is missing." He paces around me.

"Can't we go and pick them up?" I try to sound helpful, but I think a little bit of mockery seeps through.

"It. Is. Not. Our. Job." He spells out each word in the air, his face getting redder with each letter.

I look down, covering my mouth with my hand like I'm thinking even though I'm smiling. I can't help it. This is the best I've felt since I started working here.

"Who's next?" The attending throws his hands in the air. A nurse materializes from somewhere, looking shy and subdued. He must be doing an internship or something. I'm surprised Ken has allowed him to be on this floor.

"Who are you?" The doctor points to the nurse.

"I— I— I'm covering a shift. I normally work in A&E." His stuttering surprises me. A&E nurses are confident troopers. Their job doesn't allow time for timidness.

"Get out of here." The doctor waves him off.

"I'm here to help," the nurse says.

I look at him then, really look at his floppy hair and his smooth skin. His glasses and the way his scrubs are a bit too big for his body. Our eyes meet, and despite his hunched posture and stuttering, there is no insecurity there. Is he one of Sophie's people? Or another spy for the Empress, perhaps checking if I've switched sides? Or a third player?

The attending takes another call. He stomps down the corridor, hissing in the rhythm of his steps.

"So, will you need me here?" The nurse straightens. Am I supposed to know this guy?

"Uh, I'm new too, so I can't tell you. You been to this floor before?" I lean on the wall. Small talk. Interrogation. Is there a difference when you're undercover?

"I've been here since before the rebrand."

Oh. So, he's not new.

"Has the hospital changed a lot?" I ask.

He narrows his eyes for a second before smiling in a smooth, friendly way. "Yes, and some of us don't like where it's going. What do you think about this floor?"

I glance at the attending, still throwing his tantrum at the end of the hallway.

"You're too afraid to speak," the nurse says. "You know what, maybe you would find it easier with a warm meal in front of you. Come to the nurse's canteen at lunch sometime. We're a friendly bunch. Very organized too."

I blink at him. Am I being recruited? Into what? Is there an inside rebellion brewing?

I'm about to speak, but the attending's angry steps come closer. The nurse drops his head and rounds his shoulders, changing in a second from a hawk to a sparrow.

"Why are you still here?" the doctor yells at him. "Go away. We don't need you."

The nurse scurries away. The floor feels like quicksand under my feet. My previous joy is replaced by my very familiar anxiety.

"Right, that patient is a no-show. We're taking the next patient on the list," the attending barks at me.

"But she's not prepped."

"She is. They all are." He swings his arm in the direction of all doors. "That's why we keep them sedated. We have a job to do, and we need to be flexible."

"But that's—" Not suitable for all patients, is what I want to say but can't because the doctor raises a finger at me, pointing at my face.

"No backtalk because I'm about to lose my shit." He spits a little in my direction. I'm lucky I'm taller than him. "If you want the patient to be safe, make sure I'm calm and happy. Don't want to cut her up all wrong, do we?"

I press my lips together. So I won't be able to get out of this surgery. What will I have to do? The old lady's sinister face from the last room is imprinted in my memories.

Make her pretty, like you,' she'd said.

HANAKO

CHAPTER 23

Seeing Cindy safe was like taking a breath after being underwater. Showing her around the new apartment was even better. It's a simple place, with a bedroom, a living room, and a little kitchenette, but it's dry and warm and free. I took a long detour to make sure no one followed us. Then I got us takeaway coffee, and we sipped it while chatting on her new sofa.

The social worker part of me is happy. I've done my job; my client is being provided with appropriate lodging and away from the toxic environment. Next time I see her, I will be looking into finding a therapist, so she can start working on herself. There are a few jobs I think will suit her too, but all in good time.

The feeling of contentment is a warm liquid running through my veins, reaching every part of me in happy pumps. I'm giddy with accomplishment, which makes me do random nice things. I already bought and delivered a massive stack of donuts to Love and Err. Sweets won't express fully how thankful I am for Sophie's initiative, but it's a start.

Now I'm driving my car to be repainted. I'm not feeling the purple branch across its side anymore, the keyed line becoming more and more visible with each passing day. So I will have it fixed. My car will be a pristine white again by this time next week.

To treat myself, I have hired a flashy Tesla. Mathias has been trying to get me to drive an electric car ever since I met him, so I thought, why not.

I call him to let him know, but he doesn't pick up. Maybe he's still working, but doing what? Cindy didn't make it to Hale-Bopp. I hope they didn't make him do someone else's operation.

That thought puts a damper on my cheeriness. Usually, when I sort out housing, therapy, and employment for a client, or when I have a good plan for it, I'm able to let go and focus on something else.

This time, Cindy's case lingers on my mind. I know why. It's like my clients are Hale-Bopp's unfortunate patients. Mathias, who's forced to work there. It hasn't ended yet. There's no closure, so the stress continues.

When I come back home, something feels off. My mother is doing something in Mathias's room, I can hear her shuffling feet across the wooden floor. As I pass one of her paintings in the hallway, I notice it's tilted, the field of sunflowers looking like a crooked puddle of yellow. I straighten it, my eyes lingering on the little girl in the middle. Her twisted face draws the gaze, the focal point of the whole painting being her big, black eyes. Blackness seeps from them, dropping on the sunflowers around in thick glops. There is a reason why this painting isn't in a room.

I hurry to my bedroom. I want to change as fast as possible, to shed the social worker off me and rest in something soft, comfy, and pink. My room is a mess. The bed is as Mathias and I left it this morning, sheets crumpled and clothes scattered. His and mine. Although that's not the only thing.

There are actual piles of things on the floor. They are organized, but they don't belong here. I pick up an orange shirt - obviously Mathias's. His collection of shoes is behind my door. And on my dressing table, next to my skincare and hair ties, there are Mathias's neat boxes of metalworking supplies. Did he move in on his lunch break or something?

I knock on the guest room door before entering.

My mother is on her hands and knees, scrubbing the floor. Rubber gloves up to her elbows and a little cotton bandana make her look like the perfect housewife.

The room is different. Empty of character. A blank canvas.

"Did you move Mathias's things into my room?" It's hard to keep my voice even with the increasing anger simmering under my skin. It's a rhetorical question. She's doing her thing again, carpet bombing my life to feel like a mother.

"I felt he was not honest with me when I asked him yesterday." She sits back on her heels, her face arranged in a calm expression. I can't tell if she's taunting me.

"What did you ask him?"

"If he was your partner."

"He is not my partner."

She shakes her head. "I was not born yesterday, Hanako. I saw you two today. In bed. Naked."

"Things have changed since you were young." I roll my eyes. I'm about to hear some traditional love lecture. "We enjoy each other's company, but we aren't an actual couple."

There is one more who plays with us. And many more around. And you should hear the things I've done with my best friend. But I don't say any of this. I don't want to antagonize her.

"I understand being young. You must explore," she says.

"But not with Mathias?" I roll my eyes.

"Mathias is a good person. But I do not see how he can bring out the best in you." She takes off her gloves and stands up. "I am not going to be around forever to keep the Japanese part of you alive. And I cannot bear the thought of my grandchildren growing up without part of their heritage."

So this is what it's all about. "I'm only twenty-seven," I say, but it's a moot point.

"There is time, which is why I moved Mathias in with you. This passion will burn bright and strong and then disappear like a hanabi. I support you giving it a try."

"And if it doesn't disappear?" I don't know how whatever we're doing with Mathias and Connor will evolve. I don't even know if I want it to. I sure as hell wasn't ready to throw my mother's blessing into the mix. A blessing that feels very much like 'I'll get my way in the end, so I'm letting you play for now'. It's time I put my foot down.

"Sit." I go to the bed and pat the space next to me after she purses her lips and doesn't reply. The loaded silence is like a third person in the room. "What is this really about?"

"I do not know what you mean. I am looking out for you."

"You left me when I was in middle school. I'm not that child anymore." I do my best not to sound like I'm attacking her choices.

"I did not leave you. I chose a good school for you after careful consideration. I have always made decisions with your best interests in mind, even if I was not with you, physically." Her hand hovers near mine, and I take it. It would be great if we can resolve this invasion into my private life without arguments.

"I know. You helped me get a good education and this house. But we are only people. We need to talk to each other to feel close." I pat her hand with mine. It's small, with little spots marring her otherwise perfect skin. People say age shows on the hands.

"I feel close to you," she says. "We are family. I gave birth to you."

I massage her palms. It's been years since I had such prolonged skin-to-skin contact with her. I didn't think I needed it, being an adult and all, but now that I've attached myself to her, I don't want to let go.

"Let's talk now. Why didn't you call you were coming?"

Mama's hands are painter's hands - she has a prominent callus on the side of her middle finger. She wears it like jewelry - her fingers, like mine, are absent of rings, but the way her art has shaped her hands tells a story. She is silent for a long moment.

"I wanted to see how you live. Without you hiding things before I came," she says.

Now it's my turn not to speak. I would have done it. I would have curated a version of my life she would approve of. But that's what's best for everyone's comfort, isn't it?

"You do not want to listen to my life advice because you are young. But I give it only because I want you to do better than me," she continues. "I am alone now. I should have listened to my parents when they said not to run away with your father."

"But you're so successful." I shake my head. "I'm so proud of your paintings. Of how far you've made it as a woman immigrant in a world that loves to see women and immigrants fail."

She breaks free of my massage and puts her warm palm to my face. "The paintings are where I store my pain, my Hanako. People like them, but I cannot always bear to look at them. They have my life - our life - in each stroke. What was and what could have been. After separating from your father, I vowed to never betray my roots again. But I did.

"As much as America wanted to shun me away, Europe wanted to embrace me. It must seem like I was chasing money, and maybe I was. But it was more than that. I found an audience. People who enjoyed looking at my pain, who embraced it and felt it deep inside themselves. I thought I found redemption in my success. Recently, it has felt different. As I grow older, I crave to go back home; to Okinawa. I want to taste tofu, just how my grandmother made it, and go to the temple and make a wish. I want to wear colorful yukata and put the pain behind me."

Her last words trickle out like a small stream of hope. She wants me to say something. Reassure her, maybe. But I don't feel it. I've never been to Japan. Not as a tourist, not as a part-native, not as anything. I wanted to go. A dozen burned school uniforms later, and I had changed my mind.

"So why didn't you go?" I ask.

"Your grandparents would not welcome me. They told me I was not their daughter. I married the enemy. But I thought they might want to meet you instead. Okinawa people care for each other. If they see you as their own, they will love you. They will take care of you."

The pieces fall into place. Bits are still missing but I'm starting to understand.

"You want me to go there with a Japanese husband, don't you? To be accepted." I take her hand from where it's cupping my face and put it in her lap. I'm feeling something. A new thing. Not disappointment or anger, not even sadness. It's closer to the feeling I get when I play and my tops objectify me. Like I'm a tool, and my soul is floating above my body, barely attached.

"They may accept you without a Japanese husband. But Mathias will not do." She nods her head as if she's working out some cultural math in her mind. I'm a millennial. We don't do that. Being different is celebrated, welcomed, and appreciated. In my circles, at least.

"If I find a random Japanese man and go to meet your parents, will they forgive you? Give you peace?" I ask.

"Not random. It cannot be a lie. If they find out, they will never accept us."

"I don't understand why they matter so much. You say Okinawans take care of their own - why did they cast you aside? If you're a traitor for following love, they're traitors for betraying their flesh and blood." I'm having a pure brain-to-mouth moment. There is no filter; words are just tumbling out as the ideas form in my head.

I can see she disagrees, but she stays silent. The guilt that she carries around can't be dissipated with a conversation. I thought her paintings were her accepting and celebrating her turbulent past, I never imagined it was her pain laid bare on a canvas.

I feel very small next to her. All my experiences so far—the kink, the gang stuff, even my troubles with men— seem childish and insignificant, put next to this big wound of culture that my mother has sustained.

Being Japanese is important to her. She's been disconnected from a core part of herself for years. When I imagine it, my heart aches for her.

"Do not pity me," she says as she observes my face. "I cannot change the choices I make, but I can help you make better choices. You are not only American. You have to see there is this beautiful side of you that you neglect."

She talks with such fervor in her eyes, I don't dare stop her. I'm tired of this conversation, though.

"I don't neglect it. I cook Japanese food, watch Japanese television, and maintain some knowledge of the language. Yeah, I can't write and read that well, but I can speak and understand. I don't want to fight about this, Mama, but I can't give you what you want. Not now anyway."

"You choose Mathias?" She raises an eyebrow, her armor back up. She probably thinks her words didn't touch me. They did, but I can't carry the burdens of two generations before me. I need to look after myself.

"I don't. I choose me. At the boarding school you left me in, I learned to always put myself first. It's a survival thing. I know you understand because, right now, even though you say this is all for me, you're looking for a way to use me so you can get your family back. No, don't interrupt me. This family that doesn't care about you or me, sounds more important to you than the family you have here. I'm your family. And I accept you with all your pain and past choices. I love you despite everything. Why can't you look forward and be proud of me, just the way I am?"

Mama sighs, her face resigned to I'm not sure what fate. "We do not understand each other."

I bite my lips, wondering if there is anything more I can say. Nothing useful comes to mind. Continuing this is pointless, but I have one last thing prepared. It wasn't meant to be the period in a dramatic conversation, but here we are.

"I got you a present." I go to the hallway where I've left my bag. I return with a pretty white box decorated with an orange ribbon.

Mama takes it with a puzzled expression. She opens it, and then her face is awash with emotion. She loves it. I picked the fat pointed brush specifically for her style of drawing. It's long and resembles a calligraphy brush with its natural fibers and lacquered finish. But under the gloss, there are tens of hand-painted sunflowers, reminiscent of her own art.

"Try to imagine what it's like to be me. But don't use your rational brain. Put my pain on the canvas. Draw me. Alone in the boarding school, where I looked different. Or maybe draw me now, with Mathias and Sophie and everyone else. Paint me happy or paint me sad. Paint me with you, in Japan." I give her a very American hug. She doesn't hug me back, but a little hiccup of surprise tells me she doesn't hate it. "I can't wait to see it."

"Okay," she whispers. "I will paint."

"But while we're doing this discovery work, Mathias can't suffer," I say. "I will move his stuff back tomorrow, and you will sleep with me."

She nods, and as I leave her with her present, I text Mathias to stay at Love and Err tonight. *Mother emergency*, I type and hope I don't get any follow-up questions.

As I go into the kitchen to whip up something for dinner, I stare at the poppy painting again. Am I headed for similar pain? Mathias and Connor are fun, but for how long? Do I want a purpose in my life, other than the vague 'helping people' I've been feeding to myself and everyone else for years?

In a rush of feeling, I dash to my bedroom and rummage in my sock drawer. I find the rectangular red case and open it with shaking hands. The pearl necklace my mother gave me before she left me all those years ago looks as pretty as ever—a row of sparkling spheres. I run my fingers across them, feeling them. This is the only tangible thing that connects me to my Japanese roots. It was my grandmother's, a wedding present from her mother. I will wear it to work tomorrow.

CHAPTER 24

It's over. The surgery is over. I participated. I had placed the patient under and allowed the surgeon to operate on her. I did it without ever exchanging a word with her. Without seeing a signed consent document.

I'm in the locker room, shaking in my scrubs and staring at the floor. I should just grab my things and go home. I can't. Hanako will ask me how my day went, and I will have to tell her. I have no idea what I've done. It feels like a crime. I don't know if that procedure was in the patient's interest.

The OR nurses reassured me that the Brazilian Butt Lift was what the patient wanted and needed. She would wake up and love her new body. Does anyone *need* a BBL? They winked and laughed and even coaxed a smile from the surgeon, who was still angry about Cindy's absence.

The mood in the room was familiar. It had the heartbeat of a working team, doctors and nurses uniting to perform one task. I was actually impressed with how professional it all was, compared to the patient rooms. Clean, organized, efficient.

Shit, what do I do now?

I finally unlock my locker and put on my Memento Mori ring. If I had thrown a tantrum in the OR, it could have ended badly for the patient. I couldn't have prevented the operation. There was nothing I could do but keep my cover.

Right?

Right. There was no indication that anything went wrong. She will wake up, and she will be okay. I will be here bright and early tomorrow to chat with her.

I need to know what I did. Either my job as a doctor or a crime.

My hands still shake as I take my phone out and see the notification from Hanako.

Hanako: *Can you stay over at Love and Err tonight? Mother emergency.*

My shoulders slump with the weight of a feeling too hard to describe. I'm happy I don't have to tell her about the operation today; I'm sad about not holding her in my arms tonight; I'm anxious about what this mother thing will mean for us. I can bet an arm and a leg that it's got something to do with Mrs. Yagi finding us naked in bed this morning.

I change into my everyday clothes as I recount everything that happened in the OR tonight, trying to figure out again and again if there were any mistakes. I torture myself like this all the way to Love and Err, barely noticing the drive there and the rain that forces my wipers to slash across my vision with angry swipes.

Love and Err, with its bright lights and tens of voices overlapping one on top of the other, exudes a familiar, welcoming vibe that makes me release a shuddering breath of relief. I go down to the subbasement, where Damien and Thomas still live while all renovations in the club take place.

As I descend the spiral staircase I had entered from the first floor, the music and chatter fade away. I meet Damien at the lowest level of Love and Err, between walls that don't let any sound come in or out. No wandering guests here, and no distractions from the world outside. It's a cozy bunker with a dozen rooms. Only a few are kitted out, but each one holds memories for me. A time I was fighting for the greater good again and making allowances with my consciousness. Hale-Bopp isn't my first rodeo, but for some reason, it doesn't get any easier. If all goes well, it will be my last.

"Hey," Damien says without looking away from his computer.

"Hi." I sound tired even to my own ears. As I slide behind him and peer into the screen, a woman gasps, and the screen goes black. I blink in surprise. "Was that Lu-Na?"

"Diana. I had almost convinced her to show herself to you, but she's not ready yet. In any case, what happened today?"

Lu-Na are a collective of a few people who work together to help us. I know they owe their lives to Damien, like Tanya and me, but that's all. No one but Damien has ever seen them.

Diana is the star hacker. For the split second I saw her, she looked like a regular twenty-something-year-old person. I have always had questions about them all, but the way Damien always shakes his head when I start asking discourages me from getting into it now. I don't have the mental energy for another mystery rejection.

So, I tell him about the operation.

"If she didn't consent to the BBL, I can't call myself a doctor. It breaches so many rules. It's immoral," I conclude.

"You will find out tomorrow. But remember, Mathias, maintaining your cover will save a lot more people in the long run."

"In theory. Except what do I do now? Just keep putting people under, then having breakdowns after every operation? I can't. I don't know what else I can do." The memory of the sneaky male nurse who invited me to lunch slips in my mind uninvited. I could go check that out. I could but… "I think I'm done, Damien. I'm not cut out for this work. I can feel my ulcer forming as we speak."

Sophie comes in, her cheeks pink and her hair in a towel. "I swear I wasn't eavesdropping. But I did hear the last bit. Damien will say to take it easy and that you can leave if you wish to, which is true, of course. But let me play devil's advocate and give you a few reasons why you should stay undercover."

She's fresh out of the shower. Now I notice Damien's tousled hair.

"You just had sex." I smirk. It's a pathetic attempt to move the conversation along in a different direction.

Sophie winks, pats Damien on the shoulder and takes his chair after he stands up and goes to shower too. I sense a serious talk coming. My frayed nerves tingle at the edges like cut string.

"You've been helping Damien for years now," Sophie starts. "If you want out, you're out. I've been talking to Mateo Grey about him retracting his original complaint with your work so you can get your license back. I know this is why you agreed to the deal with the Arcana Empress."

I sigh. "You're just telling me what I want to hear."

"No. I don't think this is what you want to hear at all. You want me to convince you to stay." She shakes her head. It's distracting that we're leading this conversation while she is in a towel. Then I remember the various times I've seen her at the Moon Garden, in states much more intimate than this one. For the last few months, she's become a good friend. And she's been one to Hanako for years.

Hanako would encourage me to keep doing the undercover work. She would want to prevent people from getting hurt.

"You're thinking about it. Do it out loud, and I'll listen," Sophie says. She unravels her head towel and lets her hair drop in wet clumps across her shoulders. She's relaxed, and her eyes are free of judgment. Free of fear and completely lucid. She's in control, or at least appears to be.

"I'm afraid," I whisper. "That if I continue, I will take part in procedures that could cause unspeakable harm to patients. That, if I get found out, the gang might need to fight again. You've only just got on your feet after the whole Jesters fiasco. I'm scared this will somehow circle back to Hanako and Connor, or the kids. Being undercover there feels like standing on a jello cake. It makes me wobble."

Sophie nods, keeping the silence alive between us.

"I'm a coward," I say.

"From where I'm standing, it looks like you're a brave person who's very sensitive to stress. I don't mean to psychoanalyze you, Hana is much better at that, but nothing about what you've done so far has been cowardly." She pats my hand. "You treated my wounds and participated in my crazy plans to bring down the Jesters. You let Hana in your life despite perhaps feeling things were a bit hopeless on that front. You patched up anyone and everyone for free and without judging. You agreed to go undercover because you saw a way to use your skills beyond what you were taught at medical school. Maybe you're not a spy, but you're a damn good team player. You say you're a coward, but I would put my life in your hands any day. So will Damien, and Tanya, and Hanako. Maybe even Connor too."

She's shivering by the end, either from the cold or from the feelings.

"That's one hell of a pep talk." I chuckle. "But you're cold. Go put some clothes on."

"I will be back, don't run away," she says and skips to Damien's bedroom.

What I want is to feel badass. In control, like I have a hand of powerful cards to play. Hale-Bopp doesn't make me feel this way. Sophie's examples are good but don't necessarily fit. My morals weren't tested then. I knew I was doing the right thing.

In this case, I'm not so sure.

She comes back in an oversized sweater and leggings, looking a lot cozier. She looks at me expectantly. Does she think I will make a decision now?

"I'm going back tomorrow to check on the patient from today," I said. "And I will make a decision then."

"Good. Lu-Na can't seem to hack into their IT system, so they sent us this USB flash drive. If you put it in a computer connected to the hospital network, it's supposed to do something and help them. Can you do this one last thing as our spy?" She holds out a small, flat metal rectangle. "After that, whatever you decide, I'll support you."

I take the drive. It's tiny in my hands, the size of a coat button, and warm.

"I'll gladly do it," I say. Something dormant reignites in my chest. This feels right. It feels like rebellion. I may not be good at playing a corrupt doctor, but I'm good at disrupting bad people.

"You're excited." Sophie wears a quizzical expression.

"This little thing might have just saved my stomach lining." I shoot her a smile. Being on Hale-Bopp's VIP floor is lonely as hell. It's hard to remember that sometimes I'm not alone. A straightforward task that will help Lu-Na do their part is the reminder I didn't know I needed.

"I'm so confused," Sophie says.

"I'm a complicated person." It's my turn to pat her hand. They're no longer cold.

I slip the USB drive into my pocket. I'm still scared about failing and hurting people. But what if I'm successful and end up helping everyone? It's not a familiar way of thinking for my anxious self, but I roll the thought around my head, examining it like a precious stone.

Tomorrow. I will decide tomorrow.

CHAPTER 25

Things are under control. Mathias's things are back in his room, and my mother is situated in my bedroom with me. I put everything back the way I remembered it, but I will probably still have to tell Mathias about the whole thing. He's very meticulous about how he stores his things, so he'll know someone touched them.

I'm meeting Cindy today so that I can sort her out some therapy asap. It's also Wednesday, the day of our usual family dinner. I have to cancel it in light of my mother being in the apartment, but an unreasonable part of me thinks they will just have it in Love and Err without me. I know I'm not really a part of their inner gang circle anyway. Maybe I can convince them all to go out to a restaurant?

Yes, things are under control, but they're far from perfect. As soon as work matters start to improve, my personal life explodes.

I get into the borrowed Tesla feeling somewhat defeated.

The mochis I had for dessert after Mama's traditional breakfast still stick to my back teeth, making my mouth feel dry. In my office, I rinse and rinse, but the feeling doesn't go away.

Then Cindy arrives, and I pop a mint into my mouth, hoping I won't scare her off with bad breath.

"How are you feeling?" I ask.

"Much better. If you hadn't contacted those people, or organization, you know, I was maybe going to be lobotomized or something." Cindy takes a nervous sip of the water in front of her.

I try to keep my face placid. "Why do you think that?"

"When I was drugged, I wasn't completely out of it, you know. I could hear things sometimes. But when I did, my heart rate went up, and then they would sedate me more. I thought that's the end. Death. I don't even know why my partner did this. It's not like I did anything."

"A lot of the behaviors we see in men like your partner stem from the need to control. There is likely nothing that you could have done to prevent this," I say, my voice slow, measuring every word before I string my sentences. Cindy looks a bit confused. "It's not about you."

She narrows her eyes, considering what I've said. "So, is that bar part of your company?"

I blink at her. The reasons why I don't get involved in cases outside of my work come back to me like an avalanche of criticism.

"It is not. And we're not a company, we're a charity organization." I plaster a warm smile on my face, trying to hide my discomfort. What was I thinking? That we would save her, she would thank us, and that would be it? It's human nature to wonder and ask questions.

"So, was I a special case or something?" Cindy's eyes twinkle.

What is the correct answer here?

"I prioritized your safety and used unconventional methods and resources." I try to keep it vague. I'm sure I fail. Sensing where this is going, I swear in my head.

"But you do that for everyone, right?" Cindy asks in a hopeful tone. "I'm so thankful, and there are girls that could really use your help. And no female gets turned away here, right?"

What I thought would be a good deed is quickly turning into a dangerous misunderstanding.

"Cindy. This organization can help women who have suffered domestic abuse by providing them with shelter, mental health treatment, and securing a job or support from the state. The organization that took part in freeing you is not affiliated with us. I have a personal connection there, that is all."

"So you can't help everyone?" Cindy hits the nail on the head, and I almost wince. This is the main reason why I should have stayed put. But what is done is done.

"No. In your case, you were in trouble, and I had the means to help. This assistance isn't always available. It's not regulated, and it's not safe. If you are truly thankful, please keep this between us. The only promise I can make at the moment is that I'm always putting my clients' well-being first. And if there comes a time where I need to get someone to intervene like in your case, I will do my best."

"Oh." She is quiet for a moment. "So, I was lucky."

When the session ends, I'm still unsure if the misunderstanding has been cleared. I'm drained, and much of the elation of seeing her alive and well has vanished. I don't regret my decision. However, I know deep down that it wasn't the right one. Maybe for Cindy, it was, but for me as a social worker and for all the other women who won't have a chance to be saved, it was a bad move on my part. I could lose my job. Maybe even my license. And the ability to help. They say a hero would sacrifice one to save the world, but a villain would sacrifice the world to save one. What does that make me?

I press the pearls of my necklace into my skin, imprinting them like a noose around my neck. Maybe some dark chocolate will make it better.

Everyone is once again gathered around the tables in the staff kitchen area. My heart shrivels, expecting to see the big boxes of food again. I don't want to interact with people at the moment. I feel small and a bit stupid, so I beeline for the fridge where I keep my snacks. Nothing more comforting than the snap of cold chocolate.

A small green bento box sits on one of the middle shelves. I recognize it immediately. It has a cartoon panda on the lid and a tight band around to secure it closed. The band is positioned to look like the panda has a karate belt. Could it really be what I think it is? I take it out with a shaking hand.

"Did my mother visit today?" I ask no one in particular.

"She did, and she left us all food to enjoy. I can get used to this," says the main receptionist, her mouth full of fried chicken.

There is fast food scattered across the table – chicken, burgers, and a box of donuts on one side. She got my colleagues Frenzy Eats. But why? She hates fast food. Says it kills you slowly from the inside.

"Did she leave this too?" I lift the box gently, holding it with two hands now, like it's a precious baby.

"Yeah, that's your lunch," one of my colleagues replies. "I wish my mom still made me food for work. I would kill for a bowl of her chicken korma right about now."

She punctuates each word by swinging a chicken leg around. She laughs at the end. She's Pakistani; she arrived in the US when she was young. I'm envious of her easy connection to her culture. But she and I are not the same. I'm half-everything, half-nothing.

I take my bento to my office, and despite my brooding, I enjoy it all. The rice is sticky, with a sprinkling of seaweed, and the rolled omelets are moist and sweet. The vegetables are fresh, and I swear they taste like love.

Mama is meeting me halfway. She's still doing stuff I asked her not to do, but she's doing it in a way she probably thinks I would like. And because I felt shitty today and her octopus-shaped wieners made me feel less shitty, I decide I won't argue with her.

I send her a text message instead.

Hanako: *I enjoyed the bento. My colleagues say thank you for the food, too.*

MATHIAS

CHAPTER 26

The moment I'm back at the hospital, I prioritize Lu-Na's job, too afraid to check on the patient from yesterday. I don't know how I will react if I find out she's not well, so I have to make sure I do the computer stuff first, while my mind is clear.

I put the small plastic rectangle drive in the USB slot in one of the nurse's computers on the Maternity Ward. It's the only ward that I've noticed stays without nurses long enough for me to do my spy job. The reason is heartwarming - there's always a pregnant woman to be wheeled around or a baby to be checked on. They don't hang around the PCs or their phones, which works in my favor.

I message Sophie after I'm done. The whole mission is a bit anticlimactic. It just needs to go in and stay there. It will do its thing after the staff log in and use the PC as normal. Then, it's up to Lu-Na to hack the whole system.

Sophie sends me a thumbs-up emoji. I stare at it as if willing time to stop. But it doesn't stop. Two nurses whizz past me.

They're headed to the OR, the one that I don't go to anymore because I'm all about that glitzy VIP ward now.

I drag my feet up the stairs. It will be okay. It was a beauty procedure. A dangerous one, but it went well. The surgeon was alert and worked methodically. There will be no complications.

My legs start complaining by the time I reach the VIP floor. That strain is nothing compared to how my chest tightens as I press the door handle to the room with the BBL patient.

Her guardian, the creepy old lady from before, is nowhere to be seen, and I'm so thankful for that. I don't need her leering eyes on top of my anxiety.

The patient is lying on her side, her body shaking lightly. This first red flag has me moving fast toward her, my heart jumping in my ribcage as one of my nightmares takes shape in front of me.

"Hello, I'm here to check your condition. How are you feeling?" I keep my voice professional.

She's crying into her pillow, silent as death. As she looks up at me, I flinch. There is pure hatred in her eyes. A patient has never looked at me this way.

"I never wanted this," she spits out and sniffles. "I look like the hulk."

The initial shock wears off. Maybe things aren't as bad as I thought. "The swelling is quite dramatic, but it will improve in a few weeks. I understand this is not the result you hoped for, but in this case, your body needs a bit of time to readjust and heal. I would recommend lying on your stomach, so you don't put pressure on your buttocks."

She continues glaring at me. Okay, maybe that's not what she wanted to hear.

"It hurts so much. Why did you do this to me?"

"Can I confirm you consented to this procedure, Miss?" My voice is quiet. I'm back to thinking something's wrong.

"I did." She shakes her head, a rueful expression painting her tear-streaked cheeks. "And I didn't."

I drop to my knees, so my head is close to hers. I can barely hear her through the blood rushing in my head. It swishes in rhythmical waves, as if chanting, *'you did this'*.

"Did someone force you to sign the consent forms?" I whisper.

She clicks her tongue. "Why are you pretending to be nice? I'm here because my mother-in-law thought I didn't look good enough for her family. I'm sure it's in a file somewhere."

I *am* nice, I want to scream.

She makes a grab for my face, or my hair, I don't know, with a thin arm. I dodge. She's furious, but the pain and all the tubes keep her on the bed. She hates me enough to claw my eyes out. Part of me wants her to do it, to punish me for taking part in the violation of her fundamental human right. Another part knows that if I let her, she will be punished, not me. The nurses on this floor are so trigger-happy with the sedatives, I question my own place as an anesthesiologist. Requests for sedation have to go through me, but I've seen a big fat zero of them. And the whole floor is full of sedated patients.

I get up and grit my teeth. What to do now? Stay or go? Fight or flight? My flight feels more like freeze.

"Oh, there you are, Dr. Flores." A nurse I barely know has come in. Her scrubs are impeccable, hugging her figure like a sexy uniform. I struggle to remember her name, or even if I've seen her before. The air around her smells sickly sweet. She feels like a PA, not a nurse. "Mr. Rogers is looking for you."

I stifle a groan. All I want to do is go to the changing room, turn on the shower and hold my head in my hands while I contemplate what to do next. Burn my body with hot water the same way my guilt burns me inside. No such luck.

I cast a quick glance in my patient's direction. She's quiet, biting down on her lips to keep her crying silent. My heart aches for her and for my broken doctor's oath.

In a haze of self-loathing, I walk behind the elegant nurse, staring at her ponytail as it bobs side to side. When we reach the door, she gestures me inside, and I arrange my face into a calm, professional expression. The muscles of my cheeks twitch as I smile at Ken, who is sitting behind his massive desk, half facing me, half watching the bustle of Chicago through the floor-to-ceiling windows.

"Well done on your first operation," he says and claps his hands exactly three times. Clap. Clap. Clap. It feels like a gavel punctuating a sentence I'm about to receive.

Ken's face shows a range of emotions I don't feel - joy, pride, excitement. I'm assuming the news about Cindy hasn't reached his ears. I wonder if someone is frantically searching for her right now, expecting her to still attend her surgery.

"You know there's a floor above this one?" he asks.

"Yes."

"It's been under construction for the last few months. It's part of an exciting new project that will make this hospital the top place for the elite to visit." Ken swipes his arm across the air, showing me the Chicago skyline. Where is this going?

"I want you to be part of it." He points a crooked index finger at me and grins.

"What?" I blink in surprise.

"The elite want three things from their healthcare. One, quality; two, open-mindedness; and three, privacy. We provide all that here, on this floor, for adults. The profits we've made so far exceeded our financial projections. This is the future of healthcare."

"So you're opening one more floor?" I try to keep my voice steady. I will have to fight tooth and nail to avoid a future like that. Hospitals can't become the playgrounds of the wealthy.

"Yes, and it will be magnificent. The first and the best Children's VIP hospital wing in Chicago!" He throws his arms in the air, high on excitement. His head snaps up, too, leaving me a few precious seconds to compose myself.

The blood has drained from my face, and my hands are balled into tight fists.

What would Damien do in this situation? He would probably clench his jaw and talk himself down. Or maybe he would punch Ken in the face. I imagine it, and the moment becomes bearable.

I don't do violence, so that's not an option for my next step.

"What do you think?" Ken asks.

Shit, I've been silent for too long.

"It's an ambitious project. But why me?" I try to smile, but my face crumples under my effort, so I press my lips together and knit my brows, hoping I look intrigued but confused.

"You're a pediatric anesthesiologist, are you not?" Ken's reply is somewhat subdued. I'm not matching his energy, and he feels it. I bet my poorly composed expressions don't help.

What would Sophie do? Among all of us, she's the person with the most self-control. So I channel her spirit and nod.

"I am." I try to relax my jaw, so it doesn't sound aggressive. "I was only surprised because I'm new, and this seems like a big deal."

"It is the biggest of deals." Ken chuckles. It seems the spirit of Sophie calmed him. "You're new, but I've got glowing recommendations from everyone you've worked with. One of the VIPs was so taken with you, she left us a hefty tip. She's coming back in a few weeks for her cataract surgery and has specifically requested for you."

It's that creepy old lady, I'm sure of it.

"That's flattering, but that type of procedure doesn't require full anesthesia. My time will be better spent elsewhere."

"Ah, I see." Ken shoots me a sly smile. "You're not into GILFs."

"GILFs?"

"Grandmas I'd like to fuck. Come on, she doesn't look bad for 75. Might be easier to put her under if you don't want her hands crawling up your thighs during the surgery." He laughs such a hearty laugh that it knocks the air out of me. I force a chuckle that sounds like a cough.

Sophie's energy has left me, and I'm once again floating inside myself. The skillset I've cultivated so far doesn't fit the situation.

Tanya's crooked grin appears in my mind. If anyone was master at keeping herself hidden in plain sight, it was her. She knew exactly what the misogynistic clients in Club Lavender wanted to hear. She told me it was survival that pushed her forward.

What do I need for my survival now?

To leave this office, run home and get one of Hana's soothing hugs. To stop time and just be for a moment.

"I'll be there," I say. I know what to do now. I'll agree to anything, which will get him to let me leave. Then I will call Sophie and arrange a meeting with the Arcana Empress. I have done my job as a spy. I know her son's disgusting plans. I know what he lets happen on a daily basis and that he's proud of his crimes. My job here is done.

"Wonderful," Ken replies. "We will talk again closer to the Children's VIP Wing opening. For now, keep what we discussed between us and work as normal."

I nod my goodbye.

It worked. I'm out of here.

The moment I step out of his office, the walls close in on me, and I sway. A wave of nausea propels me to the staff toilets. I fall to my knees, holding the toilet bowl for dear life, and vomit everything I've eaten today.

CONNOR

CHAPTER 27

To say I feel sorry for myself would be an understatement. My foot hurts. Worse, it prevents me from living my life. I called in sick today, but I'm not feeling like I'm getting any better. My ass feels like a pancake, my back hurts in places I can't reach to soothe, and I'm hungry. Today's lunch was instant mashed potatoes and canned tuna. I ate while flicking through one of my comic books, looking at superheroes and villains, and feeling like a badly drawn person in the background.

I considered getting food delivered, then chickened out. Now I'm on the app again, salivating over pizza options, Asian food, Mexican food, and greasy burgers. I even fill my digital basket with items, licking my lips with each tap.

Just as I'm about to check out, I remember the bouncer-security guy's smile as he told me to get my foot treated. As a self-proclaimed sexual sadist, my reaction to actual sadism is not one that I'm proud of. But it is what it is.

There was always fear in me, ever since I realized I wasn't going to be 6ft tall. And being a nerd didn't help. So, I learned to make myself smaller until I was invisible to anything and anyone I perceived as a threat.

Until Laura.

She crashed into my life like a tractor plowing through a field. With a confident, constant push, she reshaped me into a part of her life. And then, she left.

The fear monster in me took that once-in-a-lifetime chance and grew. It inflated until it filled every cavity of my being. If I lost Laura, I could lose anyone. If my life didn't work out with her, it sure as shit wouldn't work out without her.

My finger is still hovering over the checkout button.

I close my eyes and press it, then throw my phone to the floor. I cradle my head in my hands. I'm so pathetic.

Laura didn't let me speak to myself this way. She would ask me if I would ever tell that to her.

"*Never*," I would always say.

And her answer was always the same. "*Then why do you say it to yourself?*"

Being kind to myself isn't something I'm good at. The only self-care I do is beat my fear monster into smaller demons. To force myself to do things that kill parts of it. Like going to the Moon Garden, playing with Hana and Mathias and anyone who would have me, or imagining teaching young people to code. The black demons in my mind shrivel up then and stay in their sad, cold corners.

I get up and hobble to the middle of the room, where my phone lies screen down on the thick gray rug. I bend down, grunting with each movement, and pick it up, my heart hammering in my chest.

The order has been approved. In twenty minutes, a person will bring me a pizza and a bottle of pop.

An overwhelming need not to be alone when that happens makes my hands shake. Who can I call?

I scroll my contacts, worrying my lower lip until I taste blood. Mathias's name looks like the correct answer to Who Wants to Be a Millionaire. I lock it in and dial.

If nothing else, he seems to have scary-looking friends. Their presence might keep the fear monster in check.

Mathias, the half-eaten pizza, and I are situated in the kitchen, the only relatively clean place.

The delivery guy was a high-school student, and I felt stupid the whole two minutes I was forced to interact with him. Then I ate my pizza in tense silence, asking myself why I let my irrational fears control me so much. It's because of Laura. Not that it's her fault, but still.

Mathias arrived about ten minutes later. He doesn't look great either, but who am I to judge?

"Have another slice," I say with a nudge of my chin.

"So what happened to your foot?" He stuffs pizza into his mouth, seeming unbothered by the state of me or my apartment.

"Funny story," I say. I scratch my head. "Kinda fucked me up, actually."

"Do you want me to take a look at it?" He puts the pizza down and wipes his hands.

"Why?" The monster twitches inside me, ready to reign free.

"Because I'm a doctor." His expression is calm, the lines of his face betraying a deep tiredness but nothing short of the truth. "I don't specialize in orthopedics, but I know enough to tell you if you need to go to the hospital."

"Wait, you're a doctor? I thought you made jewelry."

"That's to keep my hands busy." He huffs a laugh. "I forgot we don't actually know a lot about each other."

"I guess everything was on a need-to-know basis." I press my lips into one of those sad smiles.

"I wanted to get to know you. But for the most part, you left Hanako's aftercare to me. Most of the bonding happens then, really. You're a very private person. I respect that. I think Hanako does, too." He rambles a bit, then narrows his eyes. "But if you didn't call me to check on your foot, why am I here?"

"Ha. Well, I guess I'm ready to open up." I look down to my plate, the red-orange grease staining Laura's favorite set.

"Let's call Hanako and wait for her." Mathias takes out his phone, but I put my hand on his wrist before he has a chance to dial her.

"No. It's dangerous." I let my mask drop for a few moments. I let the fear monster reach my eyes.

Mathias stares back at it. He will either be my life raft or the hand that pushes me underwater.

"What happened?" he asks. "Tell me while I examine your foot."

That's enough for me. I may not know what Mathias does, how he likes his coffee, or what his favorite show is, but I know his soul. I've seen how he treats Hana when she's nothing but a puddle of tears peppered with moans. I've seen how he negotiates every scene with her and me. I trust him. He may not have seen my true self, but I have seen his. He doesn't hide his darkness the way I do. He wears it on his sleeve like expensive cufflinks. I wish I could be like him.

We sit on the sofa, opposite one another as he takes my ankle in his hands and starts his examination. As he prods the painful reminder of my time in Hale-Bopp, I let everything spill.

Mathias listens without interrupting. I conceal little, only the name of the hospital and the outcome of my work. I keep the focus on the burly men that I would rather never see again, the ones that made me afraid to go to work in case their boss needs another update.

"That's a lot. It's good you called. First, your foot needs a brace. It doesn't look or feel broken, but I would recommend an x-ray just in case. Second, I feel your pain. I struggle with stuff like that too. Cowardly high-five?" He grins.

I high-five him, though I disagree on his part. If he's a coward, I don't know what I am.

"Which hospital is this? Can you seek compensation?" He walks to a massive bag he always has with him and fishes something that looks like tape out of it. On a closer look, it's a fabric bandage.

"I'd rather have nothing to do with them."

He starts wrapping the bandage around my foot, putting gentle pressure, which makes it throb.

"Do you want protection?" His head is bowed, so I can't tell if he's joking.

I assume he isn't when I reply, "Uh, I guess I wanted to talk to someone. I was hoping you would reassure me that it's all in my head and I have nothing to worry about."

"I can only do that if you tell me which hospital it is."

What the hell does that mean? His eyes meet mine, and there is something in his gaze that makes me flinch. It tickles the fear monster like nothing else tonight.

"It's Hale-Bopp Health." I whisper it so softly, I'm not sure he's heard me at all.

His lips press into a thin line. "Did you do what they asked?"

"What?"

"Whatever they tortured you for, did you do it like they wanted you to?"

"Y-yes?" My stutter comes out as a question. Why is Mathias being so weird?

"Good. You should be fine. You can return to work. You've already given them what they wanted, right? If they come up with something else, just do it remotely and don't challenge them."

"Wait, do you know something about that hospital?"

He gets up, looking flustered. "I've heard it's not a good place, that's all."

I catch his wrist before he has a chance to escape. He shakes my fingers off. He's panicking. And now I'm panicking. Why?

"You can tell me," I say in an attempt to get something else out of him. He's holding back. I know it because his darkness is wrapped around him like a dark cloud. He doesn't hide.

"No, don't worry. You'll be fine. Can you describe the two goons who did this to you in more detail? Anything you remember."

My memory betrays me for a moment, my mind busy spiraling down a dark abyss. But their faces are down there, in the darkness of my mind, so after a few deep breaths, I find my voice.

"Tall, muscular. Buzz cuts, and they both had the same tattoo on their palm. Two crossed arrows or something." I look at him, hopeful his reply will be a revelation.

He shakes his head. "Thank you. Just stay on their good side. They don't have a reason to hurt you, remember that, and you'll be fine."

His words come fast and strong but don't comfort me at all. "Who are they?"

"Not good people. I don't know." He sits back down and cradles his head in his palms. He's having some sort of internal dilemma. I'm not close enough to be included in his doubts.

"Do you know them?" I press on.

"Yes. No." He stands up again. "My friends know of them. Listen, I need to go. You'll be fine. Go to any other hospital to get your foot checked out. And if something else happens, ring me."

You're fucking scaring me, I want to yell, but I'm too dumbfounded by his behavior. He always seems so in control of himself. Even when he was stressed, he was on top of it. What has happened to him since I last saw him? I should ask. I should, yet I don't.

I nod like a mouthless puppet and lock the door behind him. With the bandage, I can walk a little easier. I'm not hungry anymore. I talked to a friend. In theory, I should feel better.

But Mathias's strange behavior only fed my fears. He said I would be safe because I did as they asked. Except, I didn't. Shit, I'm not scared anymore. I'm terrified.

CHAPTER 28

Mathias stayed at Love and Err for a second night. I slept with my mother, expecting him to come home. When I got my phone out in the morning to call him, there was a message that he was dealing with some urgent matters and that he would call as soon as he could.

I would have been upset at the text if it wasn't for the sunflower emoji at the end of it. Whatever happens, I will see him tonight. Being apart these past couple of days has been surprisingly hard. My skin itched to tell him about Cindy's misunderstanding and ask what happened to his patient.

For every minute I'm outside work and in close proximity to Mama, she occupies my attention, so I get no chance to sneak out. She's like a child, following me around and asking thousands of questions. What I like to drink when I go out; what's my favorite type of underwear; how old was I when I first kissed; do I have a favorite client?

They're never-ending and, for the most part, annoying, but I answer them all. It seems she's really taken to heart the whole 'getting to know me' idea. I feel I should reciprocate, so I always return her questions to her, and now I have heaps of disturbing knowledge about my mother, like how she likes thongs but doesn't wear them because they can cause UTIs.

She asks me to drive her somewhere before I go to work today, and we spend the drive listening to Japanese songs from her youth. Some of them I like a lot.

I drop her off at a random bus stop.

"Where are you going?" I ask.

"Meeting a potential client." She shuts the door and walks away elegantly, stepping slowly on her kitten heels. It's like she's waiting for me to leave.

I glance at the time. If I wait, I will be late. I have an appointment first thing, so that would be bad form. I chew on my upper lip. I look around, committing the place to memory, and drive away.

It's 11 am and I'm hungry. I skipped breakfast, so I could barely disguise my rumbling stomach during the last thirty minutes of my appointment.

I'm not surprised when I hear lively voices on my way to the staff kitchen. Maybe Mama has dropped by again?

But no, when I get there, it's empty. I pick up a cereal bar from the cupboard and head toward the noise. It's coming from the reception. Weird. That place is usually deathly quiet.

My jaw drops, and my heart jumps, lodging itself in my throat when I see what's going on.

Cindy is standing in front of a row of sitting women, talking to them like a preacher. The receptionist is on the phone, probably with my manager. The other social workers are still in their own appointments.

"You don't have to wait here and worry. Your boos won't know. There's a club that does a better service, and they can get you out of trouble if you need it. Love and Err, it's called. Not too far away from the Bean, you know. And no one will know why you're there.

They have beds and all sorts. Not very good for children though; it's very loud and dark. Club vibes."

Shit. Shit. Shit. I take Cindy by the wrist and drag her to my office. She continues speaking until we're out of the reception area. Her betrayal feels like a needle piercing my lungs. I've never had a panic attack, but I'm about to have one right now.

"Cindy, why?" I ask, unable to muster anything more coherent.

"They need to know there's options. I'm sorry. We're poor people. It's nice you're offering therapies and stuff, but they don't solve the problem, do they? We still get beat up and stuff." Cindy nods her head, her eyes sparkling with zeal.

I take a deep breath. Then another one. The world spins a little, so I close my eyes for a few moments. The darkness behind my eyelids is still. No good deed goes unpunished, right?

I sit Cindy down on my sofa, look her straight in the eyes and collect every bit of authority I have in my tiny body.

"Love and Err is a sex club. It helps sex workers. It serves sex workers and their customers. It is no place for women who have been abused. It's not a healing space; it doesn't provide legal protection; it doesn't operate as a charity. We do. You're doing those women a disservice by telling them untruths."

"It's a gang, I know. Not all gangs are bad." Cindy doesn't seem convinced by my words.

"It used to be. Not anymore." I will my face to stay still, not to jump at the fact that my client is so aware. I don't lie to her, Sophie's headquarters is not the club, but she and Damien hang out there a lot.

"I don't feel safe in that apartment you got me," Cindy says.

"Why not? Has anything happened?"

"No, just, you know. When I try to sleep, it's like I'm back on that bed, half-awake. I can't sleep. I got to be awake to know I'm alive. Otherwise, I could just be there again, you know?"

"I hear you. And your reaction to what was done to you is normal. It's what your mind thinks is most productive for your survival with the tools you have. If you allow me, I will fast-track your therapy appointment. They can give you more helpful ways to deal with your feelings."

She clicks her tongue. "I don't know, sounds corny to me. I will go, but it doesn't change anything, you know, outside. I can still be hurt."

"How you perceive the outside is something that's inside you. Your perceptions are based on facts and misconceptions, and therapy will allow you to sift through those and paint a more realistic picture of your world. It's like getting glasses for your mind."

She sighs. Her eyes move around the room. My heart rate slows as I make progress. She's thinking about it, and that's the first step.

"Okay. I will do my best," Cindy says.

"Can you promise me two things?" I ask. It's highly unprofessional to ask clients to promise stuff, but I don't know what else to do to ensure she doesn't keep sending abused women Sophie's way. "You won't go back to Love and Err, and you will stop telling people to go there."

I bore my eyes into hers, trying to convey the importance of my request.

"I promise," she says. I believe her because I have no other choice.

When I open the door to send her on her way, my manager is leaning on the wall, her arms crossed in front of her, her face sporting a scowl that I've rarely seen.

My heart picks up pace again. We both exchange pleasant goodbyes with Cindy. By the time we're at my boss's office, it's like I've run a marathon. Maybe I won't avoid that panic attack after all.

"Speak," my manager, Sara, says. She looks like a big, strong momma bear on a normal day. She's six feet tall and used to be a high school football coach. Today, she looks more like an angry lioness protecting her territory.

"Is this about Cindy?" I swallow hard. The lump in my throat stays there.

"Yes, it is about your client, Lucinda. Start from the beginning and cover these topics," she glances down on a piece of paper, "the mental hospital, the escape, and the club."

What to say? Should I lie? Should I conceal some bits? I look at my lap and my bare fingers. I would be twisting and turning my rings if I had any.

"Today, please," Sara urges.

My words come out soft and slow at first, then I get into a monotonous pace, retelling what happened. I keep Sophie's gang out of the story, only mentioning Love and Err as a place that helps sex workers. I don't say anything about Lu-Na's hacking, putting the blame on the mental hospital's careless employees. I show Sara the video of Cindy getting kidnapped, hoping she would understand. I conceal how I got it. Thankfully, she doesn't ask.

"I should fire you right now." Sara sits back in her chair and steeples her fingers like a Bond villain. But she isn't one. She's the best manager I've ever had, and it breaks my heart that we're going through this now.

"I believed I acted in the patient's best interest," I whisper, though it doesn't matter. I can believe I'm a wilted flower in a field, but that doesn't make it any truer.

She narrows her eyes and inhales so loudly I prepare for her shouting at me. Every muscle in my body tenses in anticipation. Tonight, I come back jobless. My mother's questions will be firmly directed at that. I won't sneak out to see Mathias. How will I face him? I won't be able to help anyone anymore.

"Answer truthfully to the next few questions, Hana. I'm only asking because you've been my best employee for the past few years. I don't want to fire you, but if anything you say raises red flags, I will. Am I clear?" Sara leans forward. She's not shouting.

I release a shuddering breath and nod.

"Have you done this before with any other client?"

I shake my head. "No."

"Have you promised Cindy ongoing protection by these club people?"

"No, I encouraged her to engage in therapy and made sure to clear any misunderstandings."

"Have you promised anyone else they will receive a service not offered by our organization?"

"No."

"Do you still believe you acted in the patient's best interest?"

I bite my lips and look down at my lap again. I would be lying if I said I didn't.

"Yes, but," I start. Sara rolls her eyes. A red flag. "But I don't think I acted in the organization's best interests. Which is why I promise I will never do such a thing again. I know you want to hear that I regret it, but I genuinely believe Cindy's—Lucinda's outcome would have been fatal if I hadn't intervened in this way."

"And how are you going to stop yourself next time your gut feeling tells you your client is in danger?"

"I—I—" Treacherous tears well in my eyes. I'm too embarrassed to lift my head.

"Look at me," Sara says. "Eyes on me, Hana. Come on."

I look up, the tears no longer contained. "I'm sorry," I say. I'm not sure if I'm apologizing for the crying, what I did, or merely for existing right now. Following my heart has never felt so shitty.

"I get you. I saw the video. I know what Lucinda is like. I read her file. She doesn't want to commit. She goes back to her abuser. They all do until they're ready to leave for good. We can't save them all. And we can't force them to receive our help." She hands me a tissue. "Your mother is in town, right? Stressing you out?"

"A bit. I'm sorry." I pat my cheeks dry, but more liquid keeps coming out of my eyes, soaking the tissue.

"As your manager and your friend, I can tell you've lost yourself a bit. I don't want to lose you. You're a great social worker, and your heart is in the right place. But you must keep things within regulations. That's the only way we can keep providing this service."

"I understand," I whisper.

"I won't fire you. I will suspend you, however. I will take care of your clients and handle Lucinda. Four weeks. Then, we'll see."

"Thank you for trusting me." I try to smile through my tears, but it doesn't work.

"But," she points her finger in warning, "if I find out anything that doesn't align with what you just told me, I will fire you."

I nod. She gives me another tissue. We stay silent in her office for a few moments. She gives me a chance to calm down. I feel like I should fill the silence, except the lump in my throat is so big and sticky that nothing comes out.

After I leave, I take out my phone and hold it with two hands, afraid I will drop it. I message Mathias, not trusting myself to speak yet.

Hanako: *You won't believe the day I've had today.*

CHAPTER 29

After a short meltdown, a long conversation with Sophie, and a sleepless night, I'm finally where I want to be - away from the hospital and in the Arcana gang headquarters. It's a modern mansion with marbled floors and pillars and all sorts of architectural flares that hardly register courtesy of my anxiety.

I'm here to convey three things to the Empress: one, her son is in some deep shit right now, doing some horrible things on a daily basis; two, he's about to level up his horribleness, so actions need to be taken asap; and three, I'm out of this spy shit. I have barely recovered from my vomiting fit yesterday, and I'm not sure my digestive system can take any more stress.

Sophie and I are in a cozy room, which looks like something between a study and a library. The walls are lined with books and plants, and I kind of want to get up from the deep armchair I'm currently in and look around. Sophie taps her foot on the plush carpet. When our eyes meet, she shoots me a nervous smile.

"It will be fine. You did well," she says. She is probably feeling out of her depth, without Damien and Tanya, and with my anxious ass next to her, ready to flee at any point. Lu-Na left Sophie clear

154

instructions about what to say about anything IT-related but didn't offer any support today. Overall, we're on our own.

My phone buzzes in the pocket of my tailored suit, and I take it out, hoping it's Hanako.

Hanako: *You won't believe the day I've had today.*

I miss her. But I'm too embarrassed to see her until I have good news. And that's what I'm doing today. Fishing for something positive to bring home. I text her back, my fingers working quickly.

Mathias: *Ditto. We should exchange stories tonight. Safe to come back?*

It's like she was waiting for my reply because the three dots appear instantly.

Hanako: *Yes, it's your home!! Mama shares my bed now, but I'll sneak out and come to your room if I have to! You gonna miss dinner?*

I glance at the time.

Mathias: *Probably.*

The door opens, and the Arcana Empress comes in. The way she handles herself, and walks with her head high, despite her age and height, is akin to a real royal. She's about as tall as Mrs. Yagi, but where Hanako's mother prefers pearls and minimal makeup, Emilia Rogers, the leader of the Arcana gang, is all heavy golden rings and bracelets and dark makeup. Her skin doesn't hide her age, free of any interventions. She looks to be around seventy. The way she moves shows that she's kept her body in shape. She's legendary in Chicago, Damien told me, but I never found out what for exactly. Her presence in the room is like a living thing, thick and heavy with expectation.

She sits down on the expensive swivel chair behind the wooden desk and drags her cheeks out in a rehearsed smile. Her face is framed by two ferns that stand on either side of the desk. I have to crane my neck to maintain eye contact with her.

"We came here to discuss our findings at Hale-Bopp Health," Sophie says.

"Timely indeed." She nods to me. "What have you discovered, Mr. Flores? Keep it brief and to the point. Avoid emotional retellings if possible."

Wow. Well, that probably means I should try not to vomit all over her soft red carpet.

"It took your son a while to trust me, but I was eventually offered work on one of the top floors, which I can confirm is a VIP ward. Most of the patients are there against their will. They are mostly women or gender-nonconforming people. The real VIPs are their "guardians," who pay for unnecessary or dangerous treatments to be done for the benefit of their families or business. Very few VIPs are actual patients." I pause for a breath.

"Is that all?" The Empress leans back in her chair, crossing her arms.

"Not even close." A frown blossoms on my face, and I do nothing to hide it. She better listen. "Hospital records are being erased. That's something that no hospital does without explicit consent from the patient. And even if something needs to be amended, the record is annotated or archived. Never deleted. And your son knows that. Interestingly, the IT company they hired knew it too because they wouldn't provide the service for Hale-Bopp's new records software. Your son knew that, and he hired thugs to threaten the IT guy. So if you harbor any hopes that your son isn't an active part of all this, you're wrong. Furthermore—"

"Let me stop you right there, Mr. Flores. I have never thought my son was innocent. I sent you there to find out how deep his corruption is. That, and where Comet International plays into the demise of the hospital. My mistake was letting Ken occupy a managerial position he wasn't ready for. I want to know what mistakes he's making. All that you've told me so far is old news. I have other people reporting to me." She plays with a fat gold ruby ring, twisting it this way and that, showing me... what? That she's impatient? Powerful? That my words don't matter because she's familiar with the content? Well, I'm about to make her regret her approach.

"Furthermore," I continue, ignoring her interruption, "your son is about to open a VIP Children's wing. And trust me, he doesn't intend to help poor Make-a-wish kids. Problematic teenagers? No issue, sedate them to oblivion. Toddlers having meltdowns? Let's bring back the lobotomy. Don't want your heir to produce inconvenient offspring? Bring him in, and we'll give him the snip while he thinks he's getting a mole removed."

I'm panting by the end. And yes, Ken Rogers wasn't that expressive when he gave me the news. But I'm a doctor, and a worrier, and I had plenty of time to overthink what this announcement means in reality. It's not going to be good; I know it. It's going to be more of the same, but worse. Because, children.

Emilia Rogers remains silent for a very long time. Sophie keeps quiet too. We're letting the weight of my words settle between us. It covers us like the slag at the bottom of a forging pot. Then the Empress starts nodding as if she's reached a conclusion in her internal debate.

"Well discovered," she says as she puts her thin, wrinkled finger on one of the phone buttons. "Bring him in."

I turn around toward the door, expecting a security guard to enter. Or maybe even Ken. This could have been a big elaborate setup to get Sophie and her young gang in trouble. Sophie puts a hand on my shoulder.

"Relax," she whispers. "We're all on the same side."

But are we? The Empress knew what atrocities were committed in her hospital and did nothing about it.

A handsome Asian man enters in a maroon pinstripe suit that outlines his slim frame. He seems familiar.

"This is Kazuo Okada," the Empress says with an outstretched arm. "He's a military nurse, and he's been working for me for the last ten years."

He smiles at us, and I narrow my eyes.

"You can't recognize me without my scrubs, Dr. Flores?" He winks.

I straighten my back. So he's the "insecure" male nurse who met me on the day before the operation.

"You invited me to lunch," I say.

"I did. And my offer still stands. Though I can be more open here and tell you that I'm the leader of the opposition. Ever since Comet International buried their fingers into my place of work,

I have been gathering allies." The way he talks is smooth, with a baritone that clashes with his unblemished babyface. An unwelcome thought passes through my head. Mrs. Yagi would love him. His name sounds Japanese, and he doesn't lack looks or education. Hell, Hanako will probably like him too. And I know it because *I* like him. We have pretty similar taste in people.

"Kazuo hit a roadblock with his recruitment when he wasn't allowed on the VIP floor. In fact, none of the previous staff are allowed up there. One of my conditions when I gave Ken the hospital was 'no restructuring'. No firing staff. So he drowned my people with new recruits." The Empress's voice is so gentle now, I'm struggling to remember what she sounded like minutes ago when she talked down to me.

"And this is where Mathias comes in," Sophie says.

"Yes." Kazuo flashes her a dazzling smile. His canines are long and a bit crooked, making him appear like a vampire. My tongue slides across my teeth, wondering how much sharper his would feel. "Thanks to Dr. Flores's intelligence, I will be able to keep recruiting people. Scared staff might stand by when adults are being hurt. But many won't like the prospect of children under threat. So, they will join me."

I nod, partly distracted by him and partly not seeing how gathering medical workers can help.

"Are you planning a hostile takeover?" Sophie is ten universes ahead of me in comprehension, which is why she is the boss.

"In a way." The Empress leans forward, her elbows digging into the expensive leather place mat on her desk. "I don't want to reveal much about the management of the hospital, but it exists legally, despite its previous operations being directed largely toward the urgent care and rehabilitation of people in my employ. The current ownership consists of me, Ken, and the employees. If Kazuo can garner enough support, and I stand behind him, Ken and Comet International's plans can be overthrown. I would like to do it quietly. Without the media's attention or that of other gangs. No in-fighting."

"Very good plan," I say. It's like a weight has been lifted from my shoulders. "So, you don't need me anymore? I can go back to my previous life, right?"

The way Kazuo looks at me wipes the smile off my face. There's so much pity there I can almost taste it.

"It will be too conspicuous if you leave now," he says.

The Empress nods. "You're staying."

"But—but I can't. You don't understand, it's not for me. It's too much. The things they will make me do." I stand up and slam the desk, making the ferns' leaves vibrate.

Sophie takes me by the wrists and sets me down slowly. "I got this," she whispers.

"I agree with Mathias," she says in a firm voice. "We've provided you with the information you required. He can stop."

"Have you?" Emilia Rogers shakes her head, her expression collecting sternness which seems to be reserved for me. "One part of the assignment was to learn Comet International's involvement. Why this hospital? How did Ken get into such bad company?"

"You can ask him." My words come out as a whine. "He's your son."

She doesn't appreciate this. Her brows furrow, and she exchanges a glance with Kazuo that makes my blood run cold. Under the gentle exterior of an old lady, she's vicious. No one becomes legendary by being nice.

"Don't be deterred, Mrs. Emilia. Dr. Flores is a man of sturdy morals. He only wants to uphold his doctor's oath. He isn't challenging you," Kazuo says as he returns her look. I like him a bit more now.

The Empress's face mellows, and she turns her eyes back to us. "Okay. I hear you. I'm willing to forgo the investigation part into Comet International. I will use other means to learn what I need. You still have to return. Tomorrow, a VIP patient will request that you see to all of their needs. This will mean that Ken will have to find another anesthesiologist for the time being. Kazuo will work fast. This is the endgame now, so I don't foresee any complications appearing on your part. You only have to go to work and appear interested in the new development. Nothing else."

"Who is it?" I say as I exhale some of my anxiety.

"You will find out tomorrow. It's a person I trust. They have money, clout, and will protect you. They have been briefed."

"You really aren't going to tell us?" Sophie chimes in.

"They asked to remain anonymous. Respect that," Kazuo says with a smile. "But trust me, Mathias—can I call you Mathias?—you will be safe. Nothing to worry about."

More unknowns. But the prospect of not partaking in operations I don't condone makes me relax. Soon I will be done with this.

I nod to Kazuo, agreeing to some part of his reassurance. Maybe all of it. I like how my name sounds on his lips too. He pronounces it the same way as Mrs. Yagi. Perhaps it's a Japanese thing. Maybe I will ask Hanako to pronounce it this way too. But first, I need to hold her. Now that I can breathe easier, I will be able to feel more of her. I will focus on how she fits in my arms and the smell of her hair, like jasmine and her own sweet scent. And maybe I will kiss her too.

HANAKO

CHAPTER 30

Mama is snoring gently next to me when the front door opens. I hear the lock click shut, and I want to jump out and throw myself at Mathias. I've been thinking tonight, in the free moments between my mother's questions, how much I miss him.

So I don't want to reject the pull of his presence. I slip out of the bed on quiet feet; I need some alone time with him. I crave it. I'm barefoot, in my tiny satin PJs, my black hair falling free on my shoulders. I glance at my fleece dressing gown, propped on a chair on my mother's side, and decide to leave it be.

The hallway is dark and quiet. The only light comes from under Mathias's door. It calls to me like a beacon.

I knock and push the handle gently without waiting for a response. He better be ready for me because I can no longer wait.

My breath hitches in my throat when I see him. He's sitting at the edge of the bed, his crisp white shirt unbuttoned to the middle, his owl tattoo peeking underneath. He's discarded his suit jacket and his tie on the other side of the bed. Goosebumps cover my skin when his eyes lift to meet mine. They're so blue I can stare at them for eternity.

And that's what I do. I gaze at him because all words have left me. I want to touch him, to find solace in his arms.

Mathias looks tired, but his face lights up with a smile as he returns my intense look. He stands up, towering in front of me like a Greek god.

I put my hand on his cheek. The rules from a couple of weeks ago seem like they never existed. As my thumb caresses his smooth tanned skin, I have none of the anxieties I usually have when faced with the idea of letting someone in. I trust him. To do what, I'm not sure. Not break my heart? Not to betray me?

"Hello," he whispers as he takes my hand from his face and plants a soft kiss on my palm. These little moments hold the intimacy of a thousand sloppy penetrations. I'm shivering now, and not from the chill in the air.

He pulls me into his arms, holding me so tight I'm crushed against his hard chest. The owl embraces me with its wings, and I inhale the scent of him, masculine, clean, and safe.

When his arms loosen, I look up, my eyes zeroing in on his plump lips. Kink, degradation, rope—I love those things. However, they're all far away from my mind tonight. I want Mathias, just as he is, with his kinky dom persona but stressful personality, with his gentle, consistent care and his tendency toward self-neglect.

I stand on my tiptoes and press my lips to his. I'm sure he must be feeling this moment, too because his breath hitches.

My tongue tangles with his in a lazy, explorative rhythm. There's a stab of desire in my lower belly, and to my surprise, I feel an emptiness there. It's something I haven't felt in years. It makes me press my body further into his until we're flush against each other. He rolls his hips, rubbing himself against me, teasing us both.

He walks backward to the bed without letting me go. We crash on top of it, a tangle of limbs. When he releases my lips and peppers kisses along my jawline and down my neck, I moan so loudly it's like the walls vibrate.

I press my hand to my mouth, my eyes widening. He chuckles, his gaze dark with desire. But Mama is a light sleeper, so I put my palms against his chest and push myself off.

"I got suspended today," I whisper.

He adjusts himself and then scoots closer to me on the bed. "From work or in rope?"

"I wish it was rope." I crack a slight smile.

"Tell me about it." His fingers entwine with mine. I can feel the cool metal of his rings between my knuckles.

"Cindy made a scene about our charity not being helpful. And then proceeded to advertise Love and Err as the better place to get stuff sorted." I sigh.

"Ouch. And I bet your boss wasn't happy about that."

"Nope."

"Did you tell them everything?"

"Only as much as I could to keep Sophie's gang out of trouble. Nevertheless, there will be an investigation into my work, and I won't be able to see any clients for a month. I don't know what I'm going to do in the house for days on end."

"Work on your tamales?" He winks.

I chuckle. "They weren't that bad!"

He gives me a little squeeze. "I had a pretty shitty day yesterday, then today it started shitty but turned out okay. And now I think I'm in heaven."

"Oof, that's cheesy," I say, letting him scoop me up and nuzzle my neck.

We toss around a bit, giggling and poking each other, then settle under the covers. They smell like him.

"I saw Connor yesterday," Mathias says.

"Really? How come?" I ask. We don't usually see him during the week. Weekends are for play, but he's never expressed an interest outside of that.

"I'm still not sure, actually. It seemed like he needed a friend. I felt something was off when he called me, so I went to his place. Do you know what he does for work?"

"Not sure. He looks like an accountant?" I play with Mathias's tuft of chest hair. He shakes his head no. "Something with finance. No? Something with IT?"

"Yes. He's a software developer. And one of his current clients? Comet International, the new players at Hale-Bopp Health."

"You're joking." I prop myself on my arms. "He's connected to all of this?"

"He is. His work is the reason why Lu-Na were struggling so much with the system. He's good, and now he's terrified." Mathias glares into the middle distance. "And on top of that, the hospital boss wants to open a VIP Children's wing. And do god knows what in there."

"Shit. Sophie won't let that happen, right?"

"No. We went to see the Arcana leader. How much do you want to know?" He brushes some stray hair out of my face, and I marvel at his consideration. I can see he's desperate to tell me. He never did like keeping heavy secrets.

"I'm suspended. Tell me everything." I take his hand and play with his Memento Mori ring as he recounts the meeting from tonight.

When he finishes, he releases a loud, shuddering sigh.

"I feel so much better after offloading," he says with a tiny smile.

"I think your shitty thing beats mine," I reply.

"It's not a competition."

"I know. I think I made a mistake by trying to keep myself away from your undercover work. I thought I could box up our interactions. Kink on weekends, roommates on weekdays. But that didn't help. I still got all confused and ended up getting involved in Cindy's business. If I had known the whole picture with that hospital, I could have been more proactive in her care and helped you out in another way, maybe. But that's just one side of things." I look him straight in the eyes. I've thought about this for the past few days. I'm ready to say it. "I don't want you to hide a part of yourself from me. I don't want to have pieces of you and moments of your time. Somehow, I got kinda greedy, and now I want all of it. I want to be more than just play partners or roommates or whatever else we've labeled ourselves as."

His eyes widen in surprise and something else. Hope, maybe? Happiness?

"You have no idea how much I've craved to hear those words," he whispers as he pulls me close.

"Why didn't you say—" I can't finish my question because he closes his mouth on mine, devouring my words. We kiss as if the world is ending, sharing air and the sweet taste of reciprocated feelings.

When his big palms slide under my PJ vest, I moan into his mouth. He smiles against my lips, his teasing touch exposing more and more of my sensitive skin. He catches all of my moans with his kisses. I'm thankful because I can no longer hold them in. I don't have the mental strength to think about my mother sleeping in the next room or if what we're doing might bite me in the ass later. My head is full of Mathias - his tongue, his fingers, his rock-hard cock against my belly.

I'm blissfully empty again, wetness pooling in my panties. And this emptiness, it's like nothing before. It's not a hole in my soul or trauma response. It's the space inside me I've made for Mathias. It's where I will hold him and where he will live.

CHAPTER 31

She did it. She ran toward my open arms. I waited, and I hoped, and I gave her my all.

Hanako is here now, pinned under my weight, making sexy sounds, and moving like a succubus. And there's not a rope in sight. Not even a sex toy.

Don't get me wrong, I love our kinky escapades. Every single session was designed to be great. And they were. They all brought me closer to her.

But this right now, this is different. I lose myself in the feel of her silky hair and the warmth of her skin. I got under the covers with my clothes on, so now I'm melting in my shirt and trousers. They need to come off.

I break our frantic kissing and look down so I can finish unbuttoning my shirt. I get distracted by Hanako's exposed breast. It's slipped from her tank top at some point. My lips curl up, and I forget all about my own clothes. My mouth closes around her peaked nipple, and she throws her head back, her hands finding their way to my neck. She moans, and I reach up to press my hand on her mouth. We can't be waking up Mrs. Yagi. This moment is too perfect to be broken.

She rolls her hips against mine in want. I've never seen her like this. She's always been expressive, but now her limbs are all around me, and we're so tightly pressed together, we're as if one octopus. Somewhere deep inside, I realize that she was putting up walls around her inner being when she played. I thought rope brought out her most authentic self, but maybe I was wrong. Maybe she was just tending to a part of herself while keeping another one locked up, hidden, forgotten.

My teeth press into the sensitive flesh of her nipple, and she jerks a little in pleasure, curling around me like a cat. My senses are overloaded with her scent, the sounds of her heartbeat, the feel of her flesh under my touch.

I move my hands up and down her body, grabbing and pinching and kneading. There is nothing measured about the way I explore this version of her. It's just a glorious mess of feeling directing my body - desire, joy, belonging, acceptance. A feverish tranquility.

Her fingers find their way at the front of my shirt, and she pushes me slightly away to work the buttons. As each one slips open, her eyes take me in, making me feel like a god. I let her undress me down to my boxers, reveling in her taking charge. When she's done, she flops on the bed and extends her arms.

I settle on top of her, my blank mind filling with ideas about what to do next.

"I want you inside me," she whispers.

"All in good time," I say into her mouth and kiss her again. Deep and slow. I love kissing her. And I'm sure I'm going to love to stick my dick inside her, but it's not the right time. If I do it now, she will regret it later. Every moment when I wasn't thinking about the stupid hospital and the mess that is my life, I was thinking about her and about this moment. I have fantasized about entering her, inch by inch, until she's full and I am surrounded by her. And every time, those thoughts reeled back to the story she told me in the Moon Garden.

So sleeping with her is not about spontaneity and lust. It's about understanding, healing, and connection. It will happen. When she's ready. When I'm ready. But not now and not like this.

I move my mouth down, kissing down her neck and nibbling on her nipples. She shivers when I stick my tongue in her belly button. A filthy moan escapes from her mouth, and my dick twitches in anticipation. Soon.

"Be quiet now," I whisper. I hope Mrs. Yagi is a heavy sleeper. For all our sakes. My door doesn't lock, so Hanako's self-restraint is all I can rely on.

I pull her PJ bottoms down with her panties and toss them to one side. When I spread her legs and look at her, she claps her hand on her mouth and stifles a gasp. She loves being exposed, and I want to look at her like this until my eyes fall out.

I take three deep breaths, building her excitement. She's already wet for me, and I can't wait to taste her. I run my hands along the insides of her thighs, making her tremble.

Then I dive into her pussy like a hungry beast.

I suck her clit into my mouth, my fingers digging into her ass, lifting her so I can eat her like a meal. I know she's close because her trembling grows, transforming into shaking. I lick her in circles; one, two, three times. She makes a sound between a moan and hiccup, and I chuckle into her open pussy. Her breathing is ragged; I can't wait for her to come all over my face.

I dip my tongue inside her, pressing my nose into her pelvis. Eating pussy is messy business and I've missed it so much. This will need to be a regular thing.

I fuck her with my mouth; my tongue going in and out of her, and I bring one hand to play with her clit. She moans, and I hear a slapping sound. I don't look up, but I think she's put both her hands on her mouth. She might as well put a pillow on her face because I'm about to make her scream.

Her pussy is scorching hot under me, and she tastes both sweet and salty, like a summer holiday at the seaside. I love it.

I pour all of that love into my frantic mouth, and moments later, she stills, her pussy clamping on my tongue as if it wants to keep it inside forever. Then, she curls up, stifling a scream, and twitches all over.

I give her clit one last kiss that makes her jerk and climb up next to her, wiping my face with my hand.

I pull her to me, a little spoon full of post-orgasmic bliss, and nuzzle her neck. Her heart is still beating like crazy. I pull the blanket, so it covers both of us and let her gather her wits.

I'm not sure which one of us fell asleep first, but when I open my eyes next, the light of dawn paints the room a soft yellow. Hanako is facing me, our legs entwined and our hands clasped together. In my half-awake state, I imagine we lie on the bed in the shape of a heart.

"Good morning," Hanako whispers, her eyes sparkling in the semi-darkness.

"It's a great morning." I wink.

She chuckles, then sighs. "We should probably talk about this."

"Let's." I pull her closer to me, reveling in her warmth.

"Do you regret what we did tonight?" she asks.

"I definitely don't. Do you?"

"No. I'm still overwhelmed. I thought we were going to have sex, and then we didn't. Deep inside, I'm thankful. I don't think I'm ready. I was swept up by my emotions when I said what I said." She looks at me quizzically. "Why didn't you go for it?"

I lift myself up a bit and let her snuggle under my arm. I pet her hair with one hand, unwilling to let go of the physical connection between us. "It didn't feel right. Trust me, I wanted to. But ever since you told me how long it's been since you let a man have sex with you, I've been thinking that if it ever happens between us, it has to be similar to a scene. Discussed, processed in both our minds, executed with passion and care. What do you think?"

"I think that I can't wait to do it." She smiles against my chest. "What do we do about Connor? I don't like him the same way that I like you, but I love our threesome play."

"I love it too. We should keep doing it if Connor is still happy with it." I kiss her forehead, my thoughts taking me back to his messy apartment. We can't let go of him now. He's in a vulnerable place. He's been friendly to both of us, so it's time we stick by him. More so, considering we have the same enemy. "It's Friday, so let's go to the Moon Garden tonight. You're suspended, and I'm going to have an easier time in the hospital from now on. Perfect timing."

"Hmm." Her consonants rumble against my chest. "You're right. Will he be able to make it with his foot, though?"

"We can give him a lift." I pull my phone from the bedside table and shoot him a quick message.

MG tonight, play time? We can pick you up.

While I was typing, Hanako's hands have started circling my chest, playing with the hair on El Buho's head.

"Why an owl?" she asks.

"They're generally a symbol of wisdom and intuition. But in my abuelita's culture, they're also dark beings. Think night and death, bad omens, stuff like that."

She looks at me like I'm crazy. "Why would you have a symbol of bad luck on your chest? And a ring that reminds of death?"

"Doctors who work in ORs are pretty superstitious." I chuckle. "When I was thinking about what I wanted to have, I knew it was going to be a bird. Birds are free, and that's how I strive to live my life in many ways. But when I learned the folklore around owls, and specifically them being messengers of death, I knew that was my bird. See, if I have the owl trapped in the ink in my chest, it won't come for my patients. I've never had a table death."

Hanako looks both impressed and unconvinced. "Sounds legit."

"Hey, every little bit helps, you know."

"And the ring?"

Talking about the ring is different. But she's been open and honest, and I can only return that. "The night I came out to my family as bisexual, my father told me I was dead to him. My mother didn't say anything. It was after I refused to go to conversion therapy. Many years later, when I had a stable life and was finishing my med studies, I had the ring made to remind me that even when I feel most alive, I can die. I guess the whole thing taught me that I should always weigh my choices and choose wisely. There are many chances to experience tiny deaths throughout life. It keeps me humble."

"That's a lot deeper than I thought it was going to be. I guessed unresolved teenager angst." She gives me a hug.

"It kinda is. But enough about sad things." I turn and blow a raspberry on her neck. She squeals. If Mrs. Yagi wasn't awake, she definitely is now.

"I'm not used to being quiet in my own house," Hanako whispers, a naughty grin playing on her lips. "What you did to me last night was evil. I will pay you back very, very soon."

Her hand moves to my crotch. I'm still sporting a morning semi.

"As much as I want to find out what that threat entails, I really don't want your mother to walk in on us." I pull her into a crushing embrace, stopping her explorative touch mid-stroke.

Hanako grunts then giggles until I release her. "Fine. I'll go shower." Then, after a second's consideration, she adds, "Should we go together?"

She wiggles her eyebrows, and I burst out laughing. This forward version of her is highly entertaining. "Will you be quiet if we do?"

"Probably not." She shrugs, and her boobs bounce in a way that makes me regret my next words.

"Then I'll have to stay here. I can't be trusted around you all naked and wet."

"Fair enough, me neither." She plants a quick kiss on my lips, pulling away before I can stick my tongue in her mouth.

As she pulls her PJ bottoms on and skips away from my room, I sigh, trying to cleanse my brain from all the filthy thoughts that she conjures up.

I bury myself back inside the blanket, inhaling what's left of her on my pillow. My phone vibrates once. When I look at it, my mood shifts.

Connor: *I'm not going. You know why. Staying in.*

Well, I clearly didn't do a good job of convincing him that living his normal life was safe. I was in a state that night, still reeling from Ken's announcement and missing Hanako, while so desperately wanting to be out of the undercover job. It's not an excuse for perpetuating his fear, but it means now that I'm in a better place, I have to make sure he's okay.

So Hanako and I are going to Connor's tonight. To put his mind at ease and to show him he's not alone. And who knows, maybe we'll make it to the Moon Garden too.

CHAPTER 32

Mathias goes in the shower straight after me, and I head for my bedroom, wrapped in a towel. I open the door tentatively.

The bed is made, and there's no one inside. A faint smell of fresh food comes from the kitchen. Mama must be cooking. Did she hear me and Mathias chatting just now? I'm still uncomfortable after she eavesdropped on me at work. I haven't caught her doing it at home, but I'm usually still cautious. Last night and this morning, I wasn't. Mathias was too distracting. I wonder if she would have barged in if she thought we were being inappropriate.

I take one deep, encouraging breath and make my way to the kitchen. The table is set for two – there are two transparent food domes with what looks to be traditional Japanese breakfast inside. I look around the room, but unless my mother is hiding under the sink, she's not here either. I call for her a couple of times and check out the balcony. Nothing. Her shoes aren't in the hallway, so I know she's left. But where has she gone so early?

There's a note on the table.

井の中の蛙大海を知らず
A frog in a well knows nothing of the sea

Reading this is bittersweet. It might mean that my mother has realized that our lives are different and coming to terms with her shortcomings. It could also be that she's saying that about me. I choose to believe the first interpretation.

Seeing the Japanese writing makes me remember that I was once learning it. That I can read it a little bit. Maybe now that I'm suspended, I can pick up my old textbooks again and brush up on my language skills.

I peek under one of the food domes.

There's rice, miso soup, grilled fish, rolled omelet, seaweed, pickled vegetables, and a note not to forget to make tea.

I rack my brain for the Japanese words. Suddenly, I want to remember. I want to call it all by the names Mama used when she set the table. When I was young, she would put a dish, say it in Japanese, then English, then ask me to repeat it. It's a warm memory.

Gohan. Rice. Tamagoyaki. Rolled omelet. Yakinori. Seaweed.

I spot a tiny bowl of natto, fermented soybeans. I love them, but many people don't. They're an acquired taste. Oh, it's going to be funny watching Mathias try them.

I can't remember any other words. The pickles could be oshinko or tsukemono. I can't remember which. I wonder if Mama will be pleased or offended if I ask her.

In any case, I will learn again.

I put the food dome back and stare at my mother's poppy painting. It seems less sad today. But maybe it's the sunlight hitting it just right.

This is a perfect morning. Mama is making an effort to understand me, maybe, and Mathias is wet and naked one door away from me.

This gives me a crazy idea. Maybe not crazy by other people's standards, but me? I don't really do spontaneous stuff like this. It

174

must be all the happy chemicals from Mathias's tongue in my pussy last night. I've never been tongued like that down there. It was a spiritual experience I can't wait to reciprocate. I just had a shower, but whatever. My hair is still wet.

The bathroom door locks from the inside, so when I press the handle and it opens, steam wafting on my face, I know Mathias won't mind me coming in.

He's facing the wall, water running all over him. His back is tanned and more refined than I expected, his muscles flexing as he washes his head.

"Are you going to join me, creeper?" His voice is light. Did he hear me come in?

I close the door behind me. "Mama isn't in," I say. Now that I'm here, some of my confidence wanes. I bite on my lower lip, considering the situation.

"I know. That's why I left the door unlocked." He turns around, his cock already hard.

"Oh, wow." My eyes widen. I didn't expect him to be ready.

"I was actually thinking about you coming in." He grins, making me wet in a way that has nothing to do with water.

"What else?" I ask as I open my towel, revealing my chest. The way his gaze runs over me makes me squirm with pleasure.

"You said you were going to pay me back for eating you out. I was thinking about all the ways it could go." He extends an arm toward me. I take it, tossing the towel to the floor.

I'm naked, my skin covered with goosebumps, swirls of steam licking it from every direction. Mathias tugs me to him, pressing his hot, wet torso to mine.

"Keep talking," I rasp. He rolls his hips, rubbing his cock against my belly. I clench my thighs, feeling like an animal in heat.

"You could use your deft little hands on me." He takes my hand in his and brings it to his mouth. I think he'll kiss it, but he licks the tip of my index finger, then puts it into his mouth and sucks on it, his tongue twirling around it. My pussy throbs in response, remembering how he sucked on my clit last night. He does this while holding my gaze captive, and my jaw drops open. He bites a little before releasing my hand and capturing my chin with his fingers. "You said you wanted me inside you. Maybe you'll let me into your hot mouth?"

He pushes his thumb between my lips, pressing on my tongue. I try to suck, but he moves his hand down, cupping my breasts. "Or between your boobs?"

He tweaks my nipple, and I yelp softly. Unrelenting, he holds me by the waist with one arm as he pushes a finger between my clenched thighs. "Or maybe in your thigh gap?"

His finger is so close to my entrance. As he moves it in and out of the space between my legs, I adjust myself, so he rubs my clit. My eyes are still locked with his. I moan, spreading my juices on his hand. My arousal builds up, but clearly, he's not going to let me have my way this easily. In one sleek move, he turns me around, making my world spin. He adjusts himself so that his cock is between my butt cheeks. He slides it up and down as his arms encase me in a possessive hug. "Or you can use your perfect ass to get me off?"

My thoughts go fuzzy. I lose my ability to speak. I've never trusted someone to do stuff like this to me without a long negotiation first. I thought I would recoil, but the way my body responds now tells me I've been wrong. I trust Mathias. I trust him so much that I want him to push me into the wall and ram his cock into me without warning. He won't do it, though. And perhaps this is precisely why I'm here being teased by him and not anyone else.

He kisses my neck, still pumping gently behind me. I love this. Being used as an object for pleasure, where every crevice of my body can be something to fuck. I moan as his arms tighten around me even more, making my breath hitch. He bites down on my shoulder. I squirm in his grasp as the pain registers. I'm sure it'll leave a mark.

The sound of the water is far away, and I'm going into that blissful place where I'm alone and everything is perfect. Mathias's tongue moves again, and this time, he's sucking on my earlobe. A second later, his voice pulls me back to him.

"Talk to me, Yagi Hanako. What do you want?"

I gasp out of my submissive place, and his hold on me loosens enough so I can breathe deep, steadying breaths. Maybe it's the way he said my name. Maybe it was the fact that he's not doing anything now, and I crave for him to touch me. He wants me to speak. But I don't speak when I'm like this. Do I? Why not?

"Don't overthink it. Just open your mouth," he licks my neck again, "and tell me how you're going to pay me back for what I did to you."

Right. Thoughts into words. I came here to suck his dick. I wanted to drive him crazy the same way he shattered my world last night. Words. Words.

"With my mouth," I whisper.

"What are you going to do with your mouth?"

"Make you come."

He twirls me again. As I face him, he grabs a fistful of my hair in one hand and pulls so that his beautiful blue eyes penetrate mine with a look of pure desire. And care. It's a look that I've come to love. A gaze of primal lust that is soft around the edges.

Unexpectedly, more words come to my mouth. "I want to kiss you first."

"Good girl," he whispers and presses his lips to mine without releasing my hair.

The pull makes my neck sting and my pussy clench. A perfect blend of pain and pleasure. He invades my mouth with his tongue, stealing my breath, worshiping me with every move. Then he tugs at my hair, and we detach. My mouth is still open and swollen from his furious kiss when he forces me to my knees.

His cock is glorious and fits perfectly in my mouth. I haven't done this in years. A little discomfort starts in my mind. If he starts mouthfucking me now, I will probably have to call red. I'm not ready for that.

"Look at me," Mathias says. "Move your head."

He's not going to do anything. Empowered, I twirl my tongue around the tip and grasp the base with my right hand. I push him farther into my mouth until his head hits the back of my throat, then withdraw. I hollow my cheeks as I find a comfortable rhythm. He groans, his grip on my head tightening. But he never pushes into me. Instead, he puts one hand on the wall to steady himself.

"Touch yourself." His words come out between sexy groans. I do as he says, the fingers of my free hand finding my clit. I replicate the tempo of my mouth as I rub my pussy and circle my clit to when my tongue swirls around Mathias's cock.

This unlocks some kind of new submissive space within me. I'm not alone. Mathias is here with me, but nothing else makes it past. The smell of soap mixing with his natural scent is intoxicating. Droplets of water ricochet off him and land on me, making this whole thing both the cleanest and dirtiest thing I've ever done. It's the duality for me. I feed off it like a demon.

I go faster and louder. The sounds of us chasing our pleasure knock me off the edge, and I come, still sucking.

I almost collapse, but Mathias holds me steady by my hair.

He pulls out suddenly, just as I feel his balls drawing up. He comes all over my boobs, his hot cum landing on me like flowers on a stage after an outstanding performance. And hell, I feel like a star.

CHAPTER 33

When I put on my doctor's coat today, I don't feel the usual weight on my shoulders. My chest is light, and I breathe a bit easier. Knowing that I won't be operating, I leave my Memento Mori ring on. It's a small rebellion against the regulations.

I take the elevator up and hum a radio ad jingle. My endorphins are running high - my sex drive is satisfied, my belly is full of delicious food, and on the way here, I saw a flowering tree. The fact that the Empress has sorted a VIP patient, which will prevent me from going against my morals, enables me to feel all this good stuff. I'm looking forward to the time when I will get my license reinstated and be at peace with myself again.

The elevator doors open to the elegant nurse from before with the tight-fitting scrubs. She appears to be Ken's secretary. I don't know why she's dressed as a nurse.

"Dr. Flores. I've been waiting for you. Please follow me," she says in a sing-song voice.

I smile to myself. This will be about my new assignment.

I expect to go into Ken's office, but I'm instead taken to the room which had Delilah, my BBL patient, and the creepy old lady. A heatwave makes my blood bubble inside me, replacing all my endorphins with pure adrenaline. Has there been a complication? BBLs are one of the most dangerous beauty surgeries, after all.

"Dr. Flores!" Ken's voice greets me before I'm even inside.

I look around, trying my best to hide my rising panic, but the inside of the room is different than I remember. There are sunflowers everywhere, and the bedsheets are warm yellow. The coffee table has a pristine white tablecloth, and the sofa next to it has two people sitting side to side.

Ken Rogers and—Mrs. Yagi?

I blink, my brain short-circuiting from my worlds colliding in a most unpleasant way.

"Let me introduce you to Miss Tomoko Yagi, a renowned painter and art critic, and our latest VIP patient. She had requested you to take care of her specifically." Ken stands up, beaming. He comes my way, drags me closer to the coffee table, and pats my back. I look at him, puzzled. "Bow, it's an Asian thing," he whispers through his teeth.

I bow without breaking eye contact with Hanako's mother, which I'm sure is breaking all the etiquette rules, but I'm too stunned to avert my eyes. She's the VIP the Empress arranged for me? What the fuck?

Ken is oblivious to my shock. He continues talking, his voice high and friendly, grating on my nerves. "I explained that you are an anesthesiologist, so while you can be responsible for her care in the OR and at points outside, she would need a whole oncology team. Here is her record. Do familiarize yourself with it, and don't disappoint Miss Yagi or me." The last bit is for my ears only. It has an edge I'm not sure I deserve.

He scuttles out of the way like a cockroach while I remain bolted to the floor. Oncology team? Her record? It must be all made up for my sake.

"Give me a minute," I say to her as I turn around and read through the file in my hands.

For a made-up thing, it's elaborate. They've even got the correct x-rays, with the correct name and patient number. Half of the documents are translated from Italian.

"You must have a lot of questions, Mathias." She speaks in an even tone.

I join her on the sofa, my brows knit together. I can't hide from her when she says my name like that. I do have lots of things to ask. Where do I even start?

"I always call you Mrs. Yagi. I hadn't realized you're a Miss." This ridiculous, small thing comes out first.

"I do not mind. I am hardly a miss." She smiles.

This close, I can see her age. Even behind the flattering natural makeup, her eyes reveal wisdom and a tiredness that makes my chest tighten.

"Is it real?" I hold up the folder.

"As real as ovarian cancer gets."

"You must have been in pain."

"I was able to manage it with painkillers. Do not tell Hanako." She takes the file from my hand and sets it on the table, straightening it until it's parallel to the table's edges. She looks into the distance, opens her mouth, frowns, then closes it again.

"Why?" I ask. And it's a loaded 'why'. Nothing makes any sense.

"Because I do not want her to feel burdened."

"Why are you here? How did you know I would be here? Are you connected to the Arcana?" The dam holding my questions bursts under the stress of my anxiety. And these three are just the beginning. I have lots more.

"Since you are now officially my doctor, I will tell you. But what I share, is in confidence. Doctor's confidence?" She raises one brow and looks at me like a stern teacher. If she had glasses, she would be looking over them.

"Okay, I'm listening."

"I started getting period pains and bloating sometime after my menopause. I thought my periods were returning but no, it turned out to be cancer. I considered my next steps and decided my best course of action was to see my Hanako." She purses her lips and blinks as if expecting I will judge her. I don't, but as a doctor, I have questions.

"Why not have it treated there? It's not spread yet, so surgery and some chemotherapy would potentially secure a very favorable outcome."

"I'm sure you know this, but every surgery has the risk of death. I did not want to risk not seeing Hanako first."

I try to keep my face placid. I don't argue with patients, especially anxious ones. And Mrs.—Miss—Yagi is afraid despite her stern demeanor. I play with my ring as I formulate a response. Her traveling across the ocean and through a busy Chicago carries more risk than her dying on the operating table, provided her surgeon and anesthesiologist were competent.

"Delaying the surgery might have a negative impact on the overall outcome."

"I know. All of my decisions about my health are informed. I must reconnect with Hanako before I go under the knife." Miss Yagi takes a sip of water from a fancy champagne glass. I hadn't even noticed it on the table.

"I understand. You don't actually want my input. Fair enough. So why are you here, in this hospital?" I'm a little hurt that she doesn't want to tell Hanako and go for the surgery as soon as possible. Despite how much she tries to show me I'm no good for her daughter, her being around Hanako is positive. I'm sure that her newfound confidence is all because of reconnecting with her roots and actively looking into herself. She can't lose her mother after all this.

"It is for my art. And also, because Emilia Rogers reassured me about the quality of the care in this hospital."

"Only applicable if you are a VIP." I scoff and roll my eyes before I can help myself.

"Which I am," Miss Yagi says flatly.

"How much do you know?" I whisper, pressing my lips in a thin line.

"About your undercover mission? I would say everything. I also learned that my Hanako is involved in a gang and that her best friend is the leader. I have no idea how she met all of you, but I am doing my best to come to terms with it. To understand her pain and her joy."

This is a surprise. I thought Hanako's mother was all about opposing Hanako's American way of life; about bringing her back to a more tranquil existence. They must have talked while I was crashing at Damien's.

"But what you're doing right now is helping me. It's probably costing you a fortune." I scratch my head. This puzzle still has too many missing pieces.

"It is not cheap. But peace of mind rarely is." Her face softens as she peers into my eyes. "It seems you and Hanako are very close. I am not proud to admit it, but I have heard you two talk, amongst other things. You care about her."

"I do."

"That is not enough." She sighs. "Her father cared about me. I cared about him. Then as we started living together, it became apparent that we were too different. I am Japanese. He is American. It was not meant to be from the beginning."

"With all due respect, comparing your relationship to ours is like comparing apples and oranges. I don't know why you separated, but I will accept it could be because of cultural differences. However, such differences can be overcome with communication and an eagerness to learn and accept."

"Are you saying Hanako's father and I did not try to do that?"

"No, I'm saying we do it differently. This thing between Hanako and me is very new. We do not want to get married or have children at the moment. We are focusing on finding out if we can walk the same path despite our differences. And we accept that our paths may diverge in the future, and that's fine." I kinda wish there was another glass of water because my ears are burning. I'm talking out of my ass. I want to believe in what I'm saying, but the truth is, I'm still clueless when it comes to what Hanako and I are doing. It's damn great, but we haven't even told Connor about it. And seeing how Mrs. Yagi is not mentioning polyamory, I assume Hanako hasn't broached that subject yet.

"You are afraid of commitment." Mrs. Yagi narrows her eyes.

"No, our generation is just cautious." I want to add it's because we all grew up in broken families, but I don't.

"Why are you not in touch with your parents?" she asks out of nowhere.

I take a deep breath in before replying. I will be truthful. She already doesn't like me, so I have nothing to lose. "I introduced them to my boyfriend at the time, and they told me I was no longer their son."

"Ah." Mrs. Yagi nods as if she understands.

I lean my head to one side, blindsided by her simple reaction. "This doesn't faze you?"

"No. My parents also disowned me. I left with Hanako's father against their wishes." She plays with the water glass, avoiding my eyes.

"Do you miss them? Your family?"

"I do. I miss my hometown, Okinawa. The hanabi, the fireworks, in the summer were so beautiful." She seems to get lost in a memory. I envy that. I have good memories from home, of course, but they're all tainted now. I rarely think about my family. My abuelita could have passed on for all I know.

Unexpectedly, I want to share too. "I miss my abuela the most. She used to cook the most delicious food."

Miss Yagi puts a hand on mine and strokes my fingers with her thumb.

"Do not tell Hanako about my cancer. I will tell her when I am ready," she says.

CHAPTER 34

The corners of my apartment are too dark for my liking. Ever since Laura stopped living here, whenever a bulb went, I didn't replace it. Now I'm down to a few weak sources of light, giving my demons plenty of space to slide around the shadows.

I should stop personifying my fear. Yet I can't help it. If I kill them, I will kill Laura, too, and I can't do that. She seems to be the thread that's holding my sanity together. I almost quit my job today; I almost bought a plane ticket to another state. Almost, because she told me that I was overreacting and calmed me down.

This Friday is hard because usually, I would be playing in the Moon Garden. Thinking about Hana and Mathias playing without me stings a bit, but my FOMO has no leg to stand on. They invited me, and I declined.

I plop on the couch, between empty bags of chips and greasy pizza boxes. What should I have tonight? I scroll the takeaway app slowly. It's my only indulgence.

I end up ordering Chinese. Spring rolls, vegetable rice, and sweet and sour chicken. Yum.

The moment I press the button and pay for my order, there's a knock on my door. I turn around slowly, feeling like the lead in a horror movie.

No takeaway is that fast.

I drag my socked feet across the floor, as quiet as I can, and peer through the peephole.

Hana and Mathias. On my doorstep. And Hana is carrying—I squint to see better—a plant?

Mathias knocks again, rattling my brain. "One moment," I shout and hobble around in a comical frenzy, picking up discarded underwear, socks, and garbage. The place is disgusting. *I am disgusting.*

As we've been saying, the demons hiss from the dark places around me. I shake my head, chasing them away.

After the place looks a bit better, I open the door. A gust of freshness shifts the stale air of my corridor. I can't believe they're here. I look down at my sweats and t-shirt, sporting more than a few stains. My fear is gone, replaced by pure embarrassment. Ready for their looks of revulsion, I lift my head and plaster on a fake smile.

"Oh, Connor," Hanako's voice is full of pity when she takes in my state.

"She isn't pitying you, she's being compassionate," Mathias says as if he's read my mind. "We've all been there, man. So, we're here to support you."

I don't know where 'there' is. I'm not sure if I want them here, but they've already come in and shut the door behind them before I can protest.

Hanako starts taking off her sneakers, and I wave a hand. "Oh, no, no. Please keep them on."

She nods. "This is for you. It's a peace lily. They're nearly impossible to kill."

It's a plant with big, long, green leaves. I bet it will be dead within a week here.

"Do you mind if I open a window? It's not very cold outside?" she asks.

"Sure." I take the plant to the kitchen. Mathias follows me.

"Sorry for the surprise visit, but I panicked last time when you told me all about Hale-Bopp Health. I scared you even more, didn't I?" He scratches the back of his head with an apologetic smile.

The truth is, I regretted telling him. Part of me thought he would run to those guys and tattle on me. Then Laura would ask me why he would do that, and my argument would fall apart.

"Why did *you* panic?"

"It's a long story, but it's about time you heard it," he says. "I know we're only play partners, the three of us, but we should get to know each other better. And after, if you feel like we're too much, we will revisit our arrangement. Still, I couldn't let you be terrified on your own without knowing what and who we're up against."

I pour us all a glass of water, shaking a little bit. I'm not good with big conversations.

When we join Hana, she's plugged in her phone in the wall and put the torch on, using it as a lamp. The air is cooler and smells like a crisp spring evening. The couch and one of the armchairs are free of garbage. There's a neat pile of it near the table.

"I'm sorry it's such a mess," I say.

"Don't worry," Hana says. "I've seen worse."

I've no idea what that means, but it's reassuring enough. We settle around the table, and Mathias begins his story. Hana talks over him from time to time, and he takes a few breaks to ask me if I'm following. I say yes without thinking if I truly am. In the end, he asks me if what happened to me makes sense now.

I blink away my trance-like state, where I was listening like a child mesmerized by the world. In many ways, a new world did appear before me. One of danger that I would have never guessed already existed.

"Okay, so, basically, you both are kinda part of a gang, and you're investigating Hale-Bopp Health for being horrible," I start. "And them asking me to update their system by threatening me is not surprising at all considering the whole hospital is owned by gangsters. And Comet International is bad too, but you don't know how bad. And according to your estimation, this whole thing will blow over soon, and I'll be able to return to my mundane life."

"This is a perfect summary." Hana smiles at me and finishes her water in one gulp. The scene we did a couple of weeks ago, with soaking her and breaking her apart, feels as if it was ages ago. She seems so in control now, and I'm here spiraling down my demon hole.

"Mathias told me that you saw a tattoo on the men who threatened you. Was it anything like this one?" She takes out her phone and zooms in on a blurry security cam footage.

"Yeah, exactly that. Who are they?"

"Not sure yet. But the connection to Hale-Bopp and Comet International will help us narrow it down." She stands up to go somewhere.

I catch her wrist on the way. I'm ready to come clean. "Do you have an IT person in that gang of yours? A hacker, I guess?"

"Yes. Kind of. How did you know?" She looks lost for words.

"That screenshot is from CCTV footage. I thought it was unlikely you got it by asking around. Anyway, I'm not judging. I just wanted to say that... You probably think I'm too scared for what has happened." I let go of her and run my hands through my hair.

"We don't think that," Mathias says.

"Well, I didn't tell you the whole truth. I didn't really do what they wanted me to. I created an encryption around the records they wanted me to erase. Every time they 'delete' a record, it actually gets archived deep inside the system. It's still there. Your hacker could get it out and send it to the police, maybe? I don't know." My eyes flick between their faces.

"Wow, that's so cool you could do that." Hana kneels next to the sofa and pats my shoulder. "You were afraid they would find out."

"Yep," I say, popping the p.

"I agree. It's amazing. And you must be amazing because our people couldn't hack your system. They still haven't, even though they made me put in a flash drive in one of the computers." Mathias looks impressed.

I allow myself a smile. I've always been good at coding, but it feels fucking great when people appreciate it.

"I'm going to go give Sophie a call and share all we've learned," Hana says, leaving Mathias and me alone in the living room.

"I have an uncontrollable urge to clean your apartment," Mathias says with a comical grin.

"That makes one of us." I joke back, but some of the embarrassment returns. "I'm sorry. Ever since I started living alone, I haven't been the best at keeping things tidy. Laura was much better at that."

Mathias nods and keeps quiet. This is the first time I've mentioned her in front of him. I haven't mentioned her in front of people for years, actually.

"Laura was my wife," I add after the silence stretches a tad too long.

Hana comes back and plops in the armchair. I assume she's heard the last bit because she doesn't speak either. I can't tell if they're uncomfortable or just trying to create space for me to speak.

"You don't have to talk about her if you don't want to," Hana says. Are they both tuned into my mind or something? "Recently, I realized we didn't know much about each other. Mathias and I live together, so we know more, but while we gave you the freedom to share as much as you wanted, we realized you had shared nothing. If you want to change that, we're here. And if not, we'll still be here, but we'll talk about literally anything else."

She smiles that warm smile that I thought was only reserved for aftercare. It puts me at ease.

"Laura left me six years ago. It was a week before our wedding. It kinda messed me up." The words come out strained. I've never strung them in sentences like this.

"You still wear your ring." Mathias's voice is quiet like he's unsure if he should be saying anything at all.

"Yeah. They were ready and all, so I just altered mine a little bit. Hers is still in the box." My throat closes up with a feeling I've pushed down for a very long time. I'm afraid I will cry, so I look up and blink like a madman.

"Have you kept in touch?" Hana asks.

Ah. Well. In my head, yes. She's always with me, after all. But I can't tell them that. It sounds insane.

"She—she passed away, actually." A tear escapes my blinking and I swipe it off fast like the Flash. "I don't like to say it like that. But, yeah, she died."

As I say this, my demons scream in my head all at once, like I'm burning them. I can't see Laura's face. In fact, the whole world swims in my vision, like I'm drowning in it. Something violent comes out of me, shaking my whole body from the inside out. And my whole face is wet, and my hands are wet, my lips taste like salt.

Something warm circles my back, like a spell anchoring me to reality. I don't know how long I'm in this state of shipwreck, but when my vision clears, I see Hanako is crying next to me, and Mathias is running his wide palm across my back. I think I've been crying for a very long time. I can barely breathe, and my eyebrow bone hurts. My eyes sting, and my throat makes an unfamiliar gurgling noise.

As soon as I'm aware of all these things, I do my damned hardest to stop.

"Let it all out. We're not going anywhere," Mathias says as he witnesses my attempts to calm down.

And with my half-clear head, I finally know what this is all about. It's my thick, black grief. I've been nurturing it in my heart, turning it into demons. Now it pours out of me, purified and clear like my tears. And all it took was admitting to myself that Laura didn't just leave me... she died. And I can't live without her.

HANAKO

CHAPTER 35

Connor's grief hits me like a truck. I don't know what I was expecting, but it wasn't this. It's a powerful moment that leaves both me and Mathias speechless. And from what I've learned in my life about pain, grief, and crying, is that I shouldn't interfere with it. People stop when they're done for the time being. I don't offer Connor tissues; I don't want him to think I'm hurrying him along. I don't tell him it's okay because it isn't. I try to stop myself from crying back at him, but the tears keep coming. I've always been a compassionate crier, and while I've taught myself to hold it in at work, I can't do it tonight. I'm too overwhelmed, and I feel like a mirror, reflecting everything that's happening around me.

When Connor regains his ability to speak, he takes my hand that was resting on his knee and does the same to Mathias's, signaling him to stop rubbing his back.

"If it's okay, can I take you to Laura?" Connor hiccups between words.

"Of course," Mathias says for both of us.

Connor takes us through to his bedroom, which is as messy as the rest of the apartment. The air is still and smells stale.

He opens the wardrobe doors and where most people would store boxes and shoes, there is a small shrine. A photo frame of a young, beautiful woman, a small urn, like that for a pet, and a red ring box.

"There's not much left of her," Connor explains. "The black on my ring, it's an alloy mixed with her ashes. I have to redo it every now and again because I rub it off."

"She's close to you everywhere you go," I whisper. I've always thought cremation jewelry is a beautiful way to remember loved ones who have passed away.

My thoughts take me to Mama, and I try to imagine what she would say in this situation. She would probably urge Connor to take the shrine out of the wardrobe and put it in a more prominent place in the house. I don't feel he's ready to do that yet. He just admitted to avoiding words connected to her death. Healing will take time.

"I see her sometimes, in my head." He gets up and closes the wardrobe. "You must think I'm crazy; six years is a long time. Like, jeez, move on, am I right?"

He jokes about it, but it's a coping mechanism. Mathias is back to rubbing his back which seems to be his way of dealing with the difficulty of the situation. I can't stay silent, however.

"There's no expiry date on grief. It never goes away. It never diminishes. In an ideal world, you grow your life around it. It doesn't become smaller, you just get bigger," I say.

"I think I made myself very small. Sometimes it feels like it's the only thing about me." He sits down on his unmade bed.

"We're here for you but have you tried talking to someone else about it?" I sit next to him.

"Like a shrink? I mean, I feel crazy sometimes but is it that bad?" Connor scratches his head.

"A therapist can help by giving you the tools to grow your life around your grief. Mental health is hard, and they're like customer support," I reply.

He nods, considering my words. I'm pretty proud of the way I phrased my words.

"What about kink?" Mathias asks.

"A distraction. I can't forge a genuine connection with anyone."

"What about now?" Mathias pulls Connor into a side hug. "This feels genuine to me."

My phone vibrates in the pocket of my hoodie. It's Sophie. I slip out quietly and go to the kitchen, picking up all the water glasses on my way there.

"Hello?" I do my best to keep my voice steady when I answer.

"We found out who they are. We're hitting them tonight." Sophie's tone is triumphant.

"Hold up, what?" I nearly drop the glasses. "You found out who the tattoo guys are?"

"Yes. They're called Crossfire Security and joined hands with Comet International a few months ago. But listen to this, the company owners were frequent Lavender visitors. So, we know they're complete scum. And that they've avoided the investigation around it."

"That's insane. What do you mean you're hitting them tonight?" I ask.

There's a sound of ruffling papers. "Lu-Na found their headquarters and they seem to be having some sort of party tonight. We're just going to jump them there."

"You're going to kill them?" This conversation turns uncomfortable for me.

"We're going to round them up and give them to The Arcana. They've been doing lots of bad stuff on their territory, including the hospital, so they can decide what to do." Sophie's words are supposed to put me at ease. Nevertheless, I know that things like this don't always go to plan.

"Please be careful," I whisper.

"I will. We have backup from the Empress, so don't worry. I'll keep you updated. Are you still with Mathias and Connor?" she asks.

"Yes."

"Stay the night. It's safer that way. And I'm sure I'll have good news tomorrow morning," Sophie says. I can hear the smile in her words.

"Be safe," I say instead of a goodbye. Maybe if I say it enough times, the chances of it being true will improve.

I wake up from my phone's vibration. After Connor, Mathias, and I chatted for a little while and split up the Chinese Connor had ordered, we all went to sleep in Connor's king-sized bed. There was no convenient time to raise the issue of our three-way dynamic, so that's still on the to-do list.

This whole setup reminds me of a high school sleepover. We're all fully clothed, sleeping in a room that could use a deep clean.

When I slip out to pick up the call, Connor has snuggled into Mathias. Both of them are asleep, probably exhausted from the heavy conversation about Laura. Not that I'm particularly fresh about it, but I can't really sleep in unfamiliar environments. My eyes flit across the wardrobe doors. I want to open them up, so Laura doesn't sit there alone in the darkness. But it's not my place.

When I reach the kitchen, the room furthest from the bedroom, I answer the phone.

"Are you sitting down?" Sophie says, panting.

"No, are you still outside? What happened?" My frayed nerves can't take a lot.

"We got them. A few slipped out, but you're not going to believe who were the bosses of this little security firm." I hear a car door slam, and the noises around Sophie fade. "It was the Dukes. Remember I told you about them? From Lavender? Duke Harrington, who used to torment Tanya every other evening, is dead. There was an altercation, let's say, and he didn't make it."

"Is Tanya okay? Was she there?" I sit down on one of the kitchen chairs. It screeches under my weight.

"She wasn't, but she knows about it. Damien dealt with it."

Sophie is silent for a moment. That means Damien probably killed him. I press my lips into a thin line and pretend I didn't hear anything.

"So, who escaped?"

"The guy who assaulted me in Lavender. Duke Hazelton. We don't know what his real name is. It doesn't matter. I will hunt him down. It's been on my mind for a while now."

"Revenge doesn't help. Please don't become a murderer."

"I won't, Hana. I know what I'm doing," Sophie says. I want to believe her, but I can hear the adrenaline high in her voice. She's reveling in the danger again, and I hope against all hope that she'll be able to control herself when the time comes.

"So that's it?" I ask. "We can rest easy now? Connor is no longer in danger?"

"I would say you're all out of the woods. Both my people and the Arcana folk are searching for Duke Hazelton and the couple of other people who escaped. As I understand it from the Empress, a stakeholder meeting has been scheduled for early next week, so things are moving swiftly along. Kazuo has rallied quite the army of medical professionals since Mathias shared his intelligence. Oh, you should meet Kazuo. He's really hot." Sophie chuckles.

"Actually, Mathias and I progressed things a bit. We're kind of together now." I scratch my head. Is this even an appropriate time to talk about this? Probably not.

"Good for you!" Sophie sounds excited. "I can't wait to hear all the details. What about Connor?"

"It's complicated. We still have to have a chat, the three of us, but he wasn't in a good place yesterday."

"Understandable. Fucking Dukes are still ruining people's lives. I swear, I will find Duke Hazelton, and—"

"Okay, I'm hanging up. It's too early for all this revenge talk," I say and make sure to keep my tone light, so Sophie doesn't take it the wrong way. I'm not dismissing her, but I'm not good with all this illegal stuff. Ever since she became a gang leader, I can't tell if she's serious or if it's actually a joke when she mentions killing someone. I'd rather not find out.

"You probably haven't slept tonight," Sophie replies in a gentle voice. "So go get some shut-eye now. We're all safe, and we're almost done here. Love you."

"Love you," I parrot and end the call.

Okay, it seems things are reaching their natural conclusion. Which means I can maybe sleep for an hour or two. The living room is pleasantly cold from the air still blowing in from the open window. I close it quietly and lie down on the couch, putting my jacket over my chest like a blanket. Tomorrow, I will stay with Connor and clean this place up. Clear space, clear mind.

CHAPTER 36

I stuff the cereal bar I got from the hospital vending machine in my mouth and chew in silent contentment. Once Hanako let me know that the shareholders are meeting soon, I could finally see the end of my work here on the VIP floor. I would miss some parts, like the day in and day out work with patients and performing regular surgeries, though hopefully not for long. After I get my license back, I'm going to apply for jobs like my life depends on it. I guess it kinda does, as I've been burning through Damien's savings ever since he took me into the gang. In about a week, I will be out of this life and back into the mundane existence of a doctor. The prospect makes me giddy. This is the best oatmeal raisin cereal bar I've ever had.

When I go up to check on Miss Yagi, my enthusiasm dampens somewhat. She's sitting on the sofa, chatting to Kazuo Okada, and smiling like she's already his mother-in-law. Okay, I know I skipped a few steps here but hear me out. He is perfect for what she wants in a son-in-law. Handsome, successful, and most importantly—Japanese. I'm only one of those things.

Time to put on a brave face and see them both. Before I get the chance to enter, the surgeon I did my first and only VIP operation with, pulls me to one side.

"Rogers wants to see us. Something big is going down," he whispers as he pulls me down the corridor.

"What?" I whisper back.

"You know how someone hacked the system yesterday?" He stops, his face changing from one of rushing to one of conspiratorial pleasure. "Some IT guy is going to get it now. He's the prime suspect. The balls to hack into a hospital! Imagine!"

It's his gossip face. Okay, well, so Lu-Na's efforts are now confused with Connor's work. But with Crossfire Security down, what can they do? I feign surprise and continue walking.

"Wait, wait, there's more," he says. I've never understood people's penchant for gossip. Would have been useful during my initial investigation, but then again it seems Ken didn't trust him enough because of it. I stop again.

"The patient that didn't come," he starts.

"They found her?" My heart somersaults in my chest. It can't be. Hanako assured me the safe house was, well, safe. And that no one followed them there.

"No. But they found out some social worker was involved. She's in trouble too. Hah, these people really don't know who they're dealing with." He laughs and pats my shoulder.

My eyes widen and I want to slap the smile off his round face. Hanako might be in trouble too. She's at Connor's. That's secure enough. There's no one to go after them. Sophie and the others are chasing Duke Hazelton and his underlings, so even if they somehow find their way to that apartment, the rescue team will soon follow.

Having run out of gossip, the surgeon starts walking again. We reach the office in half a minute, then stay awkwardly to listen to the shouting coming from inside. I can't make out what is being said, but Ken's voice is full of rage. I bet he's spitting like mad because of the recent demise of Crossfire Security. I turn my head away to hide my smile. Maybe I will be fired for incompetence. That would be a nice conclusion.

"Should we knock?" The surgeon looks sheepish.

"You brought me," I say, emboldened by the idea of my work here being done. "Just knock. Or wait for the other people to leave."

He rolls his eyes and leans on the wall near the door. We wait, and I torture myself with the image of Hanako and Kazuo talking, laughing, kissing. A little part of me is turned on. They're both hot, and I'm pretty sure I'm falling in love with one of them. It's not Kazuo. So, if there is a scenario where Hanako is kissing him, I'm pretty sure I will be included too. Maybe Connor too. Hell, why not invite Sophie and Damien as well? I'm still constructing my dream orgy in my head when Ken's door finally opens and out comes... Duke Hazelton.

I would recognize this slimy man anywhere. His oily skin, cropped hair, and dark suit make him appear as if he's a business-man and not a lowlife. He doesn't know me, but I know him well enough. Through Lavender's cameras, I witnessed more than one of the sexual assaults he committed. My hands ball into fists, and a very undoctor-like impulse jolts me.

This guy walking around is dangerous. For all my friends. But how is he here? And looking so calm. Granted, I think he just had his ass handed to him by Ken Rogers, but still. I need to message Sophie asap.

I pull out my phone and navigate to the messaging app. Before I can start typing, the surgeon pulls me inside with him, and I make eye contact with a red-faced Ken. He looks nothing like his mother today.

"You both. Okay. Did you hear any of what I just said?" His words come out in huffs. The surgeon all but folds into himself. Pathetic.

My survival instinct tells me to do the same, but my fingers itch to finish the message to Sophie. And maybe one to Hanako and Connor. To warn them against going out or opening the front door, or—

"I fucking asked you a question!" Ken Rogers spits across the room.

"No, we didn't hear anything, Mr. Rogers. Nothing," the surgeon says.

"Whatever. You go out and prepare an operating room. And be very fucking careful because I just learned you didn't tell me a patient went missing. You have a big mouth, so how in the hell did you manage to keep that one to yourself?" Ken points a fat finger at the surgeon, jabbing it in the air furiously to punctuate his words.

"I didn't want to worry you, I—"

"Shut the fuck up and go do your job." He waves him off like he's an annoying fly.

The surgeon scuttles out of the room without saying another word. I turn to leave, too, my hand still clutching my phone.

"I need to speak to you, Flores," Ken says in a much calmer voice. It seems he still thinks I'm on his side. He's so damn wrong.

"Yes?"

"Tell me everything about this new patient of yours. Tomoko Yagi. Is she really sick?" Ken asks.

I frown. "She's really sick, yes. What's the matter?"

"Her daughter has been causing trouble. She's some social worker, and she's apparently behind the patient's disappearance. And her mother is a VIP patient here? What a fucking coincidence. I bet this is my mother's doing somehow. After she promised she would let me prove myself. Nothing I ever do is enough. Nothing!" He throws his hands in the air. So what, hurting innocent people here and playing with their lives is just to impress his cold mommy? Boo-fucking-hoo.

"I don't know. It sounds suspicious, but Miss Yagi hasn't said or done anything out of the ordinary. She's just a patient." I shrug, trying to look nonchalant. My brain is reeling now; Hanako is in real danger. Duke Hazelton has to be stopped before he gets to her and Connor.

"I saw her with one of the downstairs nurses today. There are other rumors going on, but I won't bore you with them. I just want her out of the picture."

"What do you mean?" I can't hide my shock.

"Relax. Nothing final. I don't really care if she's involved or not. But just in case, make sure she can't interfere with anything until at least the end of next week." He sits down behind his glass desk and stares at a document in front of him.

That's it? What am I supposed to do?

"I don't understand," I mutter.

"You're a sleep doctor, right? Just put her to sleep." He rolls his eyes like I'm a stupid child.

I gape at him, completely taken by surprise. I'm not doing that.

I open my mouth to explain why that's not an option, when I remember Connor. He just said okay and did his own thing.

"Right. I'll get on it," I say.

"Great. We'll get through this, you'll see. And then we'll reap the rewards of our hard work." He smiles and points at the door, now completely calm. What the hell is he talking about? What hard work?

I close the door behind me and break into a run, typing furiously at the same time. After sending my warning messages, I rush into Miss Yagi's room, hoping Kazuo is still there.

He isn't. Shit.

Miss Yagi is sitting on the sofa reading a magazine and sipping on lemon water like the world isn't just about to end.

"Grab your stuff," I whisper-shout.

"Excuse me?" She raises an eyebrow. That damned eyebrow. I don't have time for this.

I pick up her coat and shoes and shove them into her hands. Then I find her handbag and put it over my shoulder. "You need to leave. Now. Shit is going down."

Thankfully, she doesn't argue and puts on her kitten heel shoes. I hand her the bag and look out of the room to check that the hall-way is clear.

"Find Kazuo. Tell him to evacuate you and everyone about to be involved in the stakeholders meeting next week. Do it quietly.

We need to cause as little disturbance to the hospital as possible."
I push her forward toward the elevator.

"Is my Hanako in danger?" She looks at me with wide eyes, and I finally see her for what she truly is. A scared mother. A sick patient who wants to get her life in order before a risky operation. Someone who is not the enemy.

"No. Sort the evacuation with Kazuo and call her."

I pray to gods I don't believe in that I didn't just lie to her.

CHAPTER 37

I woke up late today to three 'urgent' emails from my boss. Is anything ever urgent in my job? If you stretch the meaning of the word, probably. That didn't manage to ruin my good mood. For the first time in years, I wasn't alone when I woke up. Mathias left about an hour ago, and now Hanako and I are cleaning the apartment while we wait for our breakfast waffles to be delivered. Life is good.

"I really don't mind you just sitting down while I tidy up. Having you here is motivation enough," I say to Hana as we reach for the same piece of garbage.

She plucks it from my hand and puts it in her trash bag. "I'm suspended, remember? Anything to feel useful."

We chat about small, insignificant things as we tidy up. When she suggested we do this, I thought it would feel strange, her rummaging in my stuff. But after getting to business, I realized how little 'stuff' I actually own. Most of the clutter was garbage. And isn't that sad? When I left after Laura's death, I only took her, my computer, and some clothes. A new life in Chicago that currently amounts to heaps of IT work and some kinky distractions, but nothing more. Well, maybe a couple of friends too.

"Right, I'm going down to put these in the bin." She lifts two black bags full of trash.

"I'll come with." I tie off another bag.

"Nah, no offense, but you can barely move." She winks. "Can I borrow your keys?"

"In my coat pocket," I say as I hobble to the kitchen. My foot isn't that bad.

There are two more trash bags there. How did I generate so much shit?

After I drink a glass of water and return to finish off the living room, I stop for a second to marvel at our hard work. The couch and armchairs are clean and empty. The coffee table gleams in the daylight, and the peace lily on top of it adds a homeliness to the space that was never here before. The cabinet next to the wall, which I forgot I even had, has been tidied up. The only thing remaining is to vacuum the rug and clean the floor. As I narrow my eyes at the stains on the floorboards, I understand why Hana is so adamant about us taking our shoes off in the hallway in her apartment. Maybe I'll start doing it too.

Hana's phone beeps. She's left it on top of the cabinet. Then mine vibrates in my pocket. Both of them going off? Not a great sign.

And hell, my crappy luck rears its head again.

Mathias: *You and Connor are in danger. Crossfire is after you. Lock the door and barricade yourselves.*

Well, fuck. I dial Mathias from my phone. The line rings and rings. Maybe he's in danger, too, having sent that message. What if someone saw it?

I dial Sophie next, hobbling to the door, unsure of what to do about Hana. I have to wait for her to come back, I guess, and then barricade us in. We'll have to cancel the waffles.

I sigh in relief when the lock turns, and the door opens.

"Thank god you're back. We have to—" The words die on my

tongue as the man who broke my foot comes in. He's grinning.

My fear takes over like a tidal wave, and I run, yes run, through pain and all sorts of desperate warnings in my head, toward the door. I push on it, trying to close it before he makes it through the threshold.

He simply puts his foot in front of it, and when I look out to check what's blocking me, he hits me square in the face. Behind him, I get a glimpse of another man and what appears to be Hana's lifeless body hanging off his shoulder. Then I black out.

When I come to, I'm lying on my clean couch with my hands tied behind my back. Tied badly. I can twist my fingers and fiddle with the knot, and as someone so used to tying bondage, I can undo it with my eyes closed.

I twist around to see the Crossfire Security guy sitting on the armchair next to me, his muddy combat boots spreading filth on my rug. He's eating my waffles too.

"Why are you here?" I ask. My voice comes out as a croak. Something is crusting on my upper lip. I'm pretty sure it's blood. Did he break my nose?

"Oh, because you hacked us, and Mr. Rogers didn't like that." Crumbs come out of his mouth.

"I didn't hack you. I did what you asked and then hid away here. How do you even know where I live? And where is Hana?" I flail my legs about and finally sit up. The rope around my hands slackens. My fingers are itching to untie it, but what for? I can't fight this guy.

"So many questions. I guess that's fair. I have some too." He licks his fingers, smacking his lips after each one. "Mr. Rogers emailed your boss, who said you were working from home. No foul play in obtaining your address."

My boss is a fucking idiot. If I make it out of this alive, I'm quitting my job tomorrow.

"As for your lady companion, that was a stroke of good luck. We were coming to her workplace next. Just imagine all these desperate women, and then we come in." He laughs like a maniac. I want to hurt him, but I'm terrified of his fists and his steel-toed boots. He'll vaporize me before I even breach his personal space.

"So yeah, my buddy took her so she could face the music. How do you two know each other? Did you make some sort of elaborate plan to make trouble for us?" He stands up. "Nice plant."

For a moment, I think he's going to hit my brand-new peace lily. My eyes widen, and my demons, which had been silent since yesterday, rear their ugly heads.

Don't get attached. It'll die, like your precious Laura. They snicker in the corners of my mind, shifting and turning like black snakes.

The Crossfire guy caresses a leaf between his greasy fingers and moves along. My eyes follow him, noticing the bag in the corner of the room.

"Did you tie me with my own rope?" The words are out before I can stop them.

"Oh, yeah. Why do you have so much rope?" He takes a hank and juggles it between his hands. That's going straight to the bin after.

"It's a hobby," I reply, trying to keep my face calm.

My fear has twined with my anger, giving me a strange mental clarity. Laura's face swims before my eyes. *Stay composed*, she whispers.

"You're weird," the man says. "You didn't answer my question, though. How do you know the social worker?"

"Same hobby as me," I reply. "I had no idea she was connected to your company."

"She isn't really. But it's just awfully convenient, you know, that she decided to save women or whatever at the same time you hacked us." He shrugs and sits next to me.

"I didn't hack you," I repeat. I seem to be taking the flak for Sophie's hacker.

The closeness of the guy rattles me. I try to shift away, but his hand snakes around my shoulders, and he pulls me toward his hard body.

"What did you do with the information? Did you sell it? Send it to the police?"

"I'm not a hacker." My voice is squeaky, and my bottom lip trembles. I'm so angry for my inability to protect myself.

"Help me out, little guy, or I will have to step on your other foot." He places his boot on my good foot. I jerk it away. He doesn't take that well. One moment I'm sitting there, terrified, and the next, I'm gasping for breath, the world all blurry and unstable. His fist has sunk into my belly, and god, it fucking hurts. I've never been hit like this in my life.

"I'll let you catch your breath," the guy says in a cheery voice. His breath smells like Nutella.

I cower in his embrace, taking in air like a balloon pump.

Then, out of nowhere, there's a loud crash, and the guy's grip on me slackens. He falls to his side without a sound. A big hunting knife is lodged at the back of his head, just where the spine begins.

"Dude, you scared Connor," an unfamiliar female voice says.

I turn around, dreading the possibility of more violence coming my way.

"Sorry, man. It looked like the guy was beating you up." A tall, slim guy looking at least five years younger than me is standing in my living room, looking apologetic. He's dressed in all black. His gloved fingers curl around the hilt of the knife, and he takes it out in one sharp move.

Blood seeps into my freshly cleaned couch.

"Look what you did. You have no chill." There's a woman behind him, tall and burly, almost twice my size in any direction.

"I'm so sorry. I'll clean it," the guy says and rushes to the kitchen.

I'm gaping at them, still breathing raggedly, recovering from the hit to my diaphragm.

He returns with one paper towel.

"That's not going to be enough," the woman says and shakes his head. "Connor, is it okay if I call you Connor?"

I nod.

"Connor, we will call someone who will do a deep clean here. We'll even get rid of this fella. He doesn't go well with the rest of the room." She swipes her arm across and winks.

"Who are you?" I finally manage to get some words out.

"Oh, Sophie asked us to come save you. We were right on time, man! Now, where is your friend Hanako? We have to escort you both to Love and Err, where you'll be safe." He gives me a thumbs-up.

"They got to her first," I croak. "She's not here."

"Do you know where they took her?" The woman frowns.

I shake my head. "Probably the hospital. Mathias knew we were in trouble, and it was Hale-Bopp's director that sent these guys after us."

"Okay. Thank you. We need to get to the hospital," she says to the guy. "After we drop off Connor."

"No, wait." I get up. "I'm coming with you."

"I don't think that's wise, man," the guy says.

I go to the bedroom, open the wardrobe, and look at Laura's beautiful face. Her smile comes to life, and I swear I see her nod gently at me. I move the urn and the ring box to one side and reach for the shoebox in the dark corner.

I pull out a sleek black gun. Laura's pride and joy.

I may not be able to protect myself, but she always did. And she still will. She just has to borrow my arm.

I put the gun in a backpack and walk back over to Sophie's people.

"I'm coming with," I say. "I need to see this through."

They share a look. The woman sighs.

"Okay, but you stay behind us. And if one of us says 'duck', you duck." She could be a sergeant.

"I'll try not to quack," I say.

The guy bursts out laughing, and for a moment, I forget where we're going, what mess we're in, and the dead body hardening on my couch.

CHAPTER 38

The world sways. Like a small boat in the middle of a vast, dangerous ocean. Like a car on a road full of potholes. Like a plane in a turbulent storm. I'm being carried somewhere.

My senses come to me one by one. First, there is the strong smell of chemicals and sweat. Then the sound of something ruffling next to my ears. Muffled voices. Something like shopping carts being moved around. My skin wakes, feeling the tightness of my clothes around my body. I'm wearing leggings and a hoodie. They're twisted tight around me. And there's something on my head because when I coax my eyes to open, I see nothing. I can barely breathe. It's a sack or a hood of some sort.

I've been kidnapped.

People say you never know how you would act in an emergency until you're in that situation. I always thought I would scream and cry. I thought that out of the four stress responses; fight, flight, freeze, or fawn, I would fawn my ass out. I would cry and beg and use my meek appearance to convince my attacker to let me go.

The reality is different. A feeling snakes from my head down to my body. Its icy tendrils reach my fingertips and my toes, making me go limp. My breathing slows down, and I erect a wall between me and reality.

I can't fight and can't flee. I don't feel like fawning. So, I freeze myself from the inside out. This frees up space in my mind to think.

Connor is in danger too. How did they find me in his building? Or were they there for him?

My phone remained in the apartment. I can't reach Mathias or Sophie. Lu-Na can't track me. I'm done for.

The strong arms holding me under my knees and across my back tighten as we round a corner. Or maybe we walk into a room. I'm still a sack of flesh and bones. If I move, they will know I'm awake and I really don't want them to know that.

Who even are 'they'? Sophie's reassurance from before about Crossfire Security sounds hollow in my head. It must be them. Or perhaps it's Cindy's abuser? Someone else's? The guy who keyed my car? Why the hell is my list of suspects so long?

I'm put on a soft table like a piece of meat. The hood is finally taken off my head. I keep my eyelids closed, but even through them, the light blinds me. I must pull a face because someone laughs.

"Wakey, wakey, kitten." It's a male voice, rough and mocking. I don't recognize it.

I try to reply, but there's something in my mouth. A ball of fabric that makes it hard to swallow. I crack open my eyelids in a desperate attempt to figure out where I am. There's literally a spotlight trained on my face. My body is heavy, and when I try to move my limbs, nothing happens.

"You thought you could mess with us?" The man moves around the room in circles, confusing my hearing. It's like he's everywhere.

The frost in my body melts. As tears pool in my eyes, a passing thought takes me back in time. Just two weeks ago, Mathias and Connor stuffed my panties in my mouth. It felt the same. The helplessness. The guilt and shame.

No. No, it's not the same. *Remember the hammer*, I tell myself.

I shake my head which invites another wave of laughter in the room. One on top of another. There are two people here. I lift my head, doing my damned hardest to escape the light beam and see past it. A hand comes out of nowhere and pushes on my forehead, forcing my head back on the soft table.

Then my mind pieces it together. The smells. The sounds. The spotlight.

I'm in an operating room. Probably in Hale-Bopp. I sniffle behind my gag, relief now diluting my thick, gloopy fear. Mathias is somewhere close. I know he is.

"Your skin is so smooth." The man's hand is still on my face. He runs his calloused fingertips across my cheeks, and I shudder, trying to squirm away from his touch.

"Oh, come on, kitten," he coos above me, his stale breath hitting my nose. I can't place the smell, but it's disgusting, and I gag.

A primal fear that I will drown in my vomit rises in me. Then my mind supplies another memory, blocking my senses to the here and now.

"Stay just like that, neko-chan."

"You're so beautiful, neko-chan."

"Just one more costume, neko-chan."

That's right. I've already been here. Lying like I'm paralyzed. Taking whatever someone else has in store for me like a good girl. Silent. Obedient. Submissive.

Remember the hammer. Mathias said something about a hammer. What hammer?

I need to get out of here. I need to run. I go rabid, trying to flail my arms and legs. They don't go far, stuck to like I'm a one fat tree trunk. But I don't give up. I activate every muscle in my body, and I scream behind the fabric of my gag.

"What the fuck? Hold her!"

"Is she having a seizure?"

The two male voices drip with panic now. No fawning for me. No freezing. I guess I want to fight. I thrash like a shark in a cage. If I had my teeth, I would have been trying to bite like one too.

They're stronger than me, though, so they pin me back to the operating table. But the struggle dislodges the light, and I can see them—a meathead my age and a middle-aged man in a white coat. I glimpse the tattoo on the meathead's hand. Damn it, Sophie. You should have been more thorough in the night.

After I catch my breath, I evaluate my state. I can feel more of my body now. The meathead is putting most of his weight on my torso. The middle-aged doctor only holds my legs.

I'm not going to lie and take it like a good girl anymore. Not without consenting first, anyway.

I kick out my legs, catching the doctor by surprise. My foot connects with his jaw, and he yelps like a little puppy. I feed on the sound, using it to power up my next move.

Then the door to the OR opens. Another doctor comes in. All I can tell is that he's tall. Two on one was bad odds. Three on one is just impossible.

I groan behind my gag and flop on the table. I gave it a good try.

"You ready to begin?" the Crossfire Security meathead asks the room.

No. Nope. Not ready for whatever this is. I start thrashing again.

"Keep her steady, will you? And you, Flores, do your fucking job and put her under."

I freeze. My body reacts to Mathias's name the same way it reacts to an unexpected sound in a quiet, dark, empty house.

He's here. He is, but he's not saving me yet. I twist around, trying to see his face. He's now behind me, fiddling with the equipment.

I want to scream at him. Doesn't he recognize me? Hot tears spill from my eyes.

"Remove the gag, I need to put the mask on her," he says in a flat tone. I'm too panicked to be able to tell if it's fake or genuine. Too confused.

"She's going to scream like a harpy." The middle-aged doctor mutters under his breath.

"She won't." Mathias's words come from way closer than expected. His comforting scent, like black pepper and vanilla, envelops me like a blanket. My confusion multiplies.

As the meathead's fingers peel the tape off my face and remove the gag, Mathias lowers his head to mine and talks. His words are loud as if he's talking to the whole room, but his blue eyes are trained on me, unwavering.

"I learned a new word from my VIP patient," he says. "Himawari."

My eyes widen, and when the rag comes out of my mouth, I don't scream, just as he predicted.

"No one cares," the middle-aged doctor scoffs.

But I care.

Himawari means sunflower. And sunflowers are symbols of hope.

CHAPTER 39

The fact that she doesn't scream makes me want to kiss her. That will have to wait, though, because I'm still maintaining my cover. I have to. I can't take on this massive guy. He will snap me like a breadstick.

"We've got it here," I say to him. I place the anesthetic face-mask on Hanako's face and pretend to start up the gas. She looks at me with wide, panicked eyes. I look down at her face and blink my eyes slowly. Trust me, I'm saying without speaking. And she knows this blink. It's the one I do for her while she's struggling in a scene. It signals her to take a slow blink and sync it with her breathing.

Her body visibly relaxes. I'm so proud of her courage. So thankful for her trust. There is a part of me that's stressed. I have to get us both out of here; how will I manage that?

Somehow. The OR is my domain. If nothing else, I know everything here. Like how two nurses will walk in at some point soon. And when they do, the room will be so cramped that the Crossfire brute will have to leave.

The surgeon looks at his hands.

"What are we doing? Don't you need to go scrub again?" I ask, trying to get him out of the room. Cross infection is no joke.

"I don't need full PPE," he responds, bored. "We're doing a quick prefrontal leukotomy."

For Hanako's sake, I don't react to that. Inside me, everything curdles. That's another name for a damned lobotomy. No one performs that anymore. It's barbaric.

"Uh," I mumble. "It's not a procedure I'm familiar with. Have you performed it a lot?"

I dread the answer. The grin he shoots me before replying tells me everything. "I was hired specifically for my experience with it. Don't worry, your part is not hard. Just get her under as normal. If all goes well, she will be one happy customer when she wakes up."

I nearly vomit in my mouth. Happy? If I let him have his way, Hanako will be gone. Either dead or forever changed in a horrible way. That's what happens when doctors are allowed to mince people's brains with a stick. This guy is going straight to jail after this. Or if the Empress doesn't deem that fair, then straight to the bottom of the ocean.

The big Crossfire guy finally steps away from Hanako. To her credit, she doesn't move at all. She looks sedated, subdued. But I know she's right here with me, biding her time like me, waiting for a moment to escape.

The two nurses come in with a tray of sterile instruments.

"Oh, she's already here. She doesn't look prepped," the scrub nurse says and lifts a brow.

"Just a quick little operation today. Off the record," the surgeon says.

"Uhm, I—" the second nurse starts saying something, but no one hears her. No one but me. She doesn't want to be here. Good.

The big guy looks out of his depth when the nurses move around him. He sidesteps them. "I'm going to help my boss. You going to be all right here?"

"Yeah, now that Dr. Flores has tamed the shrew." The surgeon laughs. My upper lip twitches in disgust.

I count to five after the Crossfire guy leaves. There is activity around the room, and the mood is half-cheery, half gloomy. It's obvious who's bringing what to the table.

"I don't think that's clean." I stand up and look over the tray of instruments. There's a thin, long ice pick-like tool, which I never thought I would see in a modern OR. I reach from behind the scrub nurse and pick it off the tray.

"I sterilized it," she says. I bet she pouts behind her mask.

I walk toward the surgeon, holding it in my hands as if I want to show him.

I don't do violence. I don't kill. It's not part of me. But protecting those who I love, is. Caring for my patients, is. Treating malignant conditions, is.

That's exactly what this excuse of a surgeon is. A shitstain on the doctor's profession.

"It looks fine to me," he says and reaches to take the instrument from me.

But I'm a metalworker. I have deft fingers, and they close around the handle faster than he can blink. In one perfect arch, I sink the tool into his thigh.

He opens his mouth to scream, eyes wide and wild, but I clamp my hand on his face.

Hanako takes my cue like a champion and jumps up. The nurses scream. She shushes them, and they quiet down. I don't take my eyes off the surgeon.

"I might have nicked your femoral vein, so what I want you to do now is to keep your head on. Don't pass out. The nurses will help you. Do you understand?"

He nods frantically.

I chance a look behind me. Hanako is holding a scalpel over the scrub nurse's wrist. The grip she has on the nurse's hand will surely leave a bruise. The other nurse is cowering in a corner.

"You." I nod my head up to make her come to me. "Come help out here. Don't remove the tool before we're gone. There might be lots of blood."

She walks up to me, shaking so hard she's almost seizing.

"You go help him too," Hanako says to the scrub nurse. "Do we have to tie them up or something?"

I shake my head. "They're medical professionals, not gangsters. Right? They will all stay here and tend to that injury." I point to the surgeon's thigh. He's standing still like a statue, probably afraid to move his leg. The nurses huddle around him. The scrub nurse glares daggers at me, but I don't care. I commit her face to memory so I can point her out later. Anyone willing to assist in a lobotomy should be far, far away from any OR.

I let the fact that lobotomies were performed routinely in this hospital wash over me. I can't help the past. But I can make sure the future is different.

Hanako and I make our way down the empty corridor toward the elevator. I press the button, and we wait for it to arrive. As the ten most excruciating seconds in my life tick by, I see Hanako is still clutching the scalpel.

"I don't think you're going to need that," I whisper.

"Are you kidding? I just got kidnapped. Sophie would take it with her." She leans back, hiding the scalpel with her other hand like it's a precious little thing.

"Do you know how sharp this is? Don't cuddle it."

"Okay, fine. You can hold it. Protect both of us." She hands it to me. I don't want it, but I take it anyway. I hold it like a household knife, blade down and away from my body.

The elevator arrives with a welcoming ding. It's empty. Our grand escape is turning out to be a calm, organized affair. Fine by me.

As it goes down, I look around. There's a tray attached to one side. I skim over the leaflets absentmindedly until my eyes stop on a familiar face. I grab the whole bunch.

"What is it?" Hanako asks.

"Very, very bad news for Tanya." I'm about to point to the old man in the picture when the doors open. I stuff a couple of leaflets in my back pocket, letting the others spill to the floor.

"Quickly," a male voice says.

Kazuo is ushering us out of the lift. He's abandoned his too-big bright blue scrubs for a pair of dark well-fitting ones. His hair is slicked back out of his face, and he doesn't have his glasses on. I sigh at the sight of him, this perfect Japanese man. But when I look at Hanako, she doesn't look impressed at all.

"Who are you?" Her voice drips with suspicion.

"Oh, I'm Kazuo Okada. I'm helping the Arcana and Sophie Taylor."

"Yes, Sophie told me about you." Hanako beams in response. "Sorry, I was just kidnapped. Gave me trust issues."

He laughs. She laughs. I roll my eyes.

"We were going somewhere?" I say.

"Follow me," Kazuo says. "I'll take you to Miss Yagi. She's safe in the Empress's car."

He starts walking fast toward the staff exit to the parking lot, and I step to follow when I notice Hanako hasn't moved.

"My mother is with the Empress?" She blinks, struggling to process. "Why? How?"

Oh, shit. Well, Miss Yagi won't be able to keep her secret much longer.

HANAKO

CHAPTER 40

Neither Kazuo nor Mathias explains to me why Mama is in the middle of an internal gang conflict. I had thought it was weird that she didn't call to check up on me when I didn't come back for the night; then again, it wasn't the first time she'd gone silent.

We make it to the parking lot, and Kazuo takes us to a massive black Mercedes that looks like a mashup between a Jeep and a tank. With blackened windows and massive tires, it's a menacing sight in the dark parking lot. A gangster car if I ever saw one. Is it his? He doesn't look like a guy who would drive a car like this. The Empress, whom I've never met, is nowhere to be seen. There's actually no one around.

"Where's everyone?"

"Your mom is in the back seat. I need to go back to the hospital, but you three stay here. Someone will come to get you when the coast is clear," Kazuo says.

I don't know what that means, but I don't care at the moment. I feel like I've missed an essential bit of information.

"Do you mind staying guard outside for a bit?" I ask Mathias. His face is scrunched up like he really doesn't want to be here. "What is it?"

He straightens and smiles. "Talk to your mother. I'll stay here."

I don't fight him when he pulls me into a hug and kisses my forehead. He's hiding something. It seems to do with Mama, so I let it go, open the car door and shuffle inside.

The air smells like expensive perfume and genuine leather.

"My Hanako!" My mother puts her hand in front of her face in surprise. "What are you doing here? I've been calling you."

"That's my question," I quip. Then I notice she's not wearing her regular clothes. She has a fancy hospital gown on. "Are you sick?"

"I—" She takes my hand. Not a good sign. "I wanted to help you with your investigation. When I realized the kind of enemy you were fighting, I couldn't stay idle."

"What? So, you went to Hale-Bopp for... What?" I sound like an idiot, but I'm baffled. "Start from the beginning. Where did you go that day when I left you at the bus stop?"

"That's not the beginning, my daughter." She takes a deep breath. "The beginning perhaps was when I overheard you and Mathias in your bedroom, talking about your client and his undercover work."

"So, you did eavesdrop on us." I kept checking, but I never caught her, except those two times at work.

"You have to understand, I was taught by my mother to be a quiet and respectful wife. I learned to walk in small, measured steps and not to speak unless spoken to. I learned to listen and anticipate. It was everything I knew until I came to America with your father. Some habits are difficult to shake." She looks up at me, pleading for me to see her side. I nod and keep silent.

"After I heard that it was the Arcana that was in the middle of it all, I went to visit an old friend."

"Is it the Empress?" I gape at her confession.

"I know her as Emilia Rogers. I do not know if you remember, you were small then, but my first big exhibition was in Chicago.

And one of my first benefactors was Emilia. She told me she loved my depiction of strong women. I liked her instantly; she had taken a look at my pain and called it strength. After that day, I promised myself I would be strong indeed. And I shed most of my ingrained smallness. I am still polite and quiet, but my paintings are not."

"That's amazing," I whisper.

"I wanted to help you, but it turned out the only opening for someone like me to help was to be a shield for Mathias."

"Thank you. For helping him. He was finding it really hard being there, in the hospital, witnessing the things that the patients were subjected to." Tears well up in my eyes. I don't know why.

"Yes. After our conversation in Mathias's room, I realized that my ability to listen was broken. I was not hearing what you wanted to tell me. And maybe words do not come easy when I have been away for so long. You call it eavesdropping, but I listened to you. To you and Mathias, who always tried to tell me things too and get me on your side. In time, I understood. We are different. And I cannot make you love Japan like I do. All I can do is support what you already love." She reaches her free hand to brush off a tear from my cheek.

She stays quiet, letting the words sink in. And when they do, I go saucer eyed. "Oh, you mean Mathias."

"Not only Mathias, your job and your friends, but Mathias too. I may have heard a bit too much of your love the other night." She winks.

My ears burn, and I'm so embarrassed I decide not to reply to that. I just pretend she didn't say it.

"So, you were pretending to be sick?" I ask after I gather myself.

"I came back without telling you because I wanted to see how you live. I wanted to see if I can convince you to live in a way that I thought would improve on my failings as a mother and wife." She swallows loudly, and her hand tightens on mine. "I have stage II ovarian cancer."

I'm speechless again. I wish we weren't in someone else's car where I can't process my emotions properly. I wish I could scream and sink my nails into my face. It's too much information. A rollercoaster ride I wish to get off from.

"Stage II?" I croak finally. "There are two more stages which means it's not that bad, right? Is it operable?"

"Yes. But I am afraid of being put to sleep. I am afraid I will never wake up. I cannot have the surgery until everything is in order."

This revelation knocks the air out of my lungs. I want to shout at her and tell her she's being silly, but I don't. How would that help?

"Are things in order now?" I ask instead, hoping she will get that operation asap.

"Yes. Almost. Your Mathias suggested I tell you and get the surgery. His words brought me solace. The doctor in Milan advised against traveling and postponing treatment. But I think I made the right choice." She leans forward, tentative.

I pull her into a tight hug. She returns it with equal passion. I can't remember the last time she held onto me so tightly. Maybe she did when I was a baby. I hope she did.

Tears are still streaming down my face. At this point, it's just all the confusing emotions leaking through my eyes.

We hug for a long time. For so long that I remember how comforting the smell of her neck is, how calming her measured breathing is, how warm her chest is against mine. I remember what it's like to have my mother next to me.

She lets go first, gently peeling me away and holding my shoulders while looking into my eyes. Hers are the same deep brown as mine.

"You grew up well, my Hanako. I am sorry I was not here to share your moments. But from now on, I will never be too far away. I will not smother you with my love, but my love will always be close," she says.

"I would like that." I sniffle.

"So, you and Mathias. Have you planned your future?" She smiles warmly.

I chuckle. She sure recovers fast from these emotional situations. "No plans yet. We like each other a lot. But," I hesitate for a moment, "Mathias is just one part of my life."

"Of course," Mama nods. I don't think she gets it, though.

"It was never just the two of us," I say. "There is another guy that we are more than friends with. He's called Connor. And there may be others in time, coming and going. What I feel for Mathias is the strongest I've felt for any man yet, but we're never going to be exclusive. So, for now, no plans around marriage and kids. I know it's not what you want to hear."

She blinks like a robot, her mouth pressed into a tiny line of disbelief. When she finally speaks, her voice is so quiet that I need to lean in to hear her. "This is a surprise. It is not something I am used to. I only just accepted Mathias. I mean, he is not Japanese. That is fine. So, is it like you might be a second wife or a third wife?"

"No. Nothing like that. It means Mathias and I love each other, but we might grow to love other people too. And that's good, right? More love for everyone." I'm not upset at all at her response. Right off the bat, she's trying to understand me. I can't believe it was just a few weeks ago that she was telling me I had to find a Japanese husband no matter what.

"I need to think about it," she says. "And I have to change my painting."

"The painting is happening?" I squeal. I thought she took it metaphorically, the way I meant it. But she's actually going to put all this emotional labor she's done on the canvas? "Can I see it?"

"I will show you, of course." She pulls me into another hug. Two in one night? I'm about to start crying again.

"My Hanako, my muse," she coos. "I will finish the painting and have the surgery."

CHAPTER 41

Coat, jeans, the elastic bandage on my foot, and Laura's gun in my backpack. Doesn't get more badass than that.

So when Sophie's two underlings and I enter Hale-Bopp hospital, and we stop to let an old lady pass, I'm underwhelmed in a surprisingly good way. She's in a wheelchair being taken to reception by what appears to be her daughter or granddaughter. The hospital is just... standard.

"I thought there was going to be a fight," I whisper to the young guy. I bonded with him during the car ride, despite his wish not to share his name. Another one like Sophie's nameless boyfriend, I guess.

"Ah, probably not. Sophie and the Empress are keeping it on the down-low for the patients. They don't need to be in a shootout while they're getting their colonoscopies." He winks. "There will be action upstairs in the VIP wing, though, don't worry."

We go up in the patient elevator, asking a family of five to wait for the next one. I feel like we're assholes, but also, I'm thankful that we don't take the one I rode down to the server room.

The moment the elevator doors ping open, a massive guy I'm very familiar with stands before us. It's the Crossfire bouncer sadist that was so happy when I got stepped on. I step backward, pressing my back to the mirror surface of the elevator. I came here to face my fear, but now I'm not sure what to do.

"Another one of those," the young guy says to the woman. They're both so calm that it throws me off. I also have to be calm. But how?

I twist the backpack to the front of me and fish inside for the gun.

"Who are you?" The Crossfire goon asks. Very civil of him.

"Enemies," the burly woman says. Her presence is like a shield in front of me.

I take out the gun and point it forward. "Freeze, or I'll shoot." This makes Sophie's underlings flinch.

"Hey there, my man, let's bring this down. Angela, would you deal with that thing?" the younger guy says, and I think he means me and the gun, but no, she punches the Crossfire dude straight in the face, fast like a viper. He staggers back, holding his bleeding face in shock.

This reminds me of my own crusted lip, and I palpate my nose. It hurts a bit, but I don't think it's broken.

"I can help you," I say to the younger guy as he brings my hands down and plucks the gun from them.

"This is not your gun, is it?" He asks with a pitying smile.

"No. It was my wife's."

"It kinda shows, so better keep it hidden. And if you really need to use it, take off the safety first." He winks, and I feel like a kid who just got schooled.

Okay, maybe I'm not a sharpshooter. In my defense, Laura grew up in Texas, and I was born and bred in Iowa. I put the gun back in my backpack. Angela has neutralized the Crossfire guy for the time it took me to have this small convo. He looks like a mangled mess on the floor.

"I'll put him in a room," she says. "Someone might trip if I leave him here."

"Health and safety expert," the younger guy gives her a thumbs-up and grins. "She's so thoughtful."

I nod slowly as a frown spreads across my face. These people are just built different.

After the Crossfire guy is out of the way and Angela has taken her time wiping the blood off the floor with a wet wipe she found in the room next door, we go down the corridor, and the younger guy knocks on a heavy wooden door.

Inside is a glass box of an office and four people.

"Connor!" Sophie's face bursts into a smile when she sees me. "Our guest of honor."

"What?" I'm taken aback by her words of welcome.

Angela and the younger guy nod to Sophie and clear out, leaving me with Sophie, an Asian guy, and a very expensive-looking older woman. She shoots me a piercing look, one that makes me straighten up and take my hands out of my pockets. Then she speaks.

"Mr. Jones, I've heard about what you did, and I want to commend you on your bravery and persistence to uphold your morals," she says. Her voice has a calming cadence to it. I assume she's the Empress from the gold rings and bracelets sitting heavy on her small hands.

"I don't know what you're talking about," I say.

"Miss Taylor told us all about how you refused to create a deletion tool, thus preserving vital information about this hospital's patients." She points to Sophie, whose grin spreads even farther on her face. She seems really proud of me.

"So, you'll tell the police?" I ask.

"I don't work with the police," the Empress says the same way someone might say they don't like iPhones. "But the evidence was utilized by a group of hard-working employees to convince shareholders that this hospital needs a different leader. And a name change. What kind of atrocious name is Hale-Bopp? We're one leap away from a slogan. 'Our prices are astronomically high,' would work."

She rolls her eyes, and everyone in the room laughs. Even me. I stop abruptly, surprised.

"But what about justice for everyone involved?" I ask.

"We dish out our own justice." Her voice is so cold it freezes any follow-up questions in my head. "As I was saying, my son, Ken will go back to education—"

The door swings open, and a red-faced man stumbles into the office.

"What have you done, mother?" He pants the words out, desperation dripping from him along with his sweat.

"Absolutely nothing," she says. Her face is arranged in an expression that is one lip twitch away from disgust. "We had an agreement. You lead the hospital and make yourself useful as the Arcana Magician. But in the Tarot deck, the Magician symbolizes power, potential, and unity. I let you run with this idea of a merger with Comet International because I thought you knew what you were doing. Clearly, I was wrong."

"We're making bank! Comet is good for us. Why are you interfering now? The next step of my plan was going to put us on the national map and worldwide. We would have been millionaires!" He's pulling on his cheeks, his voice shrill.

"Kazuo, close the door," the Empress says. The Asian guy obeys immediately. He's wearing fitted black scrubs and looks like he's from the 'good' part of the hospital.

"It was you!" Ken Rogers swipes to grab Kazuo by the shirt, but his hands find nothing. Kazuo sidesteps him like a boss and returns to the Empress's side.

"I will take control of the hospital until the shareholders meeting next week," the Empress continues, undisturbed. "It doesn't matter how much money we make if we're making them by committing acts I can't stand behind. No, don't interrupt me. I will highlight some, but the list is long. Refusing Arcana members free care; performing unnecessary procedures on healthy or unwilling patients; disposing of bodies by using the incinerator in the basement; threatening contractors. I'm appalled and horrified that after trying to teach you the values of our community, you were swayed by money, of all things, and turned into... this."

She swipes her hand up and down in his direction, her bracelets jangling.

"I wanted to make you proud!" He screams like a child.

I wince and almost feel sorry for him. Almost. Most people don't turn to a life of medical crime when they want to appease their mother.

"You only managed to make me disappointed." The Empress drives the message home with the icy precision of an unhappy parent. "But you're still my son. So you can choose either to go abroad and continue your management education or to leave Arcana and try to live life on your own. It seems you're not aware, but we're already millionaires. I prefer to invest in people and property, not in shady power-hungry corporations. Which reminds me, Comet International is no longer welcome. I will send them an email, but you might want to pre-warn them if you have a contact. They will erase all mention of being involved with this hospital and sell the pharmacies they own around here. I don't want to see a single supplement of theirs on my territory."

"But the deals... We'll lose so much money." Ken shuts up the moment the Empress's left brow arches. "I understand, mother. I will go study."

"Smart choice," she says. "I don't want to talk to you anymore. Leave."

He scuttles away. I'm pretty sure this is his office.

"Mr. Jones, walk with me." The Empress goes around the glass desk and puts a small hand on my shoulder. I try not to flinch because while I'm impressed by her, I'm also a bit scared. She steers me out of the office. I lock eyes with Sophie, an unspoken question on my face.

"It's okay," Sophie says. "I just have a few things to discuss with Kazuo."

In the corridor, the Empress and I stroll as if we're in a park.

"You're always welcome on Arcana territory," she says. "We

owe you, so if you're ever in trouble, come to us. If you're also looking for a job, we can always make some room in our Arcana IT team."

"Would I get a cool nickname?" I smile.

"Perhaps."

"Wait, is the IT team just some hackers in a room?"

"They're not in one room. Single offices. And they do IT support of all kinds. One of them fixed my iPad last week."

She didn't deny it. I'm not a hacker, so I shake my head. "Thanks for the offer, but I have different plans after this. Part of it is to avoid a life of crime."

"You're a good boy." She smiles and pats my shoulder again. Now I really feel bad for Ken. If it's this easy to win her approval, how did he fuck up so badly?

When we reach the elevator, we get in. I still don't know where she's taking me. There are leaflets scattered all over the floor. Despite her expensive attire and air of extravagance, the Empress squats and picks them all up. She looks at them.

"Another one of Comet International's shady dealings. I will feel so much better when they're all dealt with."

I peer over her shoulder. It's a white leaflet about a charity clothes sale, organized by a 'Rad Red Ron' orphanage. I've never heard of them. The picture is a gray building with a line of people in front of it. Two women stand like fences around children of different ages, and an old man pokes out like a tall lamppost in the middle.

"Do you think they will all leave your territory as you want?" I ask.

"Only time will tell."

The elevator doors open to the parking lot, and we walk to an all-black Mercedes G-Class. Damn, a car like this really does show she has millions.

CHAPTER 42

A knock on the tinted window interrupts me mid-explanation. I'm talking to my mother about the differences between polyamory and an open relationship with enough passion to leave her speechless and wide-eyed. She lets out a breath she's been holding on for a while after I pause to open the door and check who it is.

"Connor!" I jump out of the car, high on endorphins from being listened to and understood. High on shared familial love.

"Oh, hello!" He gives me a tight hug. Behind him, there's an older woman dressed like straight out of a Harper's Bazaar cover.

"You must be Emilia Rogers," I say and extend my hand.

She squeezes it firmly. "Wonderful to meet you, Miss Yagi Junior," she says.

"Hana is fine," I say, then correct myself, "Hanako."

She nods. "Should we set off and have some food in my house? My chef makes a wonderful lasagna. I'm sure you'll appreciate it, Tomoko."

My mother has just made it out of the car. She smiles. "I've missed Italian food."

"Italian? You've been making me Japanese food ever since you arrived," I say with a mock frown.

"That's different. Just because I prefer a grilled mackerel to a bowl of cereal for breakfast, doesn't mean I can't appreciate a good lasagna." She pats my back. It's a small gesture, but it feels familiar like we've always done it. Having her close by won't be so bad, after all. We can catch up on all the stuff we missed out on. After she recovers from her surgery, I'm taking her straight to Japan.

"And I have some pieces from Milan Fashion Week I can gift to you. Can't have an esteemed guest in a hospital gown." The Empress puts her hand under her chin in an estimating gesture.

My mother twirls like a princess. "If they're my size, of course."

They both share a gentle laugh that I've never heard before. I can't recall ever seeing or hearing my mother in a company of friends. I wonder if she was lonely when she was with my father. Alone in a new country, no friends, no family. No future, really. Maybe the decisions she regrets in her past are the same decisions that enabled her to blossom and become the force of nature that she is now.

"But I need to go upstairs first," she says. "My sketches are there."

"I got them," a breathless voice says from behind us.

Kazuo, no longer dressed in scrubs, holds my mother's massive artwork carry case.

"Oh, wonderful. You're such a sweetheart. Hanako, I hope you can find space in your polyamory network for Kazuo," she says with a proud smile.

My eyes widen, and I go bright red.

"Mo-o-om," I squeal. I don't think I've ever called her that, but the situation is perfect. I feel like I'm fifteen again, in an alternate universe where my mother said things that embarrassed me in front of my friends, and all was normal.

Everyone bursts out laughing. Mathias clamps a hand on Kazuo's shoulder, giving him a saucy wink. Oh, I think he's totally down for stuff with Kazuo. Good to know.

"Here it is." Mama's voice pulls my attention back to her. She's holding a big piece of card with confident black lines depicting one sunflower and one dahlia and a ring around them. There's writing on the ring, and I squint to read it. Memento vitae.

"Oh, it's going to be beautiful," the Empress says. "Is it about the inevitability of seasons?"

"Actually, it is the research I did when I observed my Hanako and her life. After our conversation today, however, I will have to make a few changes. Add a few flowers. Maybe a whole bouquet inside the ring." She chuckles. I'm loving this sound.

"Is it supposed to be about me marrying Hanako?" Mathias asks. He looks both confused and intrigued.

"I guess it could seem that way," Mama replies. "Art is in the eye of the beholder. You can interpret it any way you like."

"The dahlia is Mexico's national flower," he says. "And that is just like mine."

"Oh yeah, your Memento Mori ring," Connor chimes in. "Maybe she meant that you should remember to live, not just to die. Or something. You have to put a wild rose in there too, Mrs. Yagi. It's Iowa's flower."

"You're from Iowa?" I wish I sounded less surprised. "I always assumed you're a Chicagoan."

"Can't blame you, accents are close." Connor shrugs.

My mother takes a charcoal pencil and sketches a wild rose inside the rings. Then she continues sketching, adding a fourth flower, one with small petals.

"What's that?" I ask.

"Oh, a hydrangea." She continues drawing. "Kobe's flower."

"I thought you're from Okinawa." I scratch my head.

"I'm from Kobe." Kazuo lifts a shy hand.

"Oh," I draw out the o. "Too early, Mama."

"It's my art," she says as she finishes the sketch.

The final result is stunning. The sketch radiates passion and hope in its raw, black and white glory. It's definitely my mother's style but also nothing like her previous paintings.

"I love it," I whisper in her hair after I pull her into our third hug for the day.

Yep. It will be easy to get used to this.

After a hearty meal at the Empress's lavish house, Connor, Mathias, and I take a moment alone. We walk Chicago's streets, for once without fear. We move past the Arcana territory and into Sophie's like we're royalty.

"So, you and Mathias are together now?" Connor asks. He doesn't sound upset or jealous, merely curious.

"We are exploring an open relationship," Mathias says.

We discussed it briefly on the way to Connor's yesterday, so I nod and continue. "Would you like to be a part of our throuple? We still have a lot to learn about each other, and we like you a lot. We can explore it all together."

Connor smiles but shakes his head. "It's not the right time for me. I play without attachment because I'm still deeply in love with Laura. You will think I'm insane, but even now, for me, it's like she's walking here with us." He rubs his ring, his eyes shifting to its dark surface.

"It sounds like you're still grieving," I whisper.

"I am. So I've decided I'm going on a trip. Iowa, Texas, and all the places that hold the memories of my relationship. I will keep in touch, but I need to come to terms with what happened and what I've become."

"What about your job?" Mathias asks.

"Oh, fuck that shit. I emailed my resignation between the second main and dessert." He laughs. "My boss gave my address to the Crossfire goons. I'm not going to make money for him."

"Well, I hope we'll see soon. Don't be a stranger." I punch Connor's arm lightly.

"You won't get rid of me that easily."

After that, he tells us how stern the Empress was when she talked to her son, the Hale-Bopp Health's Director. It's interesting how parents can be most critical of their children while remaining lovely to everyone else. But I guess parenting isn't easy. Maybe one day I will struggle too. Or maybe not. I've learned a lot from Mama about misunderstandings and about finding my way back to a culture that I thought had abandoned me.

And modern ideas don't have to clash with traditional values. We, as people, only have to meet in the middle and take a bit of everything.

Memento Vitae.

EPILOGUE

The last few days have been full of nothing but wholesome moments and the occasional sexy time. Not sex, not yet, but so much touching it's like I can feel through Hanako's fingers.

Not having to work undercover is doing wonders for my gut health. Except when Miss Yagi cooked spicy ramen the other day, and I nearly died, but that's a story for another time. This Wednesday dinner will be special. We will have a home-cooked meal for everyone attending for the first time. No, not a meal. A feast.

I'm setting the table before everyone arrives and watching Hanako and her mother bicker in the kitchen.

"But kimchi is not Japanese," Hanako says, looking at a plate of spicy pickled cabbage.

"I am happy you know that," Miss Yagi says.

"Then why are we serving it? The theme is traditional Japanese dinner."

"Because it's tasty."

Hanako huffs and says something in Japanese, fast and confident. She's been learning it again, and it seems to be coming back to her like a tsunami. She will be fluent in no time. Miss Yagi only shakes her head.

Sophie, Damien, Tanya, and the kids arrive on time. For some reason, they have presents which they give to Miss Yagi with a promise for more. There's fruit, chocolate, and a bouquet of fresh sunflowers.

"What's that about?" I ask Hanako while everyone who doesn't know Miss Yagi introduces themselves.

"I bet Sophie's been reading up on Asian culture again." Hanako chuckles.

The mood around the table reminds me of home. I look down at my ring and play with the rotating element. Maybe it's time to make a new one.

Sophie raises her glass and clinks on it with a knife.

"So, I want to raise a toast to Mathias, Connor, and the Yagis. Although Connor isn't here with us, I have extended an open invitation to him for these dinners, and hopefully, he will join us sometime," she says. "I will be brief, but everyone's favorite male nurse Kazuo was chosen to be the new hospital director yesterday. A job is waiting there for Mathias whenever he's ready to take it. Mateo Grey withdrew the damning statement that prevented Mathias from practicing, so he's once again a fully-qualified doctor."

Everyone whoops with their glasses in the air. It's not exactly true. I have to retrain and retake my exams, but I'm on my way to getting my job back. There's nothing but procrastination in my way now. And because Hanako is suspended for another few weeks, I will take the time to procrastinate with her naked and moaning next to me.

We cheers and drink, lapsing into a comfortable silence.

"I have a few things to announce, too," Hanako says. "My mother's surgery has been scheduled for next week thanks to the Empress pulling some strings. After that, we will be visiting Japan. If anyone wants to join us, you'll be more than welcome to."

"Oh, I'm definitely going," Melanie, Sophie's sister, says.

"You've got school," Sophie replies with a mock scowl.

"Can you postpone the trip to the summer?" Melanie asks.

"If all goes well, who knows, maybe we'll go in the summer as well." Miss Yagi's voice is warm. It looks like she's finally made peace with whatever tormented her before. Hanako told me that she missed her home country, which in turn made me miss mine. I will tag along for the Japan tour, but a trip to Mexico is already being planned in my head.

"And in other good news, I got my car back. It's no longer scratched." Hanako raises her glass, and we drink to that too.

"Did you find out who keyed it?" Damien asks.

"Oh, it turns out the garage was doing the filling or filing or whatever wrong, so after a certain time, the scratches from before would show up. I still don't know who scratched it the first time, but at least I'm not scared about someone actively going after my property now."

"Underwhelming," Tanya says as she stuffs a forkful of kimchi in her mouth. She's really taken to it.

My heart twitches every time she speaks tonight. I know I'll have to break the bad news to her at some point.

When they're all leaving, I walk with her to the elevator and ask her to take the stairs with me. She side-eyes me with suspicion but doesn't protest.

"I found this in the hospital." I hand her the flyer I picked up when we're alone.

The moment her eyes focus on the picture, she freezes in place.

"I'm sorry," I say when the silence stretches between us.

She crumples the flyer in her fist and stuffs it in her coat pocket. "Have you shown this to anyone else?"

"Hanako saw it, but I didn't tell her anything."

"Forget about it. I'm out of there. You're out of the gang shit. Just focus on your life." Her mouth is tight, and her blonde hair covers half her face. "Sophie has enough on her hands with Duke Hazelton still at large. You know we never found him?"

"But maybe we could help the children," I whisper.

"Leave it," she says through gritted teeth.

I lift my hands in surrender. "Fine."

She goes down without saying another word, leaving me alone with my discomfort. I consider telling Sophie about the orphanage but then think better of it. It's Tanya's pain. If she doesn't want people poking around it, I should respect that.

On Friday night, Hanako and I leave Miss Yagi to entertain herself. Connor sent us a few photos from the beginning of his road trip and play ideas for when he's back. This only gets me and Hanako going, giddy with the endorphins of planning awesome future times.

Tonight, we go to the Moon Garden to play, enjoying the sweet feeling of victory. Because we won. Against the depravity in that hospital, against the misunderstandings between us, against the odds stacked not in our favor. We're together now, and I have one hell of an evening planned.

Hanako is wearing a red see-through bodysuit, making my dick twitch in my tight leather pants. Sophie and Damien are around too, but we don't waste time socializing with anyone. We beeline straight to the private room I pre-booked, desperate for some alone time.

After the fire here a couple of months ago, lots of rooms had to be redecorated. The moment I was in the headspace to think about kink, I got in touch with the owner with a compelling design for one of the smaller private rooms. He agreed because it fitted with the theme of the place, and I paid for the paint.

"Oh. My. God. Wow." Hanako's hands cover her open mouth when she sees the room. "Did you do this?"

"Partly." I pet her silky hair. "Here was where we really bloomed; and where I got hopeful that we might work as more than play partners-roommates."

The walls and ceiling are painted sky blue, and massive sunflowers cover each of the four walls. The floor is yellow. A single circular bed stands in the middle. There's a black leather mattress because, after all, this is a sex club, but that doesn't detract from the bright feeling of the room.

"I'm ready," Hanako says.

She turns around, her eyes glittering with emotion.

"For?" I take her chin and pull her face to mine. We breathe each other in for a few moments.

"Your cock inside me." She bites her lip, and my dick nearly bursts out of my pants.

"How romantic," I whisper as my lips brush against hers. We share a brief kiss before she speaks again.

"But I'm on top."

"You've always been, Sunflower." I tangle my fingers in her hair and push her mouth to mine.

Our tongues find a rhythm that is both familiar and the most unique, fantastic thing in the world. She tastes like everything I've ever needed, and I can't wait to have her like this for the rest of my life.

HANAKO

EPILOGUE

"But I'm on top." I can't believe I just said that.

"You've always been, Sunflower." Mathias grabs my hair and devours me in a kiss that has my knees wobbling.

He lets go only to lock the door, and then he pushes me onto the bed. It's black and round, like the inside of an open sunflower. The idea of this room, Mathias's devotion to making me comfortable, and our recent victory against the big baddies at the hospital, all coalesce into an explosion of trust.

Something animalistic overtakes me, and I growl, pulling Mathias to me. I want him with me, around me, inside me. There's no denying the empty space between my legs.

"Not so fast," Mathias whispers against my hungry mouth.

He flips me to my stomach with one smooth move and pins my hands behind my back. My submissive nature takes over, and I breathe in the scent of new leather under my face.

A minute later, he's put soft leather cuffs on me and bound them together with a little chain. I wriggle around, testing them, and receive a prompt slap to my butt. I grunt into the bed, lifting my ass in the air, begging him to hit me again.

Mathias doesn't hesitate. *Slap. Slap. Slap.* He stops only after my butt feels hot and plump under his cool palms. The faint sounds of the club music make the silence between us heavy with sticky desire.

When he touches me next, I jolt in surprise. He's dragging a sharp pinwheel across the back of my thighs. My skin breaks out in goosebumps, and I moan. The almost-pain of the little pricks goes straight to my pussy, and I soak the bottom of my bodysuit.

Taking his time, he draws lines and circles across my skin, stopping from time to time to tease me with the absence of his touch.

I want to tell him to fuck me already, but my words don't come to my mouth as usual. I groan when he replaces the sharp wheel with his fingers. He kneads my butt, each movement pushing my bodysuit between my legs. I roll my hips, greedy for any sensation, and he pulls on the fabric, wedging it between my pussy lips. I bite the inside of my cheek. It feels *so* good.

I've half-forgotten about wanting to be on top when he pulls me by the shoulders. My back flush with his chest, he wraps one hand around my neck and guides the other between my legs, forcing my knees open. His dick is hard against me, and I can't resist grinding into him.

"Mmm." His moan rumbles near my ear.

He holds me in place with a loose grip on my neck while his fingers snap my bodysuit open and find the wet, empty place that longs to be filled by him.

Teasing my entrance with one finger, his palm slides against my clit, ramping up my pleasure. My eyes roll to the back of my head as he finds a tantalizing rhythm.

I come undone in his arms, my legs shaking, threatening to betray me and have me flop on the bed like a boneless doll. But Mathias holds me upright as I ride the wave of my orgasm.

My greedy pussy opens under his touch, wanting to coax him inside, but his fingers remain outside. I'm so ready for him to fill me up and give me the release I've been longing for ever since he tongue-fucked me senseless. I twist in his embrace, so I'm facing him, my mouth finding his. We've both forgotten our words, our bodies doing the talking in a hot, basic, animalistic way.

Wrapping my legs around Mathias's waist, I jump onto him and bite his lip. He groans and twirls us so that he's sitting on the bed, and I'm on his lap, grinding on his cock through his trousers.

I put my hands around his neck, locking him in place in my embrace, my wrists still connected by the little chain. This is it now. So close. He frees his cock and guides it to my entrance, his eyes locking with mine.

I bite my lip as I hover above him and then slowly lower myself, inch by excruciating inch. His skin feels divine against mine, and I'm so happy we both got tested. I've been on the pill for a while, so now nothing comes between us, body and mind connected.

After he's inside me, I focus on kissing him, letting my pussy adjust to the size of him. His hands cup my butt, then move up and down, caressing me like I'm a work of art that can only be appreciated by deliberate, focused touch.

I roll my hips and move up, then down. I'm ready. This feels so right. The void that opened inside me when I let Mathias inside my heart is full. It's full of hope, and lust, and so much more.

This moment just scratches the surface. I have so, *so* much to explore with him. I'm going to love every second of it.

I moan, shivering, and we move as one in a field of kinky sunflowers.

THANK YOU

Thanks for reading Dark Rings. I hope you enjoyed Hanako, Mathias and Connor's story. As a child of two cultures and always struggling with belonging in this world, it was a pleasure to explore some of that in this book and share it with you.

Readers like you are my favorite people and I appreciate you so much for reading, sharing my books and leaving reviews. Thank you! <3

Any thoughts and feelings about the book, I would love to hear them. Did Ms Yagi frustrate you as much as she did me? Did you heart flutter when Mathias and Hanako finally found their way to each other? Do you think Kazuo needs his own book? Just a few questions there, because as I was editing this book, I got to experience it as a reader and I wondered what someone outside of my head would feel about this story.

Book Two will be Tanya's dark story as we delve deeper into Comet International's shady business.

SCAN TO REVIEW

NEWSLETTER

Want to be the first one to know about new releases and opportunities to get involved with my writing and my books?

Come join **Lainey's Books**.

Lainey's Books is my monthly newsletter for my dedicated fans, who are always the first to get freebies, giveaway notifications, deleted scenes, opportunities to join my advance reading teams, insights into my writing journey and many more awesome things.

As a bonus, if you join now, you will get my novelette Lust Economics for free. It's a contemporary romance, following a student who likes to attend the Moon Garden, just as Sophie and Hana do. But the Moon Garden's patrons are all wonderfully different, and each have a story to tell. *Lust Economics* is Hayley's story – about how she played too hard and failed her course. Will her quick thinking save her and the relationship she's built, or will it doom her?

Scan the QR code below to join:

ABOUT LAINEY

Lainey Delaroque started writing poems when she was stuck in a hospital with pneumonia. She was 11 years-old then and hasn't stopped writing since.

She loves dangerous, fantastical worlds and morally grey characters. She writes diverse romantic thrillers packed with action, danger and sizzling tension. When the suspense is too much for Lainey, she takes a break by writing contemporary romance stories with kinky twists.

Visit www.laineydelaroque.com or find her on Facebook, Goodreads or Bookbub.

Books by Lainey Delaroque

<u>Club Lavender Duet</u>
The Lavender Phantom
The Brigand Children

<u>Dark Things</u>
Dark Rings
Book Two (coming summer 2022)
Book Three
Dark Things Novella

<u>Moon Garden Tales</u>
Lust Economics (via newsletter)

Read on for a glimpse of the gripping beginning of Lainey's dark Chicago underworld: Sophie and Damien's story, in the Club Lavender Duet:

THE LAVENDER PHANTOM

CHAPTER 1

It is bliss. The rope around my neck tightens, hitching my breath and making my eyelids slip down. I embrace the darkness and the throbbing pain under every single strand wrapped around my body.

In this split second, there's a lot to process. A lot of rope, a lot of pain, a lot of slippery feelings. A lot of people's gazes—some I choose to ignore, some to embrace.

I whimper as a shake starts somewhere deep within me and then spreads out to my limbs. My shin presses into my right thigh. It quivers with the effort to support my body in the shape compelled by the rope. My chest dips close to the ground, held in place by another piece of rope connected somewhere above me. A stray lock of my long blond hair touches the floor as I sway gently with my efforts.

I start to slip into a familiar darkness, my heartbeat audible in my skull. Short, staccato breaths escape my lips as the air around is barred proper entry into my lungs.

The neck rope slackens and slides to the ground. I inhale, deep and soothing, and strain against the hold around my chest. The ropes dig into my ribs deliciously, embracing me with their intimate tightness, forcing me to look within myself and face the darkness there. Face the seedling of doubt that I've not quite got the adult thing together yet. That, at twenty-four, I'm still an orphan with too much responsibility to bear.

A cane connects to the inside of my other thigh, biting into my naked skin, threatening to send me off-balance. I hiss, then still. The pain takes me away from that dangerous place, and I zone my attention in on it, thankful.

My left leg extends up, held in place by two ropes. I'm exposed, but I don't mind. In fact, I let my eyelids drift up a bit and steal a look at the crowd gathered to watch. I see bare feet and stilettos, brogues and oxfords. No sneakers. Never sneakers.

My previous aches and pains from the day have evaporated, allowing me to focus on this one moment, waiting for the next hit to mark my skin. My mind empties, and I reach toward my joyous place. My eyes close again because I want to feel everything. I'm afraid I will miss some sweet, complicated feeling if I focus on something else.

A volley of cane flicks descends upon me. I bite my lip, trying to silence the small whining that has started at the back of my throat. Then I give up and let my voice out.

I squeeze my hands into fists, enduring the pain from my binds and the assault on my leg. My wrists are tied behind my back, leaving me unable to do anything but accept whatever comes my way.

As many times before, I submit to this familiar helplessness, embrace the structure it gives to my unquiet mind, accept the pain and blanket myself with it, preoccupied with the sensation. In a world where everything is loud and demanding, I put those stresses aside and concentrate on the here and now.

I pant with exertion, the eyes on me long forgotten. There is just me and the cane in a conversation of pain-bringing harmony. It tells an erotic story with each sting on my skin, and I listen. I listen until it is too much, and I let my body go limp in the ropes, giving up on my side of the exchange.

In that moment, I am no one. Not Sophie Taylor, not a respectable adult, not a woman. Just a body with tingling skin stretched, a heap of sweet surrender. There is silence now. Once I go limp, the blows stop. It seems the whole world has stopped when they start up again, a hand reaching down to catch a fistful of my hair.

Behind the cane, there is a person. This time it's a man. I can't remember his name. I can barely remember my own. I groan as our eyes meet.

"Enough?" His question is soft, for my ears only. His voice jump-starts my memory. A new guy. Connor.

Like the flip of a switch, I'm suddenly cold and overwhelmed and shake in response. "Yes," I whisper.

Connor plants a kiss on my forehead, its gentleness in stark contrast with every signal of pain my body is receiving. He gets up and starts untying me, one rope at a time; slowly, safely, letting me process the transition from partial suspension to being a soft body on the floor.

I connect to my breathing, taking deep, comforting breaths, letting the oxygen caress my every cell. As the ropes come off, my skin burns with their marks. The cold leaves me, but the shakes remain.

Connor drapes a blanket over my shoulders and presses a bottle of water to my lips. I take two brave gulps, then shake my head. He embraces me tightly. I whisper, "Thank you" and bury my head in his chest.

We stay like that for a minute or two. Having enjoyed the rope scene, I'm taking the time to come down from that intensity, to reestablish myself as part of the world of walking, thinking humans. I don't need much aftercare, but a blanket and a bear hug are essential.

As my senses return, I look around, my eyes curious to discover the state of the room. A small crowd is still gathered, quiet spectators sharing drinks and hugs. I see my friend Hanako with one of her occasional play partners. She waves at me; I wink at her and turn to Connor.

"I enjoyed this, thanks again," I say. It is the first time we have tied together. He listened well to my words before we'd started our session—my limits, my wishes for what I wanted to experience, and his as well. He's taken care to stay within the boundaries while still pushing my body to the brink of what it can take.

He is beaming. Sweating, his cheeks flushed with red, his hands shaky as he collects his ropes and starts coiling them. New to the Moon Garden, he wanted to do a session with me, a rope switch veteran, and establish himself as a trustworthy rigger. I hadn't expected much, but the scene was a pleasant surprise, and I run my fingers across my rope marks, enjoying the feel and shape of them, committing the whole event to memory.

"It was great to work with you." He gives me another squeeze.

"Do you want help getting your ropes in order?" I ask, looking at the pool of rope we are sitting in.

He shakes his head.

I nod and get up. "I'll go freshen up." I pat his shoulder. I don't like to linger after scenes and make small talk. The ultimate goal of why we converged is over, and the desire to go somewhere else and continue with my night rises like a tide inside me.

"All right," he replies. "I didn't break skin as you requested, so you should be fine."

I nod. "It will bruise beautifully though. Thank you for your hard work. I'll have only good things to say when people ask me about you."

He chuckles, shaking his head. I can see myself tying with him again if he wants to, but our meeting for today is done. I put on a satin dressing gown to cover myself and head for the locker room. On the way, I catch Hana's wrist.

"Come with me?" I say with a dip of my head to greet her partner for the night. He nods his approval. She skips behind me, her small dress lifting with each jump, flashing everyone.

My relationship with Hanako is unlike the one I have with Connor. For one, I've known her since I joined the Moon Garden a few years ago. I don't mind small talk with her. Her contagious good mood recharges me and soothes my soul like cold milk on hot skin.

Second, I'm not only her friend but her rope top. On the days I feel confident and dominant, I cover her in rope and make her suffer the way she craves. On all other days, we talk about food, pop stuff, and Moon Garden gossip.

She is slightly shorter than me and thinner. A cute Asian girl who, at twenty-seven, looks anywhere between twenty and forty. Part of that is the excellent care she takes of her skin and hair, but another part is that nature has favored her with a pretty face and a small nose, full lips, and soft jawline. Her eyes are a shade lighter than mine, brown but warm and streaked with yellow specks.

"That looked nice," she says as we enter the changing area. I need a quick shower to get rid of the sweat making my dressing gown stick to my body.

"I enjoyed it. He definitely pushed me. I was blissed out." I unlock my locker and pull out my phone. No messages from Melanie. She was supposed to drop me one when she got back home.

"Watch out for sub drop. I hate it when all the brain chemicals start to equalize and I go from being ecstatic to depressed."

"I know, Hana, don't worry. I don't usually have it very bad. Have you done anything interesting yet tonight?" I close the messaging app and open up Instagram. I find Melanie's profile and tap on the latest picture. It's a stray dog, its fur a mix of dark yellow blond and splotches of black, eating out of a discarded Frenzy Eats box. Probably enjoying some chicken bones.

"Not yet. We've just been hanging around talking to people. We'll find a private room in a bit," Hana says and heads toward her own locker. "I want to check my phone though to make sure I have no urgent appointments for tomorrow. Maybe I can have a late night and sleep in."

It is nice to chat about nothing. Comfortable.

I pick up my phone and stare at the dog photo. Melanie loves dogs. The post was made five hours ago. She was supposed to have come home or been in touch by now, but when I left, our apartment was still empty.

It is unusual for her not to be in contact, but teenagers can be volatile, right?

Something doesn't sit well with me. A gut feeling that I want to ignore but can't. I switch back to messaging.

Did you get home all right?

Placing my phone back in my locker, I start peeling the gown off my damp skin.

"Oh fuck," I hear Hana say as she rummages in the tiny purse attached to her tiny dress.

"Can't find your key?"

"No, I must have dropped it somewhere. You know this is the third time." She huffs. "Another ten dollars down the drain…"

I narrow my eyes and examine my locker's mechanism. "I can save you the money, I think. Let me try opening it. You will still have to sneak out after, pretending not to have taken a key though," I say with a smile. Moon Garden lost key penalty rules are extortionate.

"Really?"

"Give me two of your bobby pins." I put my gown back on. A conspiratorial smile blossoms on my lips without being invited.

It has been a while since I've picked a lock. I hope it is like riding a bike. I bend the bobby pins to resemble a lockpick, then insert one to act as the tension wrench and started picking the pins with the other. I empty my mind, silencing the voice that reminds me of how I gained my skills and why I stopped picking locks.

As I advance on the lock, I fight with the urge to look at Hana. Is she impressed? Bored? Is she looking at me at all? I reach the last pin and turn the lock. It clicks open with a soft sound. I smile victoriously.

Letting the door swing open, I take Hana's phone and hand it to her with a bow. "Your phone, my princess," I say jokingly.

"You opened it so quickly," she says in awe. "Where did you learn that?"

"Ah, just watching a YouTube video." Not really. On the streets of a city I have long since put behind me.

"Really? How come?"

"A party trick. To entertain." A skill I was instantly good at. To belong when I was figuring out who I was.

"I'm amazed, Sophie Taylor. I bet you could crack a safe like that. Have you tried?"

"No, that would be criminal," I say with a wink. But the answer is yes. And it *was* criminal. Just a bit.

"Awesome," Hana concludes as she scrolls through her phone. I stuff my dressing gown in my locker, press it shut, and go to shower.

"Have fun out there," I shout over the sound of water.

"You know I will," Hana shouts back. "See you later."

I scrub my body, alone with my thoughts. I'm not a criminal. In fact, I'm meek and responsible. But as everyone else, I have a past. I remember it rarely, because its contents don't fit my current life-style. My lockpicking days are behind me, and so are the days when I went looking for trouble.

My new normal is different, and that's fine. It is to be expected of a twenty-four-year-old who looks after her fourteen-year-old sister. Life changes when you get parenting responsibilities.

After I've inhaled enough steam, I come out warm and tired. It is time to head home. As I put my jeans and T-shirt on, I check my phone.

Don't w8 up not gonna b bck tonight. :)

What the hell? My eyes narrow as my fingers tickle with the need to respond with something harsh and end it with her full name and an exclamation point. But I love Melanie. I don't want to snap at her or be the super overprotective parent. She's the only reason I am who I am today.

Ok. Who are you with?

A sleepover is fine. I will just have a word with her tomorrow. I'm exhausted. My phone buzzes, and I'm proud of her for responding so quickly.

One job. Twenty thousand dollars. Reply YES to confirm.

It isn't Melanie. I huff as I delete the message, sent from an unknown number for an unknown purpose. Probably spam like all the ones I've been getting in the past few weeks. Phishing. The messages were about dating, bank accounts, new products—anything and everything. I should change my number.

I go back to the chat with Melanie. The message has been delivered. I try to remember what I was like around the same age as I wait for a reply. The memories aren't pretty. Kids can go wrong in so many ways these days. I detest my teenage self. She ran and rebelled, ignoring her loving parents, saying no because it felt *so good* to be in opposition. To be her own person. Not a child, not someone's daughter and sister. And for many, that ends up okay. But not for me.

Memories of that rainy night resurface, and I press my hands to my eyes, compressing my eyeballs, willing the images to disappear.

Melanie is not like the other kids. She's not like me, thankfully. She is good and honest. She is hardworking and bright. She has her head on straight.

Simon. gtg.

That's okay then. I have Simon's phone number and know where he lives. And he is gay, so no danger for Melanie. Well, not from Simon anyway. If she is drinking, I hope she's being responsible.

Teenagers. So difficult to manage.

I wave to a couple of people on the way out, leaving the key to my locker at the bar. The barmaid nods at me with a tranquil smile. Working at the Moon Garden must be so nice. Fetish clubs are such glorious fun.

Outside, I inhale the crisp, chilly Chicago air. Despite the calendar creeping toward spring, it's definitely still winter.

I should call Melanie back home. But tonight was a good night, and my limbs are heavy with the need to sleep. When did Melanie grow up so much?

CREDITS

Thank you to those who helped me make this book as great as it can be.

Alpha readers: Jen and Mark
Beta readers: Cécile, Dan, Emily, Shawna and Vic
Copy editor and proofreader: Lunar Editing Services

Cover image original: Alycia Fung on Pexels